John only went into  e storm. He didn't ex

And it really is love at first sight. Chris is like nobody John's ever known, and John is caught from the start. All he wants, from that very first touch, is to never let go. But John is badly burned from his last relationship and in no fit state to try again. When Chris asks him out, he ought to say no.

But what if he says yes instead?

TEA

A Cup of John, Book One

Matthew J. Metzger

A NineStar Press Publication

Published by NineStar Press
P.O. Box 91792,
Albuquerque, New Mexico, 87199 USA.
www.ninestarpress.com

Tea

Copyright © 2019 by Matthew J. Metzger
Cover Art by Natasha Snow Copyright © 2019
Edited by Elizabetta McKay

Printed in the USA
First Edition
January, 2019

Print ISBN: 978-1-949909-82-1

Also available in eBook, ISBN: 978-1-949909-81-4

Warning: This book contains sexually explicit content, which may only be suitable for mature readers.

In loving memory of David.

Chapter One

"FARK THIS," RHODRI said, "fer the ace o' farking spades."

John grunted, busy watching a Facebook slanging match unfolding on his phone. It had started to snow, which—despite Sheffield getting snow on a regular basis in the winter—ensured everyone promptly forgot how cars worked.

A fact that Rhodri backed up by leaning out of the van window and bellowing, "Who taught yer to farking drive, yer daft cunt!" at a middle-aged man in a BMW.

John snorted, grinning, and squinted out of the slush-smeared windscreen. They were nearly at the high street.

"I can walk from here," he said. "Turn around and use the ring road, if you don't want to be here all night."

"Fark the ring road," Rhodri grumbled in his thick, garbled accent. "It'll fark the suspension."

"You mean it's not already?"

Rhodri snarled a defence of his beloved, twenty-year-old death trap of a van, but John firmly stuck by his assertion as the rust bucket was hauled over to the side of the road, and the handbrake screeched like a banshee in an opera house.

"Monday for the renovation?" John asked as he curled his coat collar up.

"Yeah. Gazzer's looking fer a spring sale."

"Have a good weekend, then."

"Fark off."

John grinned and slammed the passenger door on the pseudo-affectionate dismissal. The day Rhodri Campbell started talking nice to his friends was the day hell froze over.

Mind you, John thought, squinting at the black sky, that might not be too far off.

He was supposed to meet his older sister for dinner, but she'd be at least another hour. Grimacing at the weather, John decided to find a café and settle in to wait out the snowstorm. Hunching his shoulders, he broke into a jog, aiming for the first sign he saw, and soon shouldered his massive bulk through the glass door of a tiny, heavenly warm coffee shop.

It was busy inside. Everyone else had had the same idea. The floor was crowded with shopping bags, a buggy thoroughly blocking one aisle. John's absurd size earned him some dirty looks that were hastily wiped away when he glanced back. Even the barista, when he asked for a large tea, sighed and popped her gum like it would be an *enormous* bother to cover her wide-eyed stare. The prickle of unease rose under his skin, and he forced it back down.

"Keep the change," John told her as he handed over three pounds and folded his arms to wait, knowing that— even in Sheffield—a man with biceps like the steel ropes on a suspension bridge was not going to be left waiting for long. Especially if he folded his arms.

That was when he messed up.

He stepped back to glance around for a table, and in doing so, bumped the one directly behind him. A cup banged. Someone swore. And John felt the hot flush of shame flood his face, even as he spun on his heel to try to fix the damage.

"I'm so sorry. I—"

"It's all right. I think it missed me."

"Here, let me get you another—what was it?"

And then the man looked up from patting down his jeans and T-shirt with a napkin and smiled right into John's face.

And John just *stopped*.

Staring.

The way the man smiled was...breathtaking. Literally. The air caught in John's chest, his lungs seizing for a brief moment, when a crooked smile spread across narrow features, creasing a pale face from good-looking into gorgeous. It was like the sun bursting over a still sea, like the car dashboard when the ignition was first turned in the dark. A sudden spark lit behind an attractive face to make it utterly beautiful, and John *stared*.

The stranger was tall and lean, with a halo of messy black curls that surrounded his face and threw the ethereal beauty of that smile into sharp relief. The smile itself was formed out of the most ridiculously kissable mouth John had ever seen. And the face. God. It blazed with the brilliance of that beam, and above it lay the burn of eyes the colour of an endless summer sky.

Damn.

"A mocha with peppermint and a double shot of espresso."

"A...what?" John asked, still staring stupidly.

The man chuckled, and John died. His soul ascended into heaven on the back of that sound. Jesus. Holy goddamned Jesus.

"Just ask for Chris's regular."

"T-that's you, then?"

"Uh-huh."

"Um. John. Nice to—nice to meet you."

The touch of his hand was like a cattle prod. John felt it all the way up to his brain, and the most inappropriate parts of his brain too. He had to learn how to breathe again. His heart was pounding. He wanted—desperately, stupidly, urgently—to reel Chris in and kiss him as if they were the only two people in the room.

He didn't.

Obviously.

He let go and ducked back into line to ask for the guy's regular. Tipped double. And when he took it back to the table, John knew for his own sanity and safety he should apologise once more, take his tea, and go.

Instead, he said, "Mind if I join you?" and instantly hated himself for it.

And then didn't, when Chris smiled a little wider and said, "Please."

"I am sorry about that. I'm not usually that clumsy."

"Just an accident. It sounds busy in here."

"It...is," John said slowly and frowned.

Then it clicked. That brilliant blue was as vacant as a summer sky too. And he'd never once looked John quite in the eyes. John glanced about. There was a cane leaning up against the table. A glint of a gold medical bracelet around one thin wrist. And the way Chris slid his hand across the table, heels together and fingers spread, until he found the coffee cup...

"Are you sheltering from the weather too?"

"Uh, yeah," John said, snapping out of his reverie. "It's snowing. I'm supposed to meet my sister for dinner later, but I'm stupidly early, so...here I am."

"Lucky me."

John blinked.

"What?"

"Sorry, sorry." Chris waved a hand. "Ignore me. Big important family dinner, is it?"

"No, not really. She probably just wants to have a whine about our mum. Mum's—well, *Mum*."

"Let's pretend for a minute I don't know your mum…"

John chuckled, ducking his head. "Mum's…she loves us, she wants the best for us, but her best and our best doesn't always mesh, you know?"

"Ah, one of *those*. Yes, I know." Chris raised his cup in a saluting gesture. "To parents running interference."

"She's very practical," John said. "Very—you know, we ought to all marry well-off, well-educated folks with careers and good ankles. And Nora—my sister—she's cocked that up a bit." Then he winced at his crass phrasing and started to apologise.

Chris talked right over it. "Cocked it up how?"

"Well, she's currently divorcing her well-off, well-educated, well-ankled husband for a bloke who makes sandwiches."

Chris snorted and laughed. The coffee cup wobbled dangerously before he set it down to put a hand over his mouth and laugh a little harder, and John curled his toes in his boots. A warm flush spread from head to toe. God, he wanted to touch that. Wanted to reach out and curl his fist into that wild hair and kiss him like the world was ending.

John *wanted* him.

"Well," Chris said when he'd recovered, "if your sister has a voice anything like yours, then that's the luckiest sandwich man in the world."

"Uh—"

"What about you? Ditching your missus for the maid?"

John's stomach twinged. "There's no missus."

"Or mister?"

What?

"I—no."

"Sorry," Chris said again. "I guess I'm being a little too hopeful."

Hopeful? What?

"I—are you...flirting with me?"

"Yes." Chris raised both eyebrows. "Don't tell me that doesn't happen often."

"Well...it's been a while," John admitted. "And not usually in coffee shops." Or from men. John wasn't exactly good-looking, and in his experience, it was mostly women who were into the huge and hulking thing rather than men.

"Where does it usually happen? I could always try doing it there, if you like."

John barked a startled laugh. "Er—well—clubs. Here's—here's nice though. Here's fine."

"I refuse to believe it doesn't happen often."

"It doesn't."

"Really? Hm. Local clubbers need to open their ears, then."

"I—thank you?"

"I'm making you uncomfortab—"

"No," John interrupted quickly. "I just—I'm...not used to this."

Chris turned the coffee cup around in his hands, biting his lip.

"You sounded...I don't know. You sounded like you saw something you liked. And I felt something when you shook my hand."

"You...you don't want to be trying me out," John said carefully.

Chris smiled.

It wasn't the bright, beautiful smile. It was a slow smirk, devious and dirty. And John's cock swelled fiercely in his jeans. His dick didn't care about Daniel and his damage. His dick just wanted to have that incredible body around it, and to hell with the risks. Oh, God. That was a dirty trick, and judging by the way Chris lounged in his chair, pure sex, he knew it.

"You have a voice," Chris said, "like the hot afterburn of whiskey."

"I—"

"Smooth, liquid, and so easy to bask in. Like being drunk and not caring."

John swallowed again. He was half hard. Chris spoke so slow and soft, so very deliberately, that it was turning him on even though he wasn't saying anything filthy at all.

"I'm a dumb idea," John croaked.

"So am I."

John wanted to look away. But he felt incapable of *not* looking. He was spellbound, completely captured by this stranger's wide smile and fluttering hands. They were large hands, but thin. John wanted to call them spidery. Long fingers, but narrow palmed. He wondered wildly what they felt like. John's hand were rough from his trade, but Chris had a completely smooth paleness to his skin tone, and his face was impossibly young, not weather-beaten and wind burnt. His hands, John decided, would be just as smooth. They would be cool, too, like refreshing water against John's calluses.

And then they slid over the table and hooked casually over John's thumb.

John's heart hiccuped and clenched again, and the flood of pure *want* was so powerful that his vision flexed, like a fisheye lens homing in on this stunning man. He wanted to kiss him, hold his hand, say yes, *something*. And yet he felt paralysed—moths to flames, deer to headlights, whatever. He was *caught*.

"If you're really not interested, then that's fine," Chris said. "But—"

"That's definitely not it," John muttered.

"So—you want to get dinner sometime?"

The smile softened into something sweeter. More hopeful. More—

John's dick softened. Because his heart tightened, his stomach clenched, and his throat opened.

He should say no.

He was still a mess from Daniel, still wounded after nine whole months, still unable to so much as flirt on Grindr without questioning himself, his motives, how he came off. There was no way this was a good idea. Not with anyone, and least of all this brilliant, beautiful, blind guy.

After all, if Daniel were right—

If Daniel were right, if there had been any truth in the things he'd said, then John was the last person who should be going out to dinner with a blind man.

John should have said no.

But he said yes instead.

Chapter Two

JOHN LIVED IN a small flat with his older sister in the Kelham Island redevelopment.

The redevelopment was a gentrified hipster-magnet, full of boutique coffee shops selling vegan, organic, gluten-free, lactose-free, taste-free flapjacks and thimbles of coffee for five pounds a go. John's sisters all looked the part, in one way or other, and fitted in, or at least appeared to. John, being a man who had to both duck and turn sideways to get through the average-sized door, did not.

But while being in the city centre made him feel uncomfortable—trying to squeeze down to fit into everyone's else little worlds—in Kelham Island he felt almost smug. Let any of that lot, with their three-foot words and university theses about why cars were racist or whatever, change a light bulb. It was kids like that who kept John in such good business. And with the economy in its current state, he'd out-earn the lot of them put together too.

In truth, he didn't really like living there, with pretentious neighbours and bad parking. But the flat had been cheap, in the midst of a housing crisis, and John had bought it before the development was finished. He'd originally lived with Aljaz—the closest John had ever come to finding 'the one.' But when that broke down, Aljaz moved out, and Fran, in the midst of her short spell at art college, moved in. And ever since, the flat had been a revolving door of John and whichever sister needed a room that year.

Currently, thanks to her divorce, it was Nora.

John had three sisters. Nora, at thirty-seven, was only a year older than him. Fran and Tasha, in their early twenties, could be politely referred to as surprises. All of them were blonde, less than five foot four in height, and utterly, completely, one hundred percent, in control of their stack-of-meat brother.

That was sort of a trend in John's life. He was a behemoth of a man...and everyone else in his world took absolute control. From his diminutive grandmother to the sister young enough to be his own child, everybody else ruled John. Every boyfriend had, too.

Including Daniel.

Maybe now it was time Daniel stopped ruling his life. After all, he wasn't here anymore. And John might have someone new on the horizon.

So, the first thing he did when he got home was find a bin bag and start emptying the hall closet.

All of Daniel's things, everything he'd left behind, had been rammed to the back and forgotten. Mostly. Photos, gifts, clothes. Even old climbing gear they'd bought together, back when John had been in love and thought there was something real about it all. All of it disappeared into the bag. Ugly memories of an ugly man.

His name was Daniel Ostrowski. They'd met—typically, for John's track record with men—in a gay bar in Sheffield. Daniel was exactly John's type: tall, slim, and with eyes like the sea. He lived in Doncaster, so they didn't get to spend as much time together as John had wanted, but for a whole year, John had adored him. He really had. He'd been head over heels in love, almost as much as those amazing four years with Aljaz, and he hadn't seen the signs that were so obvious now.

Like how Daniel never invited John to Doncaster to see the flat he kept bragging about. How he'd never entertained the idea of moving to Sheffield, or John moving to Doncaster, and actually setting up a life together instead of stolen weekends here and there. How, after a whole year, John had yet to meet any of Daniel's actual family.

Turned out Daniel's boyfriend might have had something to do with that.

Daniel was engaged to some other man, and when this fiancé found out about John, Daniel lied through his eye teeth and made everything so much worse. He'd tried to get away with it, tried to come out of it smelling like roses, and in doing so, had thrown John not only under the bus, but under the entire Stagecoach fleet.

He nearly destroyed John's life.

They'd split up nine months ago, yet John was nowhere near recovered. Daniel and his lies—persistent, dogged lies he spouted to anyone who'd listen and so insistently he even had John questioning if they were true—had left scars. Mental ones and, after one drunken night alone in the kitchen, physical as well. John had nearly killed himself over the whole thing, and still woke sweating in the night, hearing Daniel's accusations on a loop inside his head.

Nine months, and only now was John clearing the evidence of Daniel's existence out of his flat. Only now did he feel able.

Now, out of nowhere, it felt easy where before it had been impossible. To pick out their pictures and crumple them up. To retrieve the long-abandoned T-shirts from the back of the wardrobe and throw them away. He even found a bottle of aftershave he wasn't sure *was* Daniel's, but he couldn't remember buying it himself, so away it went.

"What are you doing?" Nora asked when she came back from her shower, standing in her plaid pyjamas and drying her honey-blonde hair with a small towel.

"Cleaning out some of Daniel's things," John said.

Nora paused.

"Oh," she said eventually. Then she frowned. "Any reason why?"

"Well, it's not like he's coming back."

She rolled her eyes. "Why *now*?"

John opened his mouth, then abruptly changed his mind. Nora was *sensible*—the only one of them who was, really—and she'd scold him just like Mum would if he told her. One coffee with a guy didn't mean it was time to move on, she'd say. One coffee didn't make a boyfriend. He was pinning his hopes on this, and so *what* if it had been nine months since Daniel. Getting rid of his things and throwing himself into a new relationship would effectively be a rebound. That was what she'd say.

And she'd be kind of right, but John didn't need to give her the satisfaction.

"I—just think it's time."

"Sure," Nora said, "but again, why now?"

John sat back on his heels, turning a jumper over in his hands.

"I—I stopped in a café today...and someone started flirting with me."

Nora made a face that broadcasted her opinion of John's mental faculties loud and clear. "You mean, you finally noticed somebody flirting with you."

"Fine, I *noticed*—he wasn't subtle—"

"Oh, *he*. I change my answer. You mean, a man flirted with you."

John threw the jumper at her. She threw it right back.

"Do you want a reason or not?"

"So-rree, princess," she drawled. "So, a man flirted with you."

"He asked me out."

"Well, that's a start. Now, we just need you to start saying yes and actually going on dates and moving on from that bulls—"

"I *did* say yes."

She stopped.

"Oh."

John grimaced.

Then, "Are you sure that's a good idea?"

"No?" John said. "But he was so—*stunning*."

"What, a random model asked you out?"

"He *could* be. Pretty sure he's not, but he *could* be."

"So, you listened to the wrong head," Nora surmised, then pursed her lips. "Well, for once, John? Good."

"Wait, what? I thought you'd be annoyed with me. Rebound relationship, and all that."

"Hey, if this guy did the asking, he's a big boy and can handle a little rebound for himself. You need to get back out there." Nora dropped her towel—and herself—onto the carpet beside him. "You're not like Fran, John. You're miserable on your own."

John bit his lip, staring at the half-full bag.

"Getting the hell away from Daniel was the best decision you ever made," Nora said. "But you've been really lonely and down ever since. So...yeah, don't pin all your hopes on this new guy, but have *fun*, okay? Get your spark back. There's someone out there for you—an Aljaz who isn't so hell-bent on going back to Croatia. But you won't find him if you're not out there looking. Okay?"

He wordlessly lifted an arm, and she tucked herself in under it to hug him. Her wet hair smelled of mangoes, and John swallowed against the lump in his throat.

"Promise me you'll go on this date with this guy, and you won't think about Daniel or any of what happened," Nora whispered in his ear.

"It's not that easy, Noz."

"I know. But promise you'll really, really try?"

John thought of Chris's bright smile, brighter eyes, and brash flirting. Maybe he wouldn't be allowed to think about Daniel. Hell, he got the distinct impression Chris would rather he didn't think at all.

"Promise," he said and hugged her until she squeaked. "But you can't tell the others yet."

"Oh, God, *really*? Nan'll have both our heads if she's not first to know!"

"That's—that's too much pressure," he admitted. "She's been bugging me about finding somebody new since we split up; she'll go all-out on Chris if—"

"Another Chris, huh?"

"—she finds—yes—out."

"Okay," Nora said. "I promise not to tell her, *unless* this turns into a not-just-one-date thing."

"What?"

"If there's a second date, the deal is off, and I spill. I'm not having her spamming my phone with 'excuse me, young lady, I have the right to know these things, blah blah blah.'"

John pulled a face.

"Fine," he said.

By which, of course, he meant fine—he just wouldn't tell Nora about a second date.

Because way in the back of his head, in the stubborn bit that resisted Daniel's crap and survived it, John already wanted a second date.

Chapter Three

JOHN HAD HAD—in total—twelve first dates.

And he'd never been so nervous.

The thing was, before Daniel, John had been a pretty confident fish in the sea. He knew his strengths. He could make people laugh, and he could make people come. Sometimes, he could even make them do both at once.

But since then—

Well, that had been before, and this was after.

Even without the before-and-after, John had never had a first date where walking in the door felt like a sucker-punch.

Chris had chosen a fancy little coffee shop that smelled of roasted beans and chocolate and was lit close and intimate like a romantic restaurant. John couldn't figure out if Chris knew that and had picked accordingly, or if it was a coincidence. Either way, it was working. John wasn't meeting for a cuppa, not in this place.

And not with this man.

If he'd thought Chris was attractive that Friday evening, it was nothing to his Saturday-afternoon-and-dating thing. The T-shirt was tight-fitting. The jeans could have been painted on. Both were black, making his skin look uniformly smooth and lickable. That glint of gold was definitely a medical bracelet, yet somehow, it gave the impression of casual jewellery. He had a silver lip ring, tucked in close to the corner of his mouth, that he hadn't been wearing last time, and John immediately wanted to get his teeth around it and feel it move under his tongue.

God, he was so screwed.

"You're not playing fair," John said weakly, and Chris grinned up at him.

"Why?"

"You look—edible."

"Oh? Well, I was going to suggest dinner later. On me?"

"Please don't," John said, sinking into the chair opposite. Chris had already bought drinks. To John's surprise, both were teas. "I had enough difficulty walking out of the last coffee shop you were in with any dignity."

"Dignity is overrated." Chris lifted the cup. "Thanks for coming though. Now, and maybe later."

"Oh, my God."

"Flirting aside, I'm genuinely glad you said yes."

John cleared his throat. "Yeah, well, I'm—glad you asked."

"You don't sound convinced."

John winced. "Er. Well. Not to—spend a date talking about my ex, but...my last breakup was...bad."

"Oh."

"Yeah."

"Hence your surprise at the flirting?"

"Yeah. And my reluctance."

Chris raised his eyebrows, and John grimaced.

"I had wood all the way through, talking to you," John confessed.

Chris's face lit up like the sun, and he laughed. The flash of pure happiness was so bright it hurt, and John's dick twitched anew at the sheer, raw, almost violent *life* in front of him.

"God," he breathed. "I'm going to get it again if you keep laughing like that."

"Sounds to me like I should keep laughing."

"Sounds to me like I'm going to develop a blood pressure problem here," John groused.

Then Chris slid his hand over John's wrist on the table, and John's skin caught fire.

"Seriously," Chris murmured, "I could listen to you read the dictionary and be turned on. So, you're not the only one."

John swallowed thickly. "Uh—"

"But, unlike you, I have no idea what I'd be eating off. Or out. Or both."

"Oh, *Christ*."

"So, fill me—in?"

"*Stop* it," John implored, and Chris grinned wickedly at him.

"Seriously. You have images. I don't. Give me some."

"If you behave!"

"Behaving perfectly," Chris sang and tapped John's wrist with two fingers. "Come on. Who does that gorgeous voice belong to?"

John swallowed. "Uh. John Halliday."

"And who's that?"

"Um. An electrician."

"Mm, no wonder there's sparks..."

"Fu—uh. Fudging hell."

"Language!"

John rolled his eyes. "God. All right. Um. I'm—tall. Really tall. Uh. And I'm broad too. I play rugby a lot, and I work out, so..."

"Could you bench-press me?"

John snorted. "Yes."

"What, really?"

"Uh, yes." Chris was tall enough, but he was skinny. Twelve stone at the absolute most.

"Mm, filing *that* information for later."

"If I don't pull my shoulders together, I can't fit through door frames."

"Holy *hell*."

"And I'm taller than most doors too."

"Shit."

"My bed's custom-made. And I have regular backaches because of the strain."

"And you're all in proportion?"

John frowned. "What?"

"You know, tall guys have big hands. Big feet. Big di—"

"Okay!"

Chris laughed again, and John groaned.

"I—yes, all right."

"Very all right."

"I'm not exactly cuddly-looking, is my point."

"You sound like you are."

John flushed. "Well. Um. Yeah."

"Really? You like to cuddle?"

"Yes."

"Oh, I'm keeping you," Chris decided. "But that's not much of an image. Big guy, I get it. So—what else? All the normal fingers and toes? Three eyes? Magical six cocks?"

John snorted, smirking. "No. Standard number of everything. Uh." He glanced down at Chris's pale fingers, white against the black of John's sleeve tattoo. "I have ink."

"You have what?"

"Ink. Tattoos."

"Oh. How many?"

Both arms sleeved, one leg the same, a huge eagle on his back, even a tiny gay pride flag on his upper thigh within about two inches of his bollocks...

"A lot."

"Is that what this line is?" Chris asked, rubbing lightly at John's wrist. John turned it over and gently moved Chris's fingers to the black eye of the snake.

"There," he said. "I had a scar before."

"What kind of scar?"

John swallowed. Daniel's scar. He wasn't going to talk about that.

"Hell if I remember."

Chris grinned and traced the snake lightly up to John's elbow. It was a huge python in vivid colours, less than six months old, and the outline still a stark groove. Chris's touch tickled. In its wake, it left a trail of raised hairs, and John's heart beat faster the higher those soft fingers climbed.

"It's a snake," he said softly.

"Why a snake?"

"I love snakes. Always have. Got a corn snake at home."

"Yeah? I've never even touched one."

"You have now," John said and flushed. He shouldn't. But he wanted to. And...

And Nora was right. He'd never be happy on his own. He'd been miserable since he left Daniel. And here was Chris, flirting and laughing and so utterly incredible—

Here was Chris, asking him to describe himself because he couldn't see.

The mental flinch, the spark of fear, was as real as if Daniel had walked right into the coffee shop with the police at his heels, and John leaned back a little until Chris's fingers slipped back down to his wrist.

Only...

Only that was sort of worse, because their hands ended up cupped about one another, soft and intimate. A sweat broke out along John's back.

Then Chris said, "I'd like to touch your snake. Your pet too," and John was startled into another laugh.

"Why—why do you want me so bad?"

Chris shrugged. "Like I said. You have a wonderful voice. And a...manner. There's something about you."

"Something like what?"

"I don't know. Something attractive, anyway."

John bit his lip, then blew upwards into his hair. "I'm not the looker here. I don't exactly beat them off with a stick."

Chris laughed. "Good, beating me off by hand is more than enough."

"Oh, for Christ's—!"

Chris's delighted cackle was like an aphrodisiac, and John suddenly felt a flash of boldness himself.

"Don't make me put you over my knee," he warned. A flash of guilt and disgust instantly followed the statement, only to be washed away by Chris's snort.

"Please, if you got hard just by my flirting with you the other day, you'd not last a whole spanking."

John shifted uncomfortably. "Yeah. Well. Might be the case again."

"Yeah?"

"Yeah."

The smile softened a little. "So, what do you say we get lunch and maybe head somewhere quieter for coffee?"

John's heart hiccuped. Christ. His body wanted to. His body wanted nothing more than to strip this gorgeous guy out of his painted-on jeans and his too-tight T-shirt and spend a whole evening sucking his cock...but his brain cringed. After all Daniel had said, after so much drilling away at John's head until John himself half believed it, there was no way he could have a one-night stand and not...

Not believe it all over again.

Not spend the next year looking over his shoulder for the cops and the court case.

"Is this— What do you want here, Chris?"

Chris's face softened.

"I want whatever you're willing to give me."

"I'm—I'm not in a place...I'm not in a place where I can really do flings," John said awkwardly.

To his surprise, Chris ducked his head and smiled sheepishly.

"I come off more confident when I flirt than I feel," he admitted. "Truth is, I don't really know what I want right now. I don't know who you are to know what I want from you yet. But I like this. Flirting and making you squirm and getting you flustered. And I'd like to do it again. And again, and again. And yeah, I want to know what it *feels* like when you squirm and get flustered, not just what it sounds like. But if you're willing to give me...dates, then I want those too."

John's ribs locked shut.

Dates?

As in—ongoing, persistent, long-term dating?

As in, go to restaurants with this guy? Have Chinese on the sofa and watch the rugby with him? Weekends at Whitby Bay, with fish and chips on the seafront? Extra keys and—

He put the brakes on. Please. One date, and he was imagining keys to Chris's flat and taking holidays together.

But...

Couldn't get to those places without dating.

And, okay, it felt like it was too soon after Daniel, but Nora was right. He had to get past Daniel's legacy. And who better to try with, than someone who could get him hard and breathless just by *smiling* at him?

Slowly, John wrapped his fingers between Chris's and squeezed.

"Dates sound good," he said and allowed himself to smile. "I'd like that."

Chris smiled as well—then it widened into a smirk, and John closed his eyes to brace against the terrible chat-up line that was bound to be coming.

And sure enough:

"I have no ethical problem with sex on the first date, though. Just so you know."

Chapter Four

JOHN WENT TO work on Sunday.

Rhodri rang as John was leaving rugby practice. Emergency call from a long-term client. Lightning strike and a lot of fried circuits. Could they sort it out?

Triple fees for the weekend, and a way of getting out of Nan's Sunday dinner with Nora smugly beaming and thereby brandishing all over the place that she knew something the others didn't?

"Yeah, sure, I'll be up in half an hour."

John was an electrician. After leaving school at sixteen, he'd trained under Tommy Whittaker, one of the best in the business. John had developed a solid reputation with Whittaker and went solo at twenty-seven. So for the last nine years, he'd made his money—and a lot of it—working on a self-employed basis. And as skilled tradesmen were in very short supply, he didn't have to put up with colleagues unless he wanted to. Most of them at the firm had been tossers anyway.

"All right, Holliday!"

Except for Rhodri. Rhodri Campbell was, like John, an excellent tradesman who'd started out as an apprentice and dogsbody. Rhodri was a bear of a plumber, who'd gone into property maintenance and renovation, and was a great source of income for John when his projects needed rewiring. So for Rhodri? Sure, why not a Sunday once in a while.

"All right, Rhod," he said, dropping down from the van. The house in question was a Victorian rectory that hadn't seen a repair since the 1890s, was now falling apart around the owner's ears, and was so far from health and safety regulations it was laughable. John wondered it had any electrics to fry in the first place.

"Thought you were off with the family this mornin'!" Rhodri boomed, clapping John on the shoulder. A loud and amiable bloke, with a permanent inability to remember John's last name properly, Rhodri was a somewhat typical labourer. That was to say, Rhodri was *entirely* under the thumb of his tiny wife, Amy.

"I was," John said. "Sunday dinner. Get one next week, doesn't matter."

"Mine too. Breaking news to the in-laws. No bloody ta."

"Nothing bad?"

"Havin' a baby," Rhodri said, and though his gruff voice didn't change, his face lit up. John grinned, the smile infectious.

"Congrats," he said, punching Rhodri in the arm. "You know what it is yet?"

"Not yet. Only ten weeks gone." Rhodri sounded rightly pleased. He'd been married to Amy for six years—John was his best man—but although they'd wanted kids, it hadn't happened. "First one should be a boy, I say. Boy first, then a girl. One of each."

John snickered. "Don't think it works like that, Rhod."

"M'just sayin'," Rhodri rumbled. "Lasses need older brothers to look after 'em. I looked out fer my little sister, and any lad o' mine will do th'same fer 'is."

John smiled faintly as they stomped down into the cellar, and the blackened wall and remains of the fuse box greeted them with a burnt stench. "You're old-fashioned," he said, and Rhodri laughed.

"You'll be th'same when you get a girl." Rhodri's rolling voice meant that *get a girl* came out closer to *gerragirl*.

John's smile didn't even twitch. "White picket fence and babies? Not a chance, mate." The façade didn't flicker. He knew better than to let things slip. Like most of the men John had worked with since leaving school, Rhodri was the traditional type. One man, one woman. Blokes could shag around, but it made a girl a slag. A girl who refused advances was a lezzer; a bloke who showed weakness was a poufter. *That* type.

John never bothered to challenge it much. It was a losing battle anyway. It made you out as an arsehole, or bent. And bent, in the building industry? Not the best of ideas. Oh, John wasn't afraid of much—he was a big sod, not many would think about trying to physically do anything. But that wasn't the only way to drive a queer out. Tools going missing, orders not coming in, work suddenly drying up. A reputation for badly done jobs. Tell the odd loyal customer not to bother with Halliday—he was a bit dodgy, bit of a nonce, know what they meant?

So, he kept under the radar. Always had. And it was easy to do when there was no boss and he could go weeks without working with anybody else. He got into the habit. Luckily, most of the lads were either much younger, or older and married with kids, so didn't see much of John outside of work. It had been easy to spin the lies. Jason had been Jess. Daniel had been Danielle. Switching pronouns was easy. Jokes about the missus were even easier. John's lack of sharing stories, and the switch from 'Chrissie' to 'Jess' and then the rapid abandonment of 'Jess' had earned him a reputation as a womaniser—much respected in that crowd—so he went by undetected.

Even by Rhodri. Which felt disloyal somehow, but John would not have risked that easy friendship for the sake of a secret. For the sake of impermanent partners and stereotypes. For the sake of—

If Rhodri had heard—if any of the old firm had heard—about what Daniel had done, they'd have believed it.

And for *that*, they'd have beaten him. His size wouldn't have protected him then.

So, when they got to work, and Rhodri asked about his weekend, John said nothing about Chris. Even a bad liar could lie well given enough time and practice, and John had had nearly twenty years of practice. So, Rhodri didn't notice.

But then, Rhodri was a Campbell, not a Halliday.

John could get away with fudging a lot of his personal details at work—but the moment he got home, at five past five that evening, Nora materialised in the kitchen doorway with two cans of lager and two eyebrows up at her hairline.

"So," she said, "you ducked out of Sunday dinner, ignored all of Nan's calls, and willingly stayed on this late? On a *Sunday*?"

"The money was good," John said defensively but took the can anyway.

"Sure. There's going to be a second date, isn't there?"

It was barely a question. Her voice was so flat, it might as well have been a statement. So much for his intentions of not telling her.

John sighed, cracked open the can, and nodded.

She *beamed*.

She might have been thirty-seven and going through a divorce, but Nora was a sucker for romance. John had tried reading her book collection once. It was stuffed with slushy novels where all the characters were called Baby or Darling and featured scenes with 'throbbing columns' and holes all over the place. Her taste in films wasn't much better. When her face lit up like that, it knocked about twenty years off her age, and John groaned as his sister shepherded him into the living room, so excited it felt like they were kids on Christmas morning.

"So," she said, throwing herself down on the sofa. "Tell me all about him. And your date yesterday. And your next one."

John coughed.

"Yeah, well, it was just coffee yesterday. Next week is a proper nice date. Restaurant and dressed up nice everything. I picked, this time."

"Hence, you put all your shirts in the dryer this morning," she said.

"Hence, I put all my shirts in the dryer this morning," John echoed obediently.

"Oh, *good*," she said. "So, tell me about him. What's he look like; what does he do?"

John's family had known he was gay since his early teens. There'd never been much issue with it, really. John was six feet tall by the time he was twelve years old, and out—though not entirely intentionally—since around the same time. He'd attracted the usual snide comments in school, and double takes as an adult when he went out with a boyfriend, but nothing serious. He was smart enough to keep his sexuality a secret from the types of people who could cause him hassle, and everyone else wasn't dumb enough to try.

Dad put it down to being raised by a domineering mother and having three sisters, never mind that John had had only one sister until he was fourteen years old and already pretty sure he wasn't into girls. Mum put it down to his interest in property programmes and home decoration, even as a little kid, but seeing as that had translated into training as an electrician and working for a building firm for most of his life, John couldn't quite follow her logic.

John put it down to being gay and had left it at that.

Generally, he knew he'd been lucky, and luck had given over to a certain amount of boldness in asking guys out when he didn't know if they swung his way. Which, in turn, had led to the old confidence he used to have before Daniel. And now, his luck could make a comeback with Chris, and that stunning, gut-wrenching smile.

So he said, "He's totally fucking gorgeous, Noz."

"John, you've said that about literally every boyfriend you've had, and none of them look alike! Come on, specifics. What's he *like*? What's he called? Craig, was it?"

"Chris," he corrected. "And he's, um. He's tall—maybe five eight?"

"Kissable height?"

"As close as I can get, yeah."

She laughed, beaming, and John grinned to match.

"He has black hair, and it's all curly and messy, a bit overlong but not *long*-long—like if you gave it the usual short back and sides, then left it for six months?"

Nora, a hairdresser for nearly a decade, nodded sagely.

"And they're quite big curls. They look soft. I wanted to run my fingers through them to see how they feel."

"What did he think of you?"

"He..."

Chris had liked his voice and touching his hands. But how could he tell Nora that without her catching on? And, weirdly, John didn't *want* to tell her about Chris being blind yet. There was some childish part of him that wanted to keep the odd secret to himself, at least in these early days.

"He liked my sleeve tattoos," he said eventually. "He says there's something about me. And he really likes my voice."

"Your *voice*?"

John winced. *Too odd.* "That's what he said. Maybe he's into music and stuff," he said. "And he thought I was charming." At least, he'd seemed charmed.

"You?"

"I charmed him into a second date, didn't I?"

All right, well, given Chris had been pushing for it, too, he hadn't exactly needed to, but John wasn't going to tell Nora that.

"How?"

"Because he likes me, that's how." John kicked her ankle. "Go away if you're going to rain on my parade."

"I'm not, I'm not!"

John grunted, eyeing her suspiciously.

She laughed. "So, come on, what's your grand plan to keep him charmed? When do we get to meet him?"

"Never?"

"Yeah, right."

"Not for a while," John capitulated. "I—I just don't want to have that pressure yet. Not so soon, not the first one after...after. He's special, Nora. I just—I feel so good with him, and he's not like any of the others. He's—I know I say that every time, but there's something different about Chris. I think there's really something special there, so...you know, I don't want Mum interrogating him about whether he's son-in-law material and scaring him off too soon. Or piling all that pressure on me and making me freak out a bit. You know what she can be like."

Nora pulled a face and nodded. "All right. But not forever."

"And don't tell Fran. She'll blab."

"All *right*. God, you suck."

"I...I want this to be the real deal," John said. "I want this to be good. And I reckon it can be. And—and after Daniel, I...I *need* good, Nora. I need this."

Nora rubbed his arm and said nothing.

Chapter Five

THIS WAS JOHN'S element.

He'd always been very good at laughter and love, and the best way to combine the two was to turn on the charm full blast and leave someone flustered, smiling, and feeling good about themselves.

And where better to do that than a no-holds-barred, dress-to-impress date?

He took his time getting ready, banishing Daniel's influence as far away as he could manage by primping and preening to perfection...or as perfect as one could make an electrician with shoulders like a front-row forward. He couldn't do anything about his massive size and spades for hands, but the tattoos could disappear under collar and cuffs, a nice tie could bring out his eyes and detract from the broken nose, and at least he hadn't shaved his head in long enough that he could comb some respectability into place.

The other step was the car. He couldn't do anything about its age. John's Volvo had seen better centuries and was running on electrical tape, superglue, and the voodoo of the fluffy dice he temporarily relocated to the boot before setting off, windows rolled right down despite the cold and snow to air it out one last time. But he'd vacuumed it out properly, put a new air freshener in, and painstakingly found a decent playlist rather than risking the braying donkey of a DJ the local radio station hired during the evenings.

It was the little things that spelled success, after all.

Chris lived in Greenhill, and the postcode he'd given John for the satnav brought him onto a potholed road lined by generous houses and long driveways. The snow had been worse here. It covered the Land Rover sitting in the driveway of number sixteen in a thick dusting of white.

The cold did nothing to cool off John's fever-high nerves as he knocked, and he felt a bit like a teenager. This was very obviously—the car, the begonias by the path, the kitten design on the welcome mat—Chris's parents' house. John hadn't picked someone up for a date from their parents' house in years, not since he was about nineteen or twenty. He fervently hoped, as he heard footsteps inside, that Chris would answer the bell and he wouldn't have to meet his folks.

The prayer was answered.

"Hey," he said, beaming when Chris opened the door, looking downright edible in a dark blue dress shirt and dark, well-fitted jeans.

"Is this smart enough for your plans?"

"That does more than well enough," John said, still grinning stupidly. "You look amazing."

A smile flickered into life. "Thank you." A hand groped over his shoulder, and then Chris was shrugging on a jacket. "We need to go now, before my stepmum realises you're here and collars you."

"Oh, Christ. Right, you ready? It's a bit icy..."

Chris's fingers were tight on the crook of John's elbow. He shouted, "Later, Caroline!" into the house before unhooking the white cane from the wall and closing the door, and then John carefully led him down the snowy drive to his cleaned-within-an-inch-of-its-life car.

"It's not a chariot," he warned, opening the passenger door and bracing his hand against the roof in case Chris didn't duck enough. "But it's better than my work van."

"I'm not much of a revhead," Chris admitted. He settled himself easily enough, fumbling for the seatbelt as John jogged around the bonnet, and then grinned when the car dipped under John's weight. "Is that the suspension or you?"

"Me," John said. "I weigh close to twenty stone, and none of it's fat."

"Wow."

"D'you live with your parents, then?" John asked, peeling away from the pavement and heading west.

"No," Chris said. "I moved out about a year ago. But— no offence, I don't exactly know you super well, yet. And Dad's a former marine. So you can know where *they* live."

John laughed. Most men would have been annoyed, but John simply felt a sharp stab of relief. He'd struggle—he *knew* he'd struggle—to prove he wasn't what he looked like. Chris was going to help him out. Chris was going to take his own precautions and make John work to be let in. Cynical as it sounded, he was doing some of John's work for him and providing his own ammunition against Daniel, even if he didn't know it.

"Sorry, I know it's probably way over the top..."

"It's not," John said. "I'm effectively a stranger. If you're still doing it in six months, maybe I'm doing something wrong or you're being over the top, but it's fine. I don't mind. Your dad's a *marine* though?"

"Former."

"Still!"

Chris chuckled, shaking his head. "He's not all that scary. Anyway, where are we going? Where are you taking me?"

"Out to dinner," John said. "Does it matter where?"

"Does if it's that dodgy Indian place on West Street."

"It's not there."

"Good. It's not very romantic either."

"No," John agreed. "It's not far, actually. I didn't realise your street—your dad's street—was this close."

The roads were empty, too, the weather having driven most people back inside. A mad cyclist was braving the elements, and a taxi was creeping about in hopes of a fare or two, but they were the only life John saw until he pulled the car off the road and into the busy parking area. The restaurant was in Dore and a right posh job that was the type of place used for proposals.

"We're here. And, um, can I make a confession?"

"Sure."

"I feel like I was dumb and awkward last time. And I'm usually pretty good at this. So, this time, I'm back in my element, and I'm going to stop being floored you asked me out in the first place, and I'm going to show you that I can be a bit of a catch if I want to be."

"Oh, yes?"

"Mhmm. So, I'm pulling out all the stops and spoiling you stupid so that you'd be daft not to give me another chance."

Chris laughed, finding the door release unerringly. "We'll see about that."

The restaurant was a nice mix of busy and quiet. John had booked a table in the corner, away from other people staring too much, and had called ahead to organise a menu that Chris could hopefully read. He pulled out Chris's chair for him and dared to stoop and kiss his temple before taking his seat and nudging Chris's foot under the table.

"You're off to a good start," Chris said mock-loftily as John ordered drinks, and chuckled when a Braille menu was handed to him. "I'm guessing...?"

"I made sure they'd have one when I booked," John agreed.

"Very thoughtful, even if it doesn't have prices on."

"They do date menus here."

"What on earth is that?" The flirtatious, low tone disappeared, and John laughed at the surprise in Chris's voice.

"It's where one of the menus has no prices on, so you can get anything you want and not think about the price. Because I'm picking up the bill."

Chris paused. "You can't pick up the *whole* bill."

"Yeah, I can."

A little line appeared between Chris's eyebrows.

"Look," John said. "It's our first proper *serious* date, and—I don't want to be rude or step on your toes or anything, but I'm betting I have a lot more money than you do."

"You're an electrician."

"Do you have any *idea* how many people don't know how to replace a fuse? Or change a light bulb?"

Chris cracked a smile, and John pressed his advantage.

"I said I was going to spoil you, and that includes taking the bill."

Chris's face hardened slightly. "That doesn't entitle you to anything."

"Of course it doesn't," John said, and the tension eased. He pushed his hand across the table and slipped the tips of his fingers between Chris's. "I'm not after anything. Just...I'm good at sweeping guys off their feet. I wanna check I've not lost the skill."

"I wouldn't thank you for that. It's disorienting." The lighter tone was seeping back in, and John slid his hand the rest of the way to squeeze Chris's.

"I *will* admit to hoping for a kiss at the end."

"That's going to take more than some water and a menu I can read."

"Yeah? Just took a coffee last time and you were offering back to yours."

"That was last time. This is now."

"What's different?"

"Dating. That could have been a fling. This has the maybe of a relationship, and I'm not putting out without some work going into that."

The attitude was back, and John laughed. "Oh my God, you're unbelievable."

"Get used to it, Johnny-boy."

John chuckled, shaking his head. "Okay. Okay, then, I'll put some work in. I have three courses and taking you home to finish the job."

"Better get moving, then." But Chris's hand and expression had relaxed, and John's heart jumped in hope. He hadn't expected such resistance to the price-free menu. Or...resistance at all, actually. On the one hand, John knew himself—he liked to spoil, he liked to lavish attention—and if Chris found it persistently disturbing, then there was going to be a problem. But on the other hand, he liked Chris's caution, same as he'd liked Chris asking for John to collect him from his parents' rather than his own house.

"I reckon I can do that," he said. "Place your order, and let me charm you."

Chris laughed and did so, opting for vegetarian dishes but shaking his head when John asked about it. "I just really like quiche."

"Okay, your taste in food is terrible, but I can deal with that..."

Chris called him an idiot, and the starter passed in easy flirting, with John firing back as much as Chris had built up on their last two café chats, and finding out—quickly—that flirts relating to Chris's appearance worked best.

"I wouldn't have taken you for shy or insecure about the way you look," John said as the starters were cleared, and Chris's face dropped slightly.

"I'm—not. Sort of."

"Sort of?"

Chris blew upwards into his hair. He propped one elbow on the table, raking a hand through his curls, and finally said, "I was...hoping we could go a bit longer without discussing this part."

John frowned. "What part?"

"Are you gay?"

The sudden gear change left John utterly confused. "Uh. Yeah. I'm here, aren't I?"

"No, I mean...gay as opposed to...bisexual, or pansexual, or something else."

"Uh. Yeah. Gay. Why does that matter?"

Chris bit his lip. He was frowning vacantly, looking anxious, and John didn't like it. He was good at this. His dates weren't meant to be anxious.

"Chris?"

"I'm—"

When the sentence stopped there, John frowned and reached over the table to touch his free hand lightly.

"Hey. Just...spit it out. Try me."

"This is the bit," Chris said lowly, "where everything is going great and we really like each other and then I say this part, and *wham*. You don't want me anymore."

John cleared his throat. "It's...going to have to be a pretty big part."

Chris snorted. "Okay. I'm trans. There you go."

John's jaw dropped. Literally. He had to shake himself and slowly close his mouth.

"This is the bit where you get all awkward and say you're not into that and you'll think about it and you'll call and then I never hear from you again," Chris said and drew back his hand. "It's fine."

"Well, it's clearly not, because I don't really fancy leaving and never seeing you again," John said. "Um. Chris, look, I'm not...I'm not really clued into this sort of thing because I don't really understand what you're telling me. You want to be a woman?"

Chris coughed a laugh. "That's very flattering, but no. Other way 'round."

"You *were* a woman?"

Chris's lips thinned. John got the impression he'd said the wrong thing.

"Sorry, I—I don't know what this means," he said hastily.

"It means," Chris said in a tight tone, "that if we were to finish dinner and go back to your place for coffee and mints and started to do what people *actually* do when they say your place for coffee and mints, I'd take off all my clothes, and you'd think you'd brought a girl home."

John frowned. "As in..."

"As in, equipment. Plumbing. Biology. However you want to put it."

"Uh. No offence, but...you have a five o'clock shadow, and I have never in my life heard a woman with a voice like yours."

A wan smile crossed Chris's features. His masculine ones. John was seriously struggling with the information. No way was this guy...well, not a guy. It wasn't possible. Was it?

"That's the hormone therapy for you."

"Does it, uh. Change other stuff too? Because—you're wearing a dress shirt. You don't exactly have, um. A chest under there."

"Oh, I do."

"You don't, I'm looking!"

"I do. I'm wearing a binder to make sure you *can't* look."

"So you're really..."

"Yes."

Silence.

Then John said, "Huh."

Chris waved a hand vaguely towards the door. "Look, just go."

"Go? Why?"

A frown crossed the pale forehead. "You're gay. You don't even get what I'm saying."

"I think you're saying that you've had shit luck with dating," John said.

"What?"

"Look, Chris, I'm floored, okay. I am. And I don't know the first thing about what it must be like to be you, but right now, I'm sitting opposite a man that I am incredibly attracted to, and more than just in terms of 'oh, hey, I bet he has a nice dick.'"

Chris spluttered with startled laughter.

"I mean—yeah, okay, I guess I was assuming you have a nice one, but...I didn't exactly look at you and think you were gorgeous because you had a cock."

"Um. Good to know."

"So—yeah, I'm pretty stunned right now, but you're still bloody beautiful. I've never...been with a woman, so I don't know physically what's going to happen there. But I want to find out anyway. And I want all the other stuff first, sex is just—nice, but it's the dessert, you know? It's the main course I'm after."

"Which is?"

"For this date, or for all the other ones?"

"Both?"

"For all of them, I want to find out if I'm right."

"About what?"

"I told my sister there might be something special here. That there might be something really good about to unfold in front of me and change the fact that the last year has basically sucked. And I could do with something special, and I want to find out if I'm right and you are that something."

A soft smile was toying at the edge of Chris's mouth.

"And for *this* date?"

John smiled and dared to reach out and catch a hand again.

"More than anything tonight," he murmured, "is that I want to be really, *really* cheesy, and take you home at the end of the evening, and kiss you under a streetlight in the snow."

Chris—

Laughed. Gasped. Sighed. All at once. It was an explosive sort of noise, but his fingers tightened around John's, and he ducked his head before the laugh won out, and then the anxiety was all washed away, and John beamed at the return of the man he'd picked up in the car earlier.

"Thank you," Chris said finally.

"So, do I get to?"

"What?"

"Kiss you under a streetlight?"

Chris laughed again, the final pinches smoothing out of his face. He looked wonderful. Whoever he was under the shirt and tight jeans, he looked utterly wonderful, and John wanted to hang the streetlight idea and kiss him right now.

"Maybe," came the reply. "But I did say it would take more than a menu and a glass of water to persuade me to put out."

"Kissing isn't putting out!"

"Maybe not for *you*."

John laughed and sat back as the main course arrived.

"Fine," he said over the descending plates. "Two more courses. I'll persuade you."

Chapter Six

IT WAS SNOWING lightly when they finally left the restaurant.

It was also far later than John had expected, and the car was frozen shut like a tomb under a thick layer of white. Chris laughed—his breath curling white smoke into the air as John struggled with the doors—and proclaimed him to be a valiant knight in shining suit-jacket when he finally succeeded.

"Next time, I'll come and pick you up on a horse, then," John said as he held the door.

"Mm, never come on a horse before..."

John closed the door a fraction too hard. Jesus. He'd been half-hard all the way through dinner, just from the play of candlelight off Chris's skin and the way he dragged a fork through his lips when eating chocolate cake. He didn't need Chris upping the ante now.

"You're going to be the death of me," he complained when he got into the driver's seat.

"Only a little death."

"Eh?"

"Little death? It's what the French call an orgasm."

"Oh, fu—um. Bugger me—"

"With pleasure."

John choked. The car choked too, the engine catching for a split second as if in agreement with him before finally turning over. Chilly air washed out of the heater and then began to warm.

"Just so we're clear," John croaked hoarsely, "I'm not actually going to, uh. You know. Tonight."

"What? Drive me home? You better."

"No, uh…"

"Kiss me?"

John inadvertently licked his lips.

"No, I'd like to do that—"

"Ah, I see. You're not going to bend me over your car bonnet and—"

"That. No."

Chris's hand crept over his thigh, and John jumped violently as it squeezed. *Christ.* He had to take a deep breath as his cock swelled, and fist his hands on the steering wheel to avoid hanging his principles, turning on Chris then and there, and screwing him like a cheap hooker in the passenger seat.

"I'm only joking," Chris said, his voice suddenly softer. "I don't quite know you well enough to drop my jeans and let you, but…I'd like you to. Soon."

John swallowed thickly.

"I, uh. I'd—like to. As well," he mumbled, and the hand squeezed once more—tight, hot, ridiculously erotic—before it retreated.

"Are you always this shy?"

The question was gentle, rather than teasing, and John exhaled as he wrenched the car into reverse and inched out of the space.

"My last relationship didn't end well," he said, carefully vague. "I guess I'm a bit gun-shy. And you're kind of…intimidating."

"Me? Excuse me, who was saying he's six foot eight and built like a brick shi—"

"I'm just a big ugly mug," John said. "You're stunning."

He said it perfectly flat and factually, yet Chris instantly blushed a violent red and spluttered.

"You are!"

"Oh, give over."

"You could be a model," John said. "And you're brilliant. Just—brilliant. So, yeah, I'm slightly intimidated, and I don't want to mess up."

"How would having sex with me be messing up?"

John flexed his fingers on the wheel as he peeled out of the car park and onto the quiet road.

"In itself, it wouldn't be," he said. "Like I said. I want to. You're incredible, and I've been...um...distracted every time I've met up with you."

"Oh, aye?"

"Hands off," John said when he spied one heading his way over the handbrake out of the corner of his eye.

"Spoilsport."

The hand retreated. John blew out a heavy breath.

"I'm good at sex," he said finally.

"Now you're just teasing."

"No, listen. I've always been good at it. It comes naturally to me, and I get off on pleasuring my partner. I could—" Oh, sod it, he was already hard. "I could go down on you and eat you out for hours and never once need you to touch me in return. I'd get just as much buzz out of it as—as being inside you."

Chris said nothing.

"But my ex was basically only with me for sex. I thought it was the real deal, turns out he just....wanted to get off. So I'm...wary."

"You want more," Chris said.

"Yeah."

"Good."

John bit his lip.

"But I still think it's unfair you just volunteered to eat me out for hours and we're not pulling over."

The tension popped. John barked a laugh, knuckles going white on the steering wheel with the effort of keeping the car under control while he cackled. When he finally snorted and subsided, Chris was smirking, more smug than any cat with any cream.

"Maybe another time."

"Promise?"

John laughed. "Promise."

"So why are you so good at sex? Have you slept with half of Sheffield or something?"

"Not really," John said as he overtook a bus struggling on the snow. "I just am. Always have been. And I'm the physical type. I like to touch."

"Touch?"

"You know. Hug, hold hands, kiss..."

"Fuck."

"Make love."

"*No*," Chris groaned.

"What?"

"No. No making love."

"It *is* making love!"

"Jesus, you sound like a pre-teen girl. Or my *mum*."

"Tough," John said, laughing. "Sleeping with you would be special, not a fuck."

"It would be a fuck."

"Nope."

"A dirty, seedy, filthy screw."

"No."

"Shagging."

"Nope."

"Boning."

"Oh, God."

"The horizontal tango."

"Are you serious?"

"The beast with two backs."

"Oh my God..."

"Beating it."

"Definitely not."

"Spanking the—"

"I will extend," John interrupted loudly, voice hoarse from laughing too hard, "to sleeping with you. And having sex."

"No making love?"

"I can make love if I want."

"Not to *this* body, you can't."

"No?"

"No. You can do any of the things I said."

"No way."

"Or you can have sex with it."

"Sleep with?"

Chris whined. He sounded like a sulky teenager all of a sudden, and it set John off into another fit of laughter.

"*Fine*. Christ. But if you *ever* say you're making love again in my presence, I'll be gone so fast you won't know what hit you."

"What's so offensive about making love?"

"It's revolting, that's what."

John grinned as he turned into the wide road on which Chris's parents lived and began to slow. "Bet I could change your mind."

"Bet you can't."

"Another time, then. We're here."

"Oh." John swore Chris sounded disappointed, and the humour drained away to leave his rapidly beating heart. "One last chance for that pulling over?"

"Mm, maybe another time," John said and got out. He heard Chris sigh gustily behind him and grinned like an idiot.

Jesus, how long had it been since he'd just *laughed* with a date like this?

"And here you are," John said, opening the passenger door and helping Chris out. The snow was even heavier here than it had been at the restaurant, and flakes settled serenely in Chris's dark curls, white flecks in inky blackness. "Safely home."

"Thank you," Chris said and held on when John tried to let go of his hand. "I had a great time."

"Me too."

"Despite the talk."

"Didn't matter," John said, stroking a curl out of Chris's eyes. "Still want to see you again."

"Yeah?"

"Yeah."

"It's the Whirlow Hall Farm Fair next weekend. Do you want to come with me?"

John had no idea what that was. But: "Yes."

Chris's smile widened. "That'd be our third date."

"Yes?"

"So...I'm thinking that you're a bit traditional, and it's only the second date."

"I have no idea where you're going with this—"

"The third date rule? Kiss me or give me the 'let's be friends' talk?"

John glanced down at Chris's mouth. Flushed pink lips against cold, pale skin. There was a snowflake melting at the very corner of them. He would taste of bitter coffee and the After Eight mints.

John's throat went dry.

And Chris was stretching up. Leaning in.

His words were a soft caress of warm air against John's mouth.

"Or can I hope for a little rule breaking?"

John kissed him.

It was supposed to be chaste. Sweet. Romantic. Supposed to be something tender and gentle, to reel this stunning, sarcastic man in and capture his attention until the next time.

Only it wasn't.

Chris's lips parted beneath his. There was a hand gripping the back of John's neck. John could taste that bitter coffee and After Eights. The car rocked as Chris's back hit it. The top of his leg was slender where it met his arse, and John spread his fingers wide to grip the cheek firmly in one palm and squeeze. His thigh was between Chris's knees. Those dark curls were soft and sensual around his fist.

And he was hard as a rock.

The realisation made John pause, and he pulled back. Barely enough to breathe. Chris followed, his teeth biting into the corner of John's mouth. He was sex personified. It was so tempting, would be so wonderful, so *easy*—

"Oh, you *are* pleased to see me," Chris whispered.

John heard his own laugh as though from very far away. As if it belonged to someone else. Quiet. Raw. A little bit jagged around the edges.

"I get it," Chris whispered.

His voice was hypnotic. Soft. So very gentle, like the fingers that caressed the shell of John's ear.

"You don't want to be used. And you're worried that's what'll happen. But you don't know what's going through my head right now."

John closed his eyes. "So tell me."

"There's this guy."

It was like listening to a story.

"He's got a voice like whiskey, burning a trail down your throat. He's enormous and can crush you into the side of a parked car when he kisses you. Your feet leave the floor when he does that, and you're helpless. It's like being branded when he touches you. You can feel his hands forever, and you don't want them to let go. And that's before you even get your clothes off. He's huge, and you're out of your depth."

John swallowed thickly.

"And yet, he fumbles over his words. He touches your hands between coffee mugs like they're something incredible, and he's scared they're not real. You can't see him staring, but you know he is. His voice isn't just sexy, but soothing too. And there's something desperate to please, but when you manage to sweep that away and he relaxes for a moment, he's got the most amazing laugh you've ever heard."

John's breath caught.

"And you make him laugh."

John licked his lips.

"And—"

Chris's mouth touched the very edge of his own. So soft, it was barely there at all. The merest whisper of sensation.

And John felt the words, more than he heard them.

"—for the very first time, you feel beautiful."

John sealed his mouth over the words and drank them away. Slid his hands up a long, slim back, to anchor between jacket-clad shoulder blades and press all that brilliance as close as he possibly could.

He could taste coffee. There was snow down the back of his collar. Someone else's hair was tickling his forehead.

And none of it mattered.

Chapter Seven

"WHA' THA FUCK is up wi' you?"

"What?" John asked, thunking his toolkit down on the bare floorboards by Rhodri's knee and grinning. "It's a nice morning, I've been to the gym, pumped and buzzing, and this renovation is easy money without any of the faking it macho bollocks you get down the firm. What's wrong with that?"

"It's bloody nine o'clock, and yer a grumpy fucker before noon and yer knows it."

John pulled a face.

"Frankly, yer look like yer've had a good shag."

Okay, *mostly* without the faking it macho bollocks. John knew for a fact that Rhodri was gaga for his missus, Amy, but he gave it the usual about the ball and chain and not getting enough the same as any of the other lads.

"So, come on, then, who was she?"

Ye-eah. She.

"Nobody."

"Bollocks."

John cracked a smile and cracked open his toolbox at the same time. "It were just the one date," he lied.

"Also bollocks. Come on. Tall, blonde, big tits?"

"Tall, dark, killer smile," John corrected, and Rhodri crowed.

"Knew it. You dirty fucker."

"If I were, I'd have had that shag," John countered.

"You mean you didn't?"

"It was a *date*. I took her out to dinner. Classy. No shagging."

"Shaggin' is perfectly farking classy," Rhodri chortled. "You need to get yer act together, Johnny-boy. Been avoidin' the game too long after your Danielle."

John winced. Yeah. 'Danielle.' Rhodri knew some stuff—like how 'Ally' had been the closest John had ever come to 'the one,' how 'Leanne' had been little more than his first fumble and entirely down to teenage lust, and how 'Danielle' had totally and utterly screwed him over. And just like before—

"She's called Chris." John let the lie ride.

"Another Chrissie or the same Chrissie?"

"Another one."

"Got a thing, you have!" It came out more like *gorratheen*, around the edge of the cigarette Rhodri shoved in his mouth. "Got a light?" *Gorralite*. John rolled his eyes and rummaged for one. He didn't even smoke.

"Not meant to smoke indoors."

"Naff off, don't count if the windows are out."

"They're not out."

"Will be Friday, Gaz is coming up wi' the sprogs fer the weekend."

"Looking forward to it?"

"Nah, gets Amy broody every farking time."

"Thought you wanted a footie team?"

"Not all at once!"

John laughed, but too soon, because Rhodri fixed him with a scowl over the cigarette smoke.

"What about you, yer shyster? Been enough farking about, en't there? You going to be settling dahn wi' this new Chrissie, then?"

John couldn't deny the jump his heart made at the idea—settling down with Chris would be nothing short of a dream—but he wasn't thick. A couple of dates didn't make a long-term relationship. They'd only kissed once. It was that new date thrill.

So he said, "God knows, Rhod, give me a chance! It's only been a couple of dates..."

"Mebbe, but I know you, Johnno. Fall hard, fall fast, that's yer trick."

John shrugged. "Well, she's smarter than me."

"Yer too bloody cagey for yer own good," Rhodri grumbled. John's gut tightened at the complaint, and he ruefully thought Rhodri didn't know the half of it. About to tell some off-colour joke and mollify him, John was waylaid by his phone suddenly ringing. He staggered to his feet and retreated to the hall to fumble it out of his pocket and answer without checking the caller ID.

So it was a pleasant shock when Chris's warm voice said, "Hey."

"Holy—hey!" John found himself grinning ear to ear. "Hey, how are you?"

"I'm okay. I wanted to thank you for dinner last night."

"Well, thank you for agreeing to come," John returned. "Anytime, seriously. I'd love to take you out again, if I didn't make too big an idiot of myself?"

Chris's laugh was deep and quiet

"No, I don't think kissing me until I can't remember my own name counts as making a fool of yourself..."

"You're seriously screwing with my resistance," John confessed quietly as his dick jumped at the tiny hint of a sex life. God, he had it bad.

"Good."

"It's not good," John countered. "You don't know me. Minute I make l—" He checked at the apparently disgustingly offensive phrase. "The minute I sleep with you, you'll never be able to get rid of me."

Something in the back of his mind cringed at the way it came out—and then Chris laughed, even lower and a little dirty.

"Maybe I don't want to. I know I suggested the fair on Saturday, but I sort of don't want to wait until then to see you."

John's throat dried.

"Uh—"

"You might have left me hanging a bit last night, and I might need a bit more of that kissing you were doing."

"Oh," John squeaked.

"Sorry if that's a bit too forward for your issues with your ex, but there it is."

"That's, um. No. That's—nice." More than. His brain wasn't convinced of the soundness of the idea, but his dick was straining. God, if Chris were here right now, there was no way John would be able to resist. "Something civilised? I'm only working this morning; we could get lunch somewhere. I could take you up to Fox House for pie and a pint? They have real fires in the hearths this time of year. I could book us a table right next to the hearth if you like?"

It all rushed out in an embarrassing gush of words, and John had to bite his lip to shut up.

"That'd be nice." Chris spoke without a trace of hesitation, and John found himself actually curling his toes in his boots. Christ, he hadn't done that since going out with Aljaz.

"So, do I pick you up from your parents' again, or—"

"Or. I'm in town. Can you get me from the library at one?"

"Yep." God, that was only three hours away. "I've got the work van, though, so you might get a bit dusty."

"It's fine. I'm not wearing anything nice."

"If it's on you, it's nice."

"Really, John?"

John winced at his cheesy line and protested his innocence before hanging up—thankfully before a *love you* could escape. Too soon.

"So when's the farking wedding?" Rhodri shouted from the next room.

"Piss off," John said halfheartedly as he wandered back, already searching for the pub's phone number. "Got to book a table."

"That were some right sappy shite." Rhodri scoffed, flicking fag ash on the floor. "Yer'll be farking drinking poncy wine next. Yer sure it's Chrissie, not summat right fancy?"

"Sod off, mate. I was at your bloody wedding, wasn't me who was calling the sausage rolls vol-au-vonts."

"Fark off with yer volly-vonts, yer can't even *say* it!"

John flipped him off and rang the pub.

After, as they stripped the burned and crumbling plaster away to find the ruined wiring—probably responsible for the fire that had gutted the room in the first place—Rhodri stubbed the fag out and somewhat less abrasively said, "Yer should hang on to this one, mind."

"What?"

"Yer've been a miserable twat since that bitch Danielle. 'Bout time you found somebody else. Classy bird that won't shag a munter like you on the first date—that's worth hangin' onto."

"Cheers. I think."

"Naff off."

But John appreciated the sentiment all the same.

And who knew? He curled his toes in his boots again. There was something here. Chris liked him—a lot, judging by last night's words and this morning's call. Maybe all John had to do was...not screw up.

And if he never gave Chris reason to think like Daniel had, then this could be perfect.

He just had to be perfect.

IT WAS STARTING to rain lightly when John pulled up outside the library. Chris was standing on the steps, sheltering under the overhang, and John had no idea how to guide him to the van by shouting, so got out and jogged towards him.

"Hey," he said, a little awkwardly, and touched Chris's arm.

The smile that spread on that narrow face was like the sun coming out. "Hey." And then fingers closed in his sleeve, a free hand walked up his arm, to shoulder, to face, and John was being kissed in the rain like something out of a romantic comedy.

And just like in the movies, he stopped noticing the rain. Time slowed to a crawl. It was little more than a chaste press of lips, yet John's entire being flexed and refocused, like a lens pulling a blurry image into crystal clarity. The lip ring was cool against his mouth. His arms caught about Chris's waist. He straightened. The drag of Chris's arms about his neck was as if his soul had been tethered, and John gathered all the warmth, never wanting to let go.

Chris pulled back with a low laugh and whispered, "You've literally swept me off my feet," into his ear.

John grinned. "Could carry you to the car, if you want."

"Mm, no thank you. Down, please."

Chris weighed nothing—but then, one of John's biceps was about the same size as Chris's thigh. John let go, relishing the feel of Chris sliding down the front of his body for a moment.

Only, Chris didn't let go of his neck.

"Could you carry me around? In theory?"

"Yeah. Easy."

"Really?"

"Uh, *yeah.*"

"Fuck." The curse was soft and tiny, and Chris's top teeth released his bottom lip in a motion that had John's pulse picking up. "So—so we don't have to *do* anything, but...do you want to maybe move this lunch plan to my flat instead?"

"Y-your flat?"

"Mm."

"Uh..."

Yes. *God,* yes. But was that really a good idea? The only reason John wasn't pressing Chris into the brickwork and tonguing him open right now was the clutch of old ladies shuffling their way down the disabled ramp into the rain, clutching their borrowed bodice-ripper novels.

Like hell they wouldn't do anything.

"Why?" he croaked.

"I make an amazing homemade pizza. And..." Fingers trailed down the side of John's neck lightly, and a hand ended up resting on his chest. "...I don't mind if you're not ready for more, but I'd like to at least progress to a little making out on the sofa."

John cleared his throat and lowered his voice.

"There—there is no way," he whispered, "that I'll be able to make out with you on a sofa and not...go further."

Chris's face lit up in a wide, filthy grin.

"Well," he breathed, "if you want to, and I want to, what's the problem?"

John's brain stalled.

Because he was six-foot-eight and had lifted Chris off his feet to kiss him without even noticing. Because he could pick him up with one arm. Because it had been so easy for everyone to believe what Daniel had said about him.

And because Daniel had been this six-foot athlete, a jiu jitsu instructor and a marathon runner, and people had still believed him. And Chris—Chris was—

Not.

"I really, really want to," John whispered, so close to Chris's mouth he could feel the swell of Chris's kiss-flushed lips when he spoke. "God, I do. But—"

But?

But?

"Third date first," John said.

Chris pinched the back of his neck, then slid his arms down John's arms and took one of his hands. His fingers were long and narrow and clutched about John's great paw like a vice.

"You're such a traditionalist," he accused, but the wide smile hadn't dimmed. "Okay. Third date. Which is this pub lunch, and you know the rules of the third date."

John laughed, a sharp stab of relief puncturing the balloon of anxiety in his chest.

"Yeah. I got it. I'll kiss you after like your life depends on it."

"Better be the way you kissed me the first time."

"How do you m—"

"I like a good grabbing."

Chapter Eight

CHRIS STRETCHED OUT in the chair by the fire like a basking cat after a good meal. John told him about how he'd come out—or rather, how Mum had marched into his bedroom when he was fourteen years old, slammed a pile of wank mags down on the end of the bed, and started lecturing him about always using a condom, and all John had wanted to do at fourteen was play basketball and beat his sister's high scores on all her favourite games to spite her. And then they were leaving, and John opened the passenger door, but Chris reached out and closed it again. Leaned against the car.

And waited.

John's breath caught in his chest.

He wanted to crack a joke, or ask permission. He wanted to crowd into Chris's space, slow and sensual, like he had on the library steps. He wanted to kiss him like that romantic comedy moment again, even though it wasn't raining anymore.

But the most incredible man in the world was standing by John's van, his dark curls wild in the wind, and his eyes blazing. And he wanted John. *Wanted* him, in every physical sense of the word.

And Christ, but John wanted him back.

His strength wavered as he reached out—

And held, barely, as John slid both hands into that wild hair, tipping its owner's head back, and kissed the open mouth with everything he had.

Chris whimpered against his lips, but before John could question it, he felt the tight clutch of fingers at the back of his coat. Hips slid up against his own. His tongue was nipped and then chased back into his mouth. An arm found his shoulders, and the extra weight was too much strain on John's neck.

That was when his resistance failed. He dropped both hands to seize Chris's perfect arse like he owned it. The sudden motion, the way Chris gasped and bucked in his hands—*God*, it was too much. John tore himself free from the kiss and lifted. Lifted until legs locked about his waist, lifted until his mouth found that long, perfect, unmarred neck—

And marred it.

"Fuck!"

The cry was breathless. Loud. Laughing. Fingers caught in John's hair and pulled him back when he tried to let go. John obliged. God, that body. That laughter. The hitch of Chris's chest under his when he bit down a second time. The way Chris shuddered when John tightened his grip around those slender thighs and perfect bum. John *wanted*, wanted so badly that his caution dissolved, and the next thing he knew was a sharp pain in his scalp as Chris prised his face away and caught his mouth in a kiss that was full of teeth and warning.

"We're getting indece—"

John sucked the last word clean out of Chris's mouth.

And then rested his nose against Chris's cheek to breathe. Hard.

"I changed my mind," Chris said breathlessly. "Yours. Take me back to yours. I want to be flat on my back in your bed and surrounded by the smell of you."

God.

God.

He had one hand down the back of Chris's jeans. Cotton briefs were soft against his palm, but the heat of smooth skin beneath them was searing. He squeezed lightly, and Chris's hand tightened in his hair again.

"Oh, God."

"I want you," John breathed.

"I can tell," Chris whispered. "Or is that an AK-47 you're digging into my leg?"

John was too far gone to so much as flinch. His hips rocked forward. Chris whimpered as he was driven slightly higher up the side of the van.

"Come back to mine," John blurted out.

He was blind with the need. All he knew was that swell of hot skin under the cotton. He wanted to sink his teeth into it, lick it, touch it, pinch it—

"Are you even fit to drive?"

Oh. "No. Christ. Um. Give me—give me a minute—"

"I'll help."

"W-what?"

"I'll help. Let me down."

John struggled. He had to force his arms to unlock from under Chris's thighs. Found himself following Chris down a little, every instinct desperate to keep his mouth right there on that incredible face.

Then buried it in that wild hair instead, when he felt fingers tugging at his fly.

"Oh, *God*—"

A hand inside his jeans. Hot and firm and so sure of itself. He should stop it. He should—he should—

He did nothing.

He simply pressed his face into Chris's hair, his body into Chris's front, and let the raw lust wash over him. Just let it. Without any of the guilt, the fear, the shame, that had shadowed every climax since the day Daniel had told the very first lie. Since the day the police had come round, the bottom had dropped out of the world, and John had started falling.

John was falling again.

But Chris's hands were there, and Chris's mouth found his once more, and maybe falling wasn't so bad. Not like this.

JOHN HAULED ON the handbrake and licked his lips nervously.

"I—I can take you home if you've changed your mind."

Chris was lounging in his passenger seat like he belonged in a grubby white work van as much as John did.

"Is that a hint that you don't want me to come over after all," he asked, "or you trying to give me a way out?"

"It's just that—"

"The truth, John."

The reprimand was soft, but it cut through Daniel's shadow.

"The second one."

"I don't want a way out," Chris said. "I want you to grab me like that all over again."

John's dick—still tired from the sudden shock of orgasm in the pub car park—twitched again. Holy hell.

"I told you," Chris said softly, his fingers tangling in the release catch on the door. "I like a good grabbing. And I didn't know I liked someone paying so much attention to my bum, so—want to try that again?"

Oh, *God,* yes.

The anxiety was choking him as he led Chris through the communal doors and up the stairs to the flat, the cane clacking calmly all the way. Chris looked as debauched as John felt. His hair was wilder than ever, his lips swollen, a purple love-bite clear as paint on his neck, and— John coughed as he fumbled for his keys.

"Uh. I've, uh. Sorry."

"What?"

"I've, um. Stained your—your jeans."

Chris bit his lip, but the smile tugged it free again.

"Well, then. I'll have to wash them here and walk around without them on."

"If you do that"—John unlocked the door and showed Chris inside—"then you won't be doing much walking around."

"Oh, good," Chris said—and dropped his jeans.

"Jesus!"

Oh, dear God.

Wow.

John stood stock-still in the open doorway and stared. Chris stepped neatly out the pile of denim on the floor, and then he was standing there only in his jacket and briefs. And those *endless* legs.

Chris was only short by comparison to John's Miracle-Gro proportions. In truth, he stood a foot shorter than John—and it was all down to those legs. Miles of alabaster skin, curving muscle, and hard edges. A tiny stretch mark disappearing into the bottom of his boxer briefs. A soft bulge inside them said he'd had the surgery. A soft hollow on the inside of each knee, where the hair didn't grow. John knew from many hours with many men that the skin there would smell of warmth and humanity and *Chris.*

John shut the door.

Pushed Chris back against the hall wall with gentle hands.

Sank to kneel in front of him.

Cupped the tops of both calves—rock hard, like a cyclist's—in his palms, and chose the first spot.

That little hollow on the inside of his left knee.

John sealed his mouth about it and *sucked*.

"Oh."

Chris's knees shivered. His hands fisted in John's hair. When John glanced up, his back had arched, and he strained up against the wall, mouth askew and eyes half-lidded. He looked like a man receiving the best head of his life.

John kissed the spot and sucked its twin on the right knee until a matching pink mark blossomed on the pale skin, hot and almost heart-shaped. He grazed his nose against wiry dark hair and moved up those slim legs with mouth and firm, supporting hands. Sucked at the soft swells of inner thighs. Scraped shallow bites along the hard edges of muscle at the outer. He took the stretch mark between his teeth and worried at it gently, nose pressing into the dark grey cotton of Chris's underwear and inhaling the deepest, basest scent of him. Above him, Chris's breath was a harsh rasp. Shaking fingers settled in his hair, and thighs shuddered under John's hands.

But John had misjudged. When he lifted one hand to cup the soft bulge in Chris's pants, he knew its texture and shift immediately to be off. So he'd not had the surgery.

John had never done this with a—

He amended the thought. He'd only sucked cock before.

Time to learn some new tricks, then. He sank his teeth into the soft sweep of flawless abdomen below Chris's bellybutton, took the cotton in both hands, and tore it effortlessly to the floor. Something thumped hard on the carpet and rolled.

"J-John—"

John pressed his nose into the wiry hair and breathed in deep, massaging that perfect arse in both hands. Chris whined. He was shaking almost violently in John's hands, and John could feel the tiny, self-aborted thrusts as clear as though the hips in his hands had belonged to his own body.

And yet his name was said again. High. Thin. Uneasy.

"Do you want me to stop?" John asked softly, glancing up.

Chris shook his head.

"You sure, babe?"

The endearment slipped out of its own accord. Chris huffed a little.

"Floor. Please. Do me on the floor."

John laughed and dragged Chris down the wall without hesitation. Twisted both of them to the side. Spread those mile-long legs on the floor and sucked on an exposed jut of hip before returning to his place, settling his weight firmly over Chris's legs.

He'd never done this before.

And he was going to explore *exactly* how this all worked.

"Tell me what you like," he breathed, kissing the bite-bruised stretch mark. "Tell the whole *building* what you like. I want—I want to give you a whole new level of pleasure. Okay?"

"O-Okay."

John kissed the stretch mark one last time—then focused.

And learned.

God, did he learn.

When he licked at every inch of hot, wet skin he could find, Chris lay gasping and shivering under him. When John wrapped his lips about the head of his swollen clit, the gasps turned to stuttering whimpers and disjointed words. When he created a rhythm—a deep, hard massage of the perfect arse still cupped in his hands, rocking it up into hard, almost brutal sucks—the words turned into only one word, repeated again and again.

Please.

The abandon was intoxicating. The scrabble of fingers on the carpet like claws. The way Chris thrust up into his lips. The way he moaned and whimpered. The desperate, shameless abandon of that sharp wit, brilliant mind, the *trust*—

The trust.

Oh, God, that trust.

That he'd dissolved in John's hands, let John of all people see this, smell it, hear it—

Feel it.

He slipped his hands lower, to push Chris's thighs up and expose him a little more. John had never tasted this before, and he dragged his tongue against Chris's lips. He tasted oddly sweet. The whimpers eased into breaths again—displeased. John returned his mouth to its former home and spread the sweetness on his fingers instead, stroking and exploring until he found the source.

Gently, he pushed.

Chris tensed immediately, and the tightness made the truth obvious. This was new for both of them. John coaxed a little relaxation with his mouth, and when the breathy sighs started up again, began to gently rock his index finger against that slickness, massaging rather than truly penetrating.

But what would it feel like—

This would be like no climax John had ever caused before. And he needed to know, suddenly. A fierce, almost primal, urgency demanded that knowledge. What would it be like, to be buried deep inside when Chris reached the peak? What would it feel like, look like, sound like, *taste* like, even? Could John do that? Could he do all of it, again and again and again, until Chris was utterly spent?

He redoubled his efforts. Sucked hard, until a groan turned into a yell and a hand fisted in his hair, forcing him down harder until he could suck on it like any cock he'd ever had.

"More."

Chris only said it once.

But once was enough.

John pushed.

His finger slipped into slick heat, dizzyingly tight and searingly hot. When he crooked the knuckle and stroked that fascinating softness inside, Chris's words disappeared entirely. A silent reel of pleasure that John felt radiating through damp skin and clutching hands.

Now.

It had to be now.

So John slid his hand beneath the debauched body below him. Found a cheek. Cupped the soft warmth of it. Firm. Sure.

And did three things, all at once.

Sucked.

Squeezed.

And stroked.

And the peak was like nothing he had ever known.

Chapter Nine

JOHN HARDLY DARED to breathe.

He certainly didn't dare to move. Simply breathing seemed an act of sacrilege, as every inhale made Chris's head and hand rise, and every exhale made them fall.

The world could have ended, right then and there, and John would not have made a move to stop it.

They had retreated to John's bedroom after that mind-blowing mess on the floor. Turned out, Chris was a sleeper after sex—they had exchanged some lazy kisses, and then he had simply tucked his head against John's neck and more or less passed out.

And John hadn't moved a muscle since.

He was still fully dressed, bar his open jeans and soft cock hanging free. He had jerked off to the intense beauty of Chris in the afterglow, and then Chris had destroyed him by sucking the mess off John's fingers.

Chris, by contrast, was still entirely naked from the waist down. One bare thigh was resting between John's legs, pressing lightly up against his balls. It left his legs so temptingly open, and John's hand was resting almost possessively on that ridiculously perfect arse. John was daring to hope, once Chris woke up, that he'd be allowed to play down there again.

But it wasn't the position that had reduced John to this frozen, barely breathing statue.

It was the gentle wash of breath against his neck.

Chris's breathing.

Chris, half on top of him and half-naked, and fast asleep.

The trust was almost as incredible as the way he looked when he came. His hand was bunched into a fist, the fingers curled about the neck of John's T-shirt. John had no idea where the other arm had gone. His curls tickled.

And John felt on top of the world.

All his hesitations, all Daniel's lies, seemed like they were a million miles away from this. As though they had never happened. Sure, he'd been grabby at the van—and then Chris had grabbed back, just as hard, and demanded more. There was no amount of mental gymnastics John could do to convince himself that Chris hadn't wanted every second. And a whole lot more seconds too. And maybe when he woke up, John would hand over some more seconds.

Or, he thought as he dared to carefully shift his arm and slide a single finger into Chris's loose fist and tease the hand flat again, maybe not. Because maybe then, Chris might start to think this was just sex, maybe start to handle it like what Daniel had obviously wanted John for—his cock and nothing else. Lying in the mess of his bed with this half-naked beauty draped over him, John found his thoughts straying so strangely away from sex.

And onto other things. Like the gentle fan of Chris's eyelashes, dark on his pale face. Like the soft clutch of his hand as it tightened again. Like the—

Bang.

"Ow!"

—smash of his fist into John's chin when the front door slammed.

"Whoa!" John yelped, and caught Chris's elbows before he could fall off the bed entirely. "Whoa, whoa, it's just me. Just me."

Chris blinked wildly—then relaxed as suddenly as he'd started.

"Shit," he said. "Shit, I'm sorry. I—I think I forgot where I was."

John rubbed his jaw with a wince—Chris could certainly throw a punch, that was for sure—but laughed quietly anyway.

"No worries. I think my sister's home."

Sure enough: "John! D'you want dinner?"

"I'll sort my own!" John bellowed back, and Chris chuckled, shifting on his knees, and—

"What kind of dinner?" he asked.

—straddling John's denim-clad thigh.

"Uh."

Chris was very warm and very wet.

"Um," John said as Chris slid a little closer and began to kiss his neck. "I'm easy."

"Mm, good."

Chris's mouth found his jugular, and John decided food-food could wait. He slid both palms around to that gorgeous bum and gripped it, dragging Chris as close as possible. Chris laughed, shed his coat, and pushed at John's.

"I want to feel those biceps properly."

"Yeah?"

"Mhmm..."

John managed to shuck off the coat without disturbing the sensual ride of the half-naked guy on his leg, and then found his mouth caught in eager teeth. The way Chris sucked on his tongue went straight to John's cock. Hot, wet, and so damn *intense*. Both of Chris's hands were wound into his hair, his entire body rubbing against John's front, and it left John with a thousand possibilities, all more incredible than the last.

And John had no idea which one to choose.

That long back was trapped in a T-shirt and an undervest, but Chris refused to be separated from his assault on John's tongue. His tightness from earlier said making love wasn't going to be mutually enjoyable. And John was so hard, just from that wet patch Chris was leaving on his jeans, that he wouldn't last long enough to *make* it possible.

Focus.

He needed to focus.

He wanted to watch, this time, and there was no way he'd be watching if Chris got off first. So—

He shifted the weight in his lap until Chris's gentle rocking brushed his cock too. Until John could trap his aching dick between hand and hip, and crudely, rudely use Chris's own sinuous motion to rub himself off. John tore his mouth away to watch and stared. At the ripple of muscle in lean thighs. At the shift of hips under alabaster skin. At the gleam of sweat and sex under the shadowed curls of hair.

Chris bent forward again, and his teeth sank into the lobe of John's ear.

And he *sucked*.

John grunted as he came. The sudden rush of fluid coated his fingers. His vision shivered—and then, when it cleared, he smoothed the slick mess over both hands and began to paint with it. Smoothed it into skin and hair. Buried a hand into the wet heat between Chris's thighs and massaged it with his own pleasure.

And Chris shivered.

Just froze in place for a split second, and shivered.

John bit his shoulder and moulded them together until Chris was high on his knees, and his messy desire rubbed against John's belt. Until John could cup his arse in one hand, and hold him tight, and finger him with the other. Rub his thumb across violent heat and gently breach that wet warmth with another.

"Oh, fuck. Fuck-fuck-fuck!" A hoarse whisper and nothing more. The slow, sensual motion shivered, then sped up. Chris rode John's fingers like he was born to do it, and John looked up.

Only just in time to see his features seize, and then—

That long body twisted. Shook. Shuddered in his arms in silent ecstasy.

And *relaxed.*

John caught the breathy sigh with his mouth and squeezed one thigh with his hot hand.

"Beautiful," he whispered when he let go.

Chris's only reply was a whimper when John lightly touched his clit again.

"God, you're so beautiful."

"I want—"

"Anything," John promised rashly, still caught by the sheer, mad brilliance of him. How could simply touching him to completion have John so spellbound? It was little more than a handjob. Barely even that—it was obvious Chris would have climaxed on his own, with or without John's help.

But would it have been quite so incredible?

"M'not ready yet," Chris murmured, catching John's head in both hands and kissing him fiercely, like they were drunk. "Not ready. But I want you to fuck me."

John's brain tried to change gears without a clutch and stalled.

"Uhhh."

"Feeling you inside me is fucking incredible, and I want more of it. All of it. And I'm not ready yet, but you're going to help me get ready soon. Right?"

"Oh my God, right."

Chris laughed quietly, then—and quite suddenly—slid sideways off John's lap and crashed into the sheets and pillows with a thump. John laughed and leaned over to kiss him. He looked a complete mess in a rumpled T-shirt and his socks, only wearing the messy result of their sex between the two.

"You're gorgeous."

"Mm, thank you," Chris murmured, stroking his fingers over John's jaw.

Then his stomach rumbled, and he laughed, retracting them.

"I'm also starving. You wore me out."

"Dinner, then?"

"Your sister's out there!"

"And your clothes are in here. You can, uh, wipe off with a T-shirt if you want."

Getting dressed was not as orderly or simple as John would have liked. Chris stood by the bed, bold as brass, as he wiped off with one of John's old shirts. The sight of him made John want to do exactly what Chris wanted—to get inside him in every way possible. As it was, he was unable to resist snatching kisses, so it took an extreme amount of effort on John's part to step out of reach long enough to change out of his sex-soaked clothes and into something more suitable for a kitchen.

So long, in fact, that he heard the front door close before he ever managed to open the bedroom one.

"Ah," he said.

"What?"

"Nora's gone out again."

"I see."

"Do you—" John swallowed, throat suddenly dry. "God, stay the night. Please."

Chris's face twisted. "I'm sorry," he said. "Can't. Got a doctor's appointment in the morning, and I haven't got my medication here."

John bit back his disappointment. Chris must have heard it, though, as he stretched up on his toes to kiss John's cheek.

"Take me home via a takeaway and stopping in a lay-by for dinner and dessert," he whispered. "And next time you bring me over, I'll bring an overnight bag."

John let out a breath.

"Saturday is the farm fair, right?" he croaked.

"Uh-huh."

"Bring an overnight bag."

Chapter Ten

SATURDAY ARRIVED BRIGHT and icy cold.

Or maybe it just felt colder, as John was usually at rugby training or the gym on Saturday mornings, not trying to park his car in a mudbath of a field.

He'd never been to Whirlow Hall Farm. It was, shockingly enough, a farm, nestled into the Whirlow area of Sheffield. Whirlow was a bit too fancy for the likes of John, and he'd never so much as been to a farmer's market in a city centre before, never mind a Christmas version on an honest-to-God farm.

Apparently, he was the only one. It was only ten in the morning, but it was *heaving*.

To his surprise, nobody looked twice at the enormous bear walking up the muddy, single-track road from the field to the farm buildings. A couple of old ladies even asked him directions, and John realised that in his Timberland boots, hi-vis vest, and black hoodie, he must look like one of the farm hands. Ruefully, he imagined that the hoodie covering up even his neck tattoo probably helped matters.

Chris was waiting on a stone wall shy of the gate—and John paused on the corner, licking his lips nervously. *Bugger*.

He was waiting with someone.

It could have been worse. It could have been his mum or dad, but she was obviously a friend, a pretty black girl probably around Chris's age or even younger. She had a dog on a lead, which was snuffling eagerly at Chris's hands. But Daniel's legacy had left John a little nervous even of friends, and he had to shove his hands in his pockets to hide their sudden shake, and take a deep breath.

"Okay," he told himself. "Go."

She was just a friend. Just a friend.

"Chris!"

Chris's head turned, though his hand didn't pause in ruffling the dog's ears, and then he smiled when John called again.

"Hey," he said and lifted both hands almost like a kid asking to be picked up. John beamed, the rush of warmth erasing his anxiety, and stooped low to kiss him quickly.

"Sorry. Had to find somewhere to park we'd not need to swim to later."

The girl giggled, and John flashed her a nervous smile.

"I'm Gina," she said and held out a hand. "I'm one of Chris's college friends."

"John."

She shook his hand with a smile, then nudged the dog and introduced it as Lulu. John relaxed as he stooped to pet her. Dogs were easy. And people who kept dogs were easy. If the dog liked him—and most dogs liked John fine—then Gina wouldn't get twitchy either.

"I'll leave you lovebirds to it, then," she said, sliding down off the wall. "But by *eleven*, Chris, or there won't be any left."

"Any what?" John asked as she loped away up the track with the dog, disappearing into the throng heading for the top barn.

"Chutney," Chris said. "Her mum makes Caribbean-inspired jams and chutneys. They're *really* good. I always get Dad some, so she's saving me a few jars."

"And we have until eleven to pick them up?"

"Yep." Chris beamed up at him. "Can I get a proper kiss now?"

There were advantages to being bigger than a doorframe. John knew full well that he earned several displeased looks and sideways glances as he leaned down, cupped Chris's chin between finger and thumb, and kissed him until they both ran out of air. But like hell anyone was about to say anything within a hundred miles of him.

"Better," Chris murmured when John let go, and stood up from his perch. John found his hand and folded it up into the crook of John's elbow. "Thank you. I'm okay 'round here, but I'm slow. Ground's all uneven."

"That's fine," John said. "I've never been, so gives me the chance to look around a bit. I have to ask though. College?"

Chris laughed. "Oh, yeah."

"Please tell me I didn't go down on an eighteen-year-old in my flat..."

"Not quite."

"Not *quite*?"

"I'm twenty-four."

John coughed. Okay. Same age as Fran. That had always been John's rule—younger than his baby sisters was too weird for him—but, *Christ*, that was young.

"You've gone quiet. What's wrong with twenty-four?"

"Nothing. I'm just...a bit older than you."

"How much older?"

John blew out his cheeks. "Uh. Twelve years."

"Oh, that's fine."

John blinked. "Really?"

"Yeah."

"It's a bit of a gap..."

"My stepmum is fifteen years older than my dad; it's not that big."

John whistled.

"I don't mind if you don't," Chris said, squeezing his elbow. "Anyway, I'm not in college anymore. It was sixth form college. Gina and I were in the same French class."

"You speak French?"

"Oh, sure. *Voulez-vous couchez avec moi*, and all that."

"What?"

Chris stopped dead and stretched up on his toes. John bent to hear the whisper—and got his ear licked.

"Jesus!"

"It means, do you want to sleep with me?"

John coughed. "Uh. Well. You know. Maybe."

"Maybe?"

"Fine, yes."

Chris laughed and began to walk again. "Better. I don't speak French anymore though. I didn't even like it, and I never finished the course. But me and Gina stayed mates."

"That's nice," John said.

"What about you?"

"Dropped out at sixteen and got an apprenticeship with a builder's firm," John said, shrugging. "Been on construction sites and changing fuses for most of my life."

"I don't work. Can't. I used to help Gina's mum with the bottling sometimes, but she went off me when my voice dropped, and I had to start shaving."

"You what? Why?"

"She doesn't want me getting trans in the jam jars, I imagine."

John scowled. "Oh, for fu—God's sake."

"Fuck's sake," Chris corrected.

John rolled his eyes.

"Yeah, Trisha doesn't like me. That's why I always go and get the jars Gina's saved for me from the stall. She could bring them over anytime after work, but I always get them here because it drives Trisha nuts."

"Smearing your queer hands all over the jars?"

"Yep. Shame she doesn't know her daughter's a lesbian."

"Seriously?"

"Yep. That's how we made friends."

"What, because Gina's a lesbian?"

"She kept changing all the people in the textbooks into women so she could pull girls in French. And I kept changing them back so everyone would stop calling me a girl. It was chaos."

John laughed. "Oh, Christ. When I was in school, I gave another kid a handjob in the bike sheds. I didn't go rewriting the textbooks."

"Yeah, well, when you're not six hundred feet tall, passive-aggressive is the way to go." Chris tucked himself closer as an army of five-year-old choristers marched past in disturbingly tidy Brownies uniforms.

"So, basically, this Trisha woman doesn't want your hands all over the jars and giving people new genders or whatever, but there's lesbian all over them anyway?"

"Yep."

John licked his lips. He'd been lucky growing up. For all her faults, his mum had never batted an eyelash at his bringing home boys instead of girls, so he'd never really gotten into any hot water about it. Even his old-fashioned granddad had just grumbled that it was all this modern fast food and said nothing more about the matter. But he'd had boyfriends who'd not been so lucky. And by the sound of it, Chris and Gina hadn't totally missed the bigotry either.

"So," John said. "If I were to suddenly develop this really intense urge to kiss you, and we just so happened to be at this Trisha's stall…"

Chris snorted with laughter.

"…would it be unreasonable of me to put my hands in your back pockets and kiss you?"

"I think, given how busy the top barn is, and how big you are, it would be rude of you *not* to put your hands in my back pockets and shield me from all the other shoppers."

"My mum always raised me not to be rude."

"Good. Be polite right now, then."

John grinned and did as told. His hands found those back pockets—and, completely coincidentally, the perfect swell under them—and his lips found Chris's. Even when Chris's grin warped the kiss a little askew, it felt all the better for it.

"I could totally train you," Chris murmured against his mouth, and John laughed, breaking it off.

"You kidding? You could have me on the end of a lead if you chose."

"Mm, not my kink, but I'll bear it in mind. Come on. I can smell the hog roast, and I'm hungry."

Quite unexpectedly, John found himself enjoying the fair a little. The choir were crap, reminding him of Fran belting out her favourite carols with the same wild disregard for the actual tune or words, and both barns were crammed with stalls selling overpriced knick-knacks and weird food. It wasn't his thing at all.

And yet…

The Christmas decorations kept bouncing colour off Chris's face. He had a tendency to tuck himself against John's side to talk to people or touch the crafts. The look of rapture on his face as he twisted a leather cord with a metal charm hanging from it through his fingers was so intense that John silently bought it and tucked it into his own pocket for later. And when he initially decided against a pulled pork sandwich, saying he didn't want to make a mess, John promised to personally kiss him clean. He capitulated in such a painful mix of shy and sexy that John could have stayed all damn day at the market without a single extra bit of incentive but Chris's presence at his side.

Plus, there was an upside. Mum was into pointless ornaments and collected owls in particular. John found her a two-inch barn owl hand-carved out of wood, and a couple of bottles of craft ale for Dad, who was always moaning he couldn't get any decent beer in France. He even managed to find a pretty glass charm for Nan to hang in her kitchen window. So, it was three weeks until Christmas and he hadn't done any of his shopping yet, so what? He'd officially started now.

They stopped by Gina's mum's stall. Little cubes of bread were laid out, with taster pots of jam and chutney. John tried out a few, got a jar for Nora's sandwich-making boyfriend, and surreptitiously watched the heavyset stall owner frowning at Gina and Chris as they made their exchange—a too-tight, too-long hug for a carrier bag full of little jars.

Then Chris gestured in John's direction, frowning, and John grinned.

"Gotcha," he said, catching the hand. "Where to?"

"You need to check out the glass flowers," Gina said helpfully, pointing away to the very back of the barn. "They're gorgeous. Chris's mum would love one of the roses."

"Help me find a rose," Chris said, turning.

Turning right into John's front.

Well, it was crowded. And Gina's gay-hating mother was watching. And John couldn't possibly be rude, not on a third date and in public.

So he slid his hands smoothly into Chris's back pockets and leaned down to kiss him. The sweet traces of a thousand flavours of jam. Peach, somewhere in there. The coolness of that lip ring. The smirk that smoothed away to simple enjoyment—and the hand that caught at the back of his belt, firm and fierce.

God, John could have stood like that forever.

But he backed up, pressed their noses together lightly for a moment with his eyes closed to savour it, and turned them away towards the glassware stall.

"Is she scowling at us?" Chris whispered once the cane had pushed over ten metres or so of straw and rough ground.

John glanced back and grinned.

"Oh, yeah."

"Good. Bitch."

"Gina's giving me a look."

"What kind of look?"

John's stomach clenched. "A kind of...I don't know. Like she's trying to work me out."

"Oh, she's weighing you up."

Oh, crap.

"I didn't tell her until this morning," Chris said.

"And if she doesn't like me?" John said hesitantly.

"So what? I *hated* her last girlfriend. Didn't make any difference. Come on. I need a rose for Mum."

There weren't actually any glass roses, but they found some incredibly intricate water lilies instead, casting rainbows against the wooden eaves high above them, and Chris bought one of those. John, not usually one for ornaments, liked the splay of rainbows. Casting gay all over the place. He picked up a glass heart strung on a ribbon and decided to hang it in the window at home, see if he couldn't use it as a kind of subtle, surreptitious little pride flag.

"Can we drop these off in your car?" Chris asked as they made their way out of the barn. "I'm scared of dropping them."

"Yeah, sure. You want to wait here while I go over though? The field's a death trap."

"I'm going to get another hot dog. Leave me at the foodie places."

John laughed, sliding a hand to the small of Chris's back. "Okay."

And then the unthinkable happened.

"Chris!"

The voice rang out not ten feet from the top barn, and then a woman in wellies and a woolly jumper, a jauntily high brown ponytail swinging behind her head, descended on them and dragged Chris into a tight hug.

"You didn't say you were coming up, darling. I'd have given you a lift!" she scolded, then released him and did a double take at John. "Oh! Hello! Oh, I *see*."

Chris pulled a face and sighed. "John, this is my stepmum, Lauren. Lauren, John."

Stepmum.

Oh, God, *stepmum*.

John's chest seized up tight. His fingers started to shake. She was—she was doing the face. The little frown between her eyes. The glance back and forth between them. The pinch at the corner of her mouth.

She wanted to know what he wanted with Chris. Why he was here. What his intentions were. She doubted him. She thought—she thought—she thought—

She thought like Daniel.

"I came with Gina, and I'll be going with John," Chris was saying, but his voice sounded like it was coming from underwater.

"Oh, and should we not be expecting to see you for Sunday lunch tomorrow?"

"Mm, I wouldn't bet on it."

"Well, I'll get out of your hair. Ah, but, here, before I forget, take this. It's my present for Caroline, but you know what she's like. Stash it at your flat for us, eh?"

A small paper bag with something soft inside appeared and disappeared again, and then Lauren and her lime green wellies were vanishing into the top barn—and Chris was squeezing John's hand.

"John?"

John bit his lip and closed his eyes to breathe.

"John? You okay?"

"I—just—give me a sec."

Chris hesitated. Then his shoes nudged John's on the cobbles, and his hands were sliding around John's ribs in a hug.

"John?"

His voice was very soft and uncertain, and John exhaled heavily. He bent to rest his lips against the crown of Chris's head and simply breathed.

God, that had been—bad. *Bad.* But so stupidly, unnecessarily bad, too. She'd said hi, hugged her stepson, and gone again. That was *normal.* She hadn't freaked out or started shouting or—

Well, no, of course not. She was a tiny little woman in her fifties, and John was *John.* She'd wait until later. Get Chris on his own. Grill him about this massive hulk, and how obviously thuggish he was, and was Chris *sure,* had they *done* anything, what had *happened*—John fought to keep hold of his certainty, when they'd been tangled up in his bed and on top of the entire world, but—but—

But it slid through his fingers like sand, and that balloon in his chest wouldn't damn well *burst*.

"Talk to me," Chris whispered. "You're freaking me out a little here."

"Sorry."

John's voice sounded wrong, even to his own ears.

"What was that?"

"I—I—"

"You sound...panicky."

John laughed. It was a high, harsh sound, and Chris made a soft noise.

"I take that back. You *are* panicky."

"I—I'm okay." He was. Chris's firm hug was helping. Lauren had gone. The crowd swelled and surged around them, uncaring.

"Why did Lauren cause that?"

John swallowed. So Chris *had* noticed.

"I'm—I'm not so good with...with families."

A pause.

Then: "Why?"

"My—my ex."

"Oh."

Another pause.

And John knew it was coming, but felt the hot burn of tears threatening when Chris said, "Why?" again.

"It's...hard to explain."

Chris sighed. "Okay."

Then he backed up, fisting both hands in the front of John's hoodie.

"This isn't the first time you've been a little funny about this ex of yours," he said. "And I know something's up. And that something is affecting the way you handle me."

John took a shaky breath. "It—it'll affect every relationship I ever have, Chris."

"So—maybe this is something we need to talk about."

John swallowed.

Talk about it? Tell Chris exactly what people thought when they looked at John? What they thought when they saw him with Chris? What *Lauren* thought?

And why it had been so easy for everyone to believe every word that Daniel had ever said?

The instinctive answer was no.

But—

But now, Chris's stepmum had seen John for herself. If John didn't tell Chris the truth, she'd tell Chris the lie.

It was now or never.

Chapter Eleven

CHRIS SUGGESTED ENDCLIFFE Park. He knew it like the back of his hand, and John needed neutral territory. Somewhere they could both walk away, somewhere neither of them would feel trapped, but also, in a savage act of self-defence, somewhere busy enough that Chris wouldn't want to cause a scene.

So they went to a park that Chris knew, bought massive cups of tea and coffee, respectively, and found a bench.

And John said, "You don't know what I look like."

Chris sighed. "No."

"Have you—do you— God, can I get a pass for asking dumb questions right now?"

"I guess so, if it'll help you tell me what happened with Lauren back there."

"Have you always been blind?" John blurted out.

"No."

"When—when did—"

"I was six. And we're not talking about that; we're talking about you."

"Okay. Do you remember what anyone looks like?"

"Not really."

John licked his lips. "So—so you don't know what it's like to just look at someone and be afraid?"

Chris paused.

"I know what it's like to hear someone and be afraid," he said.

"Yeah, but there's no shouting or violence or—"

"There doesn't have to be," Chris said. "The same way you could read me the phone book and I'd be happy, there are people who could read me the phone book and I'd be afraid."

John chewed on his lip.

"Are you saying you're one of those people?"

"People look at me," John said, "and they see a thug."

The worst of it was that John hadn't always minded. His type in guys—twinks who demanded to be worshipped—tended to like a big, rough-looking bloke. And being a wall of muscle and ink was a really good thing walking home at night, or going to fix fuses in the less desirable parts of the city. It used to just irk him, once. Just make him roll his eyes and think the hipsters round his flat were hypocrites for all their non-judgemental equality rallies, and then crossing the road to avoid him when he was out for his morning run.

Then along came Daniel.

"I look hard," he croaked. "I look mean. People are afraid of me. And I never used to really mind, because, you know, screw what they think, what did I care, right?"

"Right," Chris said firmly.

"Then I met Daniel."

"The ex?"

"Yeah."

"So, what changed?"

"He—we were together for a while. He lived over in Doncaster, wasn't out to his family, said his dad would kill him, so it was all really quiet. Stolen weekends now and then. He met my family a couple of times, but never the other way around. He was training as a hairdresser, said he wanted to finish his course, and then he'd leave Doncaster and come and live in Sheffield with me, and it would all be okay."

"And you believed him."

Chris's voice was so quiet, so sympathetic, that John wanted to cry.

"Yeah," he mumbled instead.

"How much of it was bollocks?"

John barked a harsh laugh. "He did live in Doncaster. He was training as a hairdresser. The rest was all lies. He was *engaged*. He was going to get married to this other bloke, some accountant or something."

"Oh, the son of a—"

"He'd mentioned this salon a couple of times, so I'd figured out where he worked, see, so I went over, intending to surprise him after work and take him out for dinner or something. It was our one-year anniversary. I was thinking, you know, it had been a year, his course was bound to be finishing soon, so what harm could it do if I picked him up and we came back to Sheffield and celebrated where his bigoted family couldn't see us, right?"

"Oh, God."

"Only, I turned up and caught him as he was leaving, and he walked straight into the arms of this twat in a suit, and I—I caused a right scene, started shouting in the middle of the street at this suited idiot and saying I was Daniel's partner, and who did he think he was. And he said he was Daniel's *fiancé*."

Fingers crept over John's hand, warm from the polystyrene cup. John squeezed them and took a shaky breath.

"I cleared off after that. I realised I'd been the other man, and I cleared off. And the next—the next thing I knew, there's the police at my door, and I'm being arrested."

"For what?"

"For—"

He couldn't say it.

His throat stuck on the word. If he said it, Chris would go. Anybody would go. Hell, *John* would go, in their position. People didn't do what Daniel had done. They didn't tell those kinds of lies. They *didn't*.

"For what, John?"

"He—he told—he told his fiancé—that we'd pulled at a party, it was this one-night stand he'd regretted ever since, but I kept—I kept coming back. That I'd—I'd r—"

The word stuck again.

"That I made him do it."

There was a long, awful pause.

Then:

"Do what?" Chris whispered.

"Everything. That our whole relationship *wasn't*. That—that we'd had this one-night stand, and then I kept calling him and threatening him and saying if he didn't come over and have—do it again, then I'd tell everyone."

He could hardly breathe. The air was too thin. Slowly, John let go of Chris's hand and bowed to press his forehead to his own knees. There wasn't enough *air*.

"And what's your version?" came the softest question in the world.

"It was a relationship, Chris. It *was*. We went to gigs and hiking and did normal bloody relationship things. We *did*. It wasn't—it wasn't anything like what he said, it *wasn't*."

"So—"

"Only he kept *saying* it."

The lie had been bad enough. The lie had been horrible and heartbreaking—but in itself, only that John had misjudged Daniel so badly. He'd thought himself in love, only for that love to turn out to be a heartless, cheating c—c—word that John wouldn't ever say out loud.

The worst of it hadn't been the original lie—but the way Daniel had repeated it. Over and over and over again.

"The minute he said I'd made him sleep with me, his fiancé called the police. And Daniel told them the same story. And they arrested me, and I spent hours in this interview room with some free lawyer and this detective telling them it wasn't true."

He could still hear the policewoman's slow, careful questions. He could still smell the lawyer's perfume.

"I told them everything, and I thought that would be the end of it. I mean, I had text messages of us flirting on my phone, and I had a selfie of us at a gig, and Nora came down and gave a statement saying he'd come to family dinners and had been at Nan and Granddad's anniversary celebration. I thought it would be dead in the water."

"Only it wasn't."

"He just kept saying it, kept coming up with new stuff, kept lying— He'd give them things like his STI check results and say the dates meant something, and he got all these people like his mum and whoever to say he wasn't the type to cheat, and he just kept on and on and on, and—and do you know what it's like, when you *know* something's true, but someone insists so hard and so long that it's not that you start believing it too?"

John's voice cracked then. He could feel tears on his face. The questions were circling around his head like vultures, the shadows of the damage Daniel had left behind. When he was arrested, he knew the truth. Knew it was a load of lies, from beginning to end, and not one bit of it had been true. It was a desperate attempt by a pathetic little man trying to get out of getting caught.

And then, over the next four months—four *months*—of the same lies, over and over and over…

He'd started to question. He'd started to wonder if he was losing his mind. If he'd remembered it right after all. If, if, if.

Four policemen had come to his door to arrest him, not one or two like normal people got. The detective frowned at him all the way through that original interview. The lawyer kept telling him to say 'no comment,' like he was guilty. They took his clothes away so he'd not be able to hang himself. The judge only granted bail because he'd never been arrested before.

Because he'd pulled Daniel when they were both drunk in a nightclub. Because maybe a big lad like John drunk *was* too scary to say no to. Because maybe he *was* intimidating. Because maybe—maybe—maybe—

He'd lie awake at night, replaying every sexual encounter he'd ever had in his mind, looking for the fear, the coercion, the force. Looking for the moments when his boyfriends wanted to say no, but couldn't. Looking for the hints he'd missed. Looking for the r—

Two months after that initial interview, he worked himself up so badly that he sat in the kitchen all night, with a knife and a packet of pills, trying to work up the courage to do it. To end it. It had gotten so bad he'd tried to end it all.

"Even Tasha started looking at me funny," he croaked. "My own *sister* thought I could have done it. That fiancé thought I could have done it. I had to quit football. And every time someone so much as looked at me funny in the street, I wondered if they knew, if they were thinking I could do something like that, if they thought I was this dangerous r—"

Chris's hand smoothed down his back and disappeared.

John closed his eyes, and the wracking sob that tore at his frame was the first since that shell-shocked, terrified cry in a police station cell, nine months ago.

"What happened then?"

"W-what?"

"You're not in prison. So what happened then?"

"Police decided there wasn't any evidence of what he was saying. Dropped it. I never heard from him again."

"Good," Chris murmured. "So, when you saw Lauren..."

"I thought— God, Chris, my own sister started avoiding me. So ever since, when people give me funny looks, it makes me think of what happened. Everyone thinks I'm this massive monster, and I must be dangerous. And families— what kind of family are going to want me anywhere near their son? And you—"

He stopped, scrubbing at his face.

"Me, what?"

"Don't—don't get angry with me."

"Depends what you're about to say," Chris said warily.

"You—you're worse."

"Worse how?"

"You're—Daniel—you're   more..."   *More   what?* "...vulnerable than he was."

"Meaning?"

John blew out heavily. "Meaning people are going to look at me, this brick outhouse of a man, with you, this—this blind, trans guy who needs a cane to get around, and—and think even *more* that I'm an abu—ab—bad."

Chris sighed.

For a long moment, there was silence.

And then Chris said, "Do you believe them?"

"What?"

"Do you believe you're bad?"

John opened his mouth—and paused.

"*John.*"

"I never meant to be," he said fervently. "I've never—I'd never, not ever, force anyone to do anything on *purpose*. But I'm—you've felt me, Chris. People are scared of me. How—how do I know nobody's ever done something because they're scared to say no? How do I know when yes actually means yes when I'm like this?"

"Trust."

"W-what?"

"Sounds to me," Chris said softly, "that Daniel's not only damaged the way you see yourself, but the way you trust your partners."

"How do you mean?"

"You don't trust that they mean what they say when you're doubting things like that."

John swallowed spasmodically.

"Guess not."

"So, what now?" Chris murmured.

John blinked at the blurry ground.

"Sorry?"

"What now? You can't have a panic attack like this just because my stepmum shows up."

"I—you're—you still want to—"

"Okay. *Okay.* Listen."

Chris slid off the bench with a heavy sigh and went to his knees, guiding himself between John's feet with tiny touches of his fingers. Once there, both arms came up around John's neck, and John found his face buried into the warm shoulder of Chris's coat.

"You're not dangerous, John."

It was like a punch in the chest. His eyes burned. With a choked noise, John burrowed harder into Chris's shoulder and brought his arms up to cling back.

"Not going to deny you're a massive motherfucker, but you're not dangerous."

John laughed wetly.

"When I'm with you," Chris said softly, "I feel safe."

The tiny word was like a shiver in John's soul.

"And maybe there's a couple of things you ought to know. I have a GPS tracker on my phone *and* in my cane—in case I get into bother, or I'm lost—so my dad can find me again. Gina was in that café with us at another table, on our coffee shop date. She told me what you look like afterwards, so I might not really get how that means you're dangerous—well, except maybe your size—but I could describe you to someone else if I had to. I've never *actually* dated someone I didn't already know before; you're the first time I left that comfort zone. I'm cautious. And yet—I have a condition that can literally knock me out in your presence, but it was only the lack of medication that had me going home after that night in your flat."

John felt a whole new wave of tears, but for a whole new reason, welling up.

"My point is, I'm cautious as hell, and yet I still feel safe with you. I feel good with you. You make me feel happy, confident, sexy, beautiful—and yes, I know what it's like for everyone to tell you something you know isn't true, and for it to get inside your head. I know I can bring a lot to a relationship. I know I want one. I know that someone out there—maybe someone right here—could be a great thing for me, with me, and there's nothing about me that makes me undateable. But when you're trans, when you're disabled, everyone else tells you otherwise. You get this on repeat from the wider world that you're this ugly, fucked-up freak, nobody will ever want you, and you've no right to want these things."

"That's—"

"Bullshit, I know. But it doesn't stop me believing it when I'm down. It's hard to resist what everyone else says is true."

It wasn't the same. The two situations—they weren't comparable, yet they kind of were. Chris kind of got where John was coming from. What it was like to know something was a lie, but to half believe it anyway.

Chris sat back on his heels. John let go, only to find his face cupped in cool hands and lips brushed against his cheek.

"Let me be very clear," Chris said. "If you ever, *ever* try and make me do something I don't want to do, this is over. No second chances. No excuses. But you'll know about it. I promise you, I am a noisy bastard when I'm not happy. There's no way you'll be missing it and wondering later if you read the signs right."

John's lip wobbled. Chris must have felt the shake, for his mouth stopped it, steadied it, with the softest kiss in the world. John closed his eyes and focused on the feeling.

"You're kind of a little fucked up in the head," Chris whispered. "And I think you need a bit of professional help to maybe untangle that. But you don't scare me. You didn't scare Gina. And you know, you won't scare my family either."

"You don't know that," John whispered.

"Oh, I do. My dad's the best in the business when it comes to reading people. He's going to take one look at you and write you off as a pussy."

John choked with laughter.

"Trust me," Chris murmured. "If you need to take things slow with the whole meeting the family thing, then okay. But don't do it out of some fear they're going to rush me off to a safe house and have you arrested for daring to put your hands in my pockets. And—maybe think about getting some counselling or something, 'kay?"

John scrubbed both hands over his face and exhaled heavily.

"You're—" he started.

What?

Perfect? A godsend? A blessing? An angel in skinny jeans?

"I—"

"What do you need?" Chris murmured.

"I need to go home," John croaked. "And I'm—God, I'm so sorry, but right now, I don't think I could handle you. I'd second-guess if you meant yes about having salad for lunch at this point."

"Oh, hey, spoilers, that's a hard no right there," Chris quipped and stood. "Okay. Tell you what. You run me back up to Whirlow Hall Farm, I'll join Lauren doing whatever the hell it is she's doing, and you go and get your space and call me tomorrow, yeah?"

John reached out, slid both arms around Chris's waist, and hugged him hard. Buried his face against Chris's stomach, feeling the hard thump of a pulse against his nose, and inhaled.

God. "I love you," he mumbled into the fabric, saying what he'd started to only a moment before.

"What?" Chris asked, stroking his hair with gentle hands.

John unburied.

"Nothing," he mumbled and caught one of the hands to kiss them. "Come on. I'll take you back up."

Chris kissed him on the mouth, soft and sweet, and John closed his eyes and caught at that wild dark hair to deepen it.

As though maybe he could hold on.

As though maybe Chris would let him.

Chapter Twelve

SUNDAY WAS A day of ritual.

In the morning, John had rugby training. At eleven, he jogged home and showered, then fired up his battered chariot of a car, drove around half the city fetching various sisters, and drove the lot up to Hathersage for Sunday dinner at one with Nan and Granddad. And woe betide any of them if they dared to miss Sunday dinner.

Which was why he was surprised to get home, still steaming from the pitch and the run, and find Nora searching for her car keys.

"Why are you taking yours?" John asked as he toed his filthy shoes off.

She blinked at him. "Well, you're not coming, are you?"

"Uh. Yes?"

"Really?"

"I've only missed one," John said, stupefied. "Why would I miss today?"

She flushed a little. "Well, it's just—you've been out all the time with Chris, I assumed you'd be out today too."

John bit his lip. "Oh. No."

She paused in her rummaging. "John? Everything okay?"

"Yeah. Fine. I just need to shower. Ten minutes."

Ten turned into twenty, but he felt better for it and rehearsed what he had to say. He didn't want to totally jump in head first and tell the whole family about Chris, or he'd end up married before he knew what had happened. But yesterday's talk was burning around the edges of his mind, and he needed to unload it.

So, he went for it and said, "I told Chris about Daniel," as he wandered back into the hall.

Nora dropped her shoe.

"I told him everything," John said. "And he didn't walk away."

"Oh, *John.*"

"He said—" The lump in his throat was back, and John mentally cursed. "He said he'd never been afraid of me, and—and he's really overcautious usually, but he f-felt—"

Nora's hand caught him at the back of the neck, and he buckled down into her hug, sniffling against her shoulder like a little kid.

"Good," she murmured in his ear. "Good for you, finally landing yourself a guy who has a brain between his ears."

John choked a little laugh and squeezed her back until she squeaked.

"D'you want me to drive?" she asked softly, and he snorted.

"God, no, you screw up the seat," he mumbled. He let go and scrubbed his hands over his face, giving her a watery smile. "I needed space after telling him everything. I had a bit of a meltdown on him."

"I'm not surprised," she replied and then nudged him with her elbow. "So? I'll have to drive anyway, right? There's no room in the car for him too."

"Give over. He's not coming."

"Aw, why! He's obviously a keeper!"

"Yeah, which is why he's not coming."

"We'd be nice."

"Okay, firstly, no, you wouldn't. Secondly, *you* aren't the problem."

"You're right, but now I know he's a keeper, do you *honestly* expect me to keep him a secret?" she asked airily, and John groaned.

"Nora—"

"Nan'll guess anyway, you know."

"What? Why?"

"You not moping around like a wet weekend and the obsessive phone-checking you were doing last week? She'll notice. If you don't want her to know, you better come up with a convincing lie, and fast."

John groaned again.

"And if she asks me, I'm telling her the truth."

"Nora!"

"I'm not getting the blame for you keeping secrets!" she argued, popping open the front door. "Now, come on, Fran's already started texting me."

John pulled a face and obligingly bitched his way down to the car in Nora's wake, but was already quietly planning. He couldn't spring the whole family on Chris just like that. Chris was bright and breezy, but he was also a little bit oddly shy sometimes. And John's family could be pretty full on. Especially Fran and Nan.

Nan especially was going to go nuts.

John's grandparents had very different approaches to, well, grandparenting. His parents had retired to the South of France the minute they were able to and not come back— and Nan had been appalled. Swanning off to France and leaving their precious babies? The *nerve*.

Granddad was just like John's dad, really. Their duty to the family was over when the kids had jobs and had permanently moved out to their own homes. They weren't fathers and grandfathers anymore until a new generation sprang up. Dad puttered about France birdwatching. Granddad shuffled about in his garden, coaxing mint and tomatoes out of the soil.

But Nan was a completely different kettle of fish.

Nan was all about marriage and children. The apron strings came off when somebody else's were ready to replace them. Single was not an option for a happy, fulfilling life— no matter how many bitter arguments Fran brewed up on the matter. Nora had been blissfully free of Nan's fussing until she'd announced she was getting a divorce. John, Fran, and Tasha were still firmly—*very* firmly—under the cosh. After the Daniel fiasco, Nan had been pretty intent on John getting a new, better boyfriend.

She was going to eat Chris alive, so John had to play this carefully.

Not that Nora gave him much chance. The minute they stopped by the flat and Fran wriggled into the back seat, Nora turned right around to grin at her and announced, "John's got a new boyfriend!" like the nasty, evil, cruel older sister that she was.

"Nora!"

"Yes!" Fran whooped, kicking him in the back.

"Ow!"

"What's his name? Where is he? We're picking him up too, right? Look, I'll squish up; he can sit between me and Tash—"

Fran had a habit of cosying up to John's boyfriends. She liked gay men, apparently. And as she was the same age as Chris, she'd probably love him even more. John rolled his eyes again and said no.

"Why not?"

"Because it's not that serious yet."

"Bollocks it's not," Nora said, and John grimaced.

"You're hiding him," Fran accused, and kicked him again. "Don't be such a queen; he'll love us. Let's go and get him."

"Can't," John said as he peeled out into the traffic. "Don't know where he lives."

"Call him and ask."

"No." Thank God, his phone was in his jeans pocket, trapped tight against his thigh so Fran couldn't steal it.

"What's wrong with him that you don't want to bring him to Sunday dinner?" Fran demanded.

"Nothing wrong with him. Plenty wrong with *you*."

"Hey!"

Nora fended off the attack—probably reckoning John would crash and kill them all—and John called them both some unsavoury names as he dropped down through Netheredge to reach Abbeydale Road and the grubby little flat that Tasha called home.

John and Nora, in their mid-thirties, were the planned children. Mum was all for a white picket fence, one girl, one boy, and lace curtains in the kitchen window. Fran had been an anniversary surprise, judging by her birthday being eight months and twenty-eight days after Mum and Dad's crystal anniversary. She'd been so much of a surprise that Mum had presumed her to be menopausal weight gain for the first six months. Only, it turned out menopausal chubbiness didn't kick. Then there was a baby in the house, and John could be described as a big brother in age as well as physical stature.

When Tasha turned up, not even a full year later, Mum sent Dad to get the snip.

Sometimes, though, John kind of got where Nan was coming from with her fussing, when he looked at his baby sisters. Fran, kicking him from the back seat, had blue hair and was doing evening classes in nude portraiture and Urdu. She had a job in a chippie and a different sexuality every month. Tasha, smoking a cigarette on the curb in front of a shabby computer repair shop probably covering up a money laundering scam, lived in a one-room bedsit with her baby and never quite hid her track marks well enough. Fran was wild and waxed lyrical about the world; Tasha was wild and weighed down by it.

So, yeah. Sometimes John sympathised.

But then, Nan would go on at him about 'letting' Aljaz slip through his fingers, and John would roll his eyes and grumpily point out that he had a good job and a nice flat and mates at the rugby, and he didn't want to move to Split with anyone, not even Aljaz.

"John has a new boyfriend, and he's keeping secrets!" Fran bellowed as Tasha slid into the car.

"Oh," said Tasha.

"What's his name?" Fran demanded.

"I'm not say—"

"Chris," Nora interrupted.

"Oh my God, you've met him?"

"No," Nora said. "He came over once, but there were *noises*, so I went out for dinner again."

John flushed hotly as Fran cackled and ruffled his hair from behind.

"I hate you all," he whined.

"What do you know?" Fran demanded, seizing Nora's arm.

"He wears trainers and he speaks English," Nora said immediately and then shrugged. "Nothing else. I didn't even see him—thank God, judging by the sound effects."

"Oh, screw you," John groaned.

"Mm, no, I got the impression he was scre—"

"Shut up!"

All three women sniggered at him. John loudly wished they were brothers, or dead, and got smacked by three different hands for the cheek.

Boyfriend aside, it was a fairly typical drive out to Hathersage.

Nan and Granddad had lived out here as long as John could remember, in a neat little cottage wedged into the hillside just shy of the village centre. In the summer, it commanded glorious views over the Peak District. In the winter, it nestled in thick snow, almost impassable, and John had to drive everyone out crushed into his work van.

Granddad controlled the outside of the cottage—the lavender bushes lining the gravel path, the black metal gate, the ivy scrambling eagerly up the side of the porch—but Nan controlled the inside. The smell of wood shavings—potpourri, Nan insisted, but Rhodri called them wood shavings, and John liked his version better—and the paper flowers tucked around their great-grandma's old crucifix on the wall were as familiar as the feel of his own skin. This was home, to John. This was where his soul had been born.

"There you are!"

Nan was like her granddaughters: short, blonde, and round. She was a dumpy little woman, firmly in the grip of that almost stereotypical grandmother look. Her hair was permed, her hands were wrinkled, and her wardrobe full of flat shoes, sensible skirts, and woolly cardigans. They were both in their eighties, but while Granddad looked a hundred, frail and thin, Nan looked seventy, fat and energetic. Her hugs were soft and smelled of the same lavender Granddad grew outside. After every one, she would step back and visually examine the recipient, then pat them on the cheek and move on. John had never quite decided if it was endearing or annoying.

And she was sharp as hell, despite the fluffy cardigans and devotion to her knitting, because she took one look at John and said, "Something's changed."

John sighed. *Three. Two. One.*

And Fran chirped, "He has a boyfriend!"

Nan's face lit up, and she looked to the door as though John had left him in the car by mistake. "Have you really?" It wasn't exactly a question. "Well, when do we get to meet him? What's his name? Where did you meet him? What—"

"Granddad, can I drown Fran in the duck pond?" John shouted.

A grunt emanated from the living room.

"That means yes," John decided. Fran shrieked and fled into the kitchen.

"Shoes, young lady!"

John managed to escape a little in the chaos. Granddad had to be corralled out of his armchair to come and sit at the table with the rest of them—where he promptly hid behind his newspaper again—and for a little while, Nan was distracted by despairing over Fran's new tattoo and holding court over the new vicar at church.

"And do you know, he's supportive of gay marriage, isn't that good, John, dear?"

There it was. Smooth as anything, they were back to his new boyfriend. John grimaced.

"I guess so."

"It'd be lovely if you could get married in church," Nan said brightly. "It's never too late, you know! What's this new young man of yours like?"

Young. She'd not like that.

"Er—"

"I think it's still a bit new and shiny, Nan," Nora said, finally being helpful. "I've not even seen him yet."

"Yeah," John mumbled. "It's—I'm not even sure I can say 'boyfriend' yet. It's only been a couple of dates."

"Everyone starts somewhere," Nan said, waving a hand. "What's his name?"

"Chris."

"Oh!"

"Not the same Chris," John added quickly.

"Well, good, never did like that boy."

She had, in fact, utterly adored him, until John didn't anymore and they split up. Then, he became the devil incarnate. Which was harsh, in John's view, as the original Chris hadn't been a bastard or anything. Just...boring. But that was how Nan worked. Unfailingly supportive, until the prospective grandson-in-law was dumped again, at which point he'd never been good enough to join the family anyway.

"What's he like, then? How did you meet?"

"Um. In a café."

Her smile dimmed a fraction. "Oh. Does he work there?"

"Uh, no."

"What does he do?"

Nothing. But Nan wouldn't like that. She abhorred laziness, and John wasn't sure it was all right to go around telling other people about disabilities.

"Uh—"

"Who cares what he does?" Fran chirped. "What's he *look* like? Is he gorgeous?"

"Yeah. He's stunning. Proper model material. And he asked me out. I was staring like an idiot, could hardly string two words together. He's, um. He's tall, he's got dark curly hair, he—" *kisses like he could come on the spot from that alone.* "—uh. Looks great."

"*Very* new, is it, dear?" Nan said diplomatically.

"Yeah. Very."

"You'll simply have to bring him next weekend. And—"

John was rescued by the grace of his phone ringing.

"Shit, it's probably Rhodri, let me—"

He stumbled up from the table. Nan's lips thinned a little, but she waved him away, her dislike of phone calls at the table outweighing her dislike of leaving it without permission. John slipped into the living room and closed the door behind him when he saw Chris's name on the display. *Ears burning or what?*

"Hey, babe."

"Hey yourself." Chris's voice was low and warm. "Just wanted to check in after yesterday. You okay?"

John found his mouth curving into a smile. "Yeah. I'm okay. Thanks—thanks for listening. And calling. And...not running for the hills."

"You're welcome, I guess?" Chris sounded mildly amused. "Are you busy?"

"At my grandparents' for Sunday dinner."

"Oh, sorry, I'll let you g—"

"No, no, it's fine. It's good, actually. Nora kind of let slip about you and me, so Nan's interrogating me."

"Oh, God, am I going to find a horse's head in my bed?"

John laughed. "Doubt it. She wants me to bring you over so she can talk you into marrying me in the family church."

"Mm, don't do church. Or weddings, for that matter. Maybe next time."

"If you were free next Sunday," John said, "I might have to skip coming up here for your important plans."

"Oh, really?"

"Mm."

"Then your granny would think I'm leading you astray."

"We-ell."

"Oh, I see. You *want* to be led astray?"

"Maybe by you."

"In which case, want to lead yourself over to my flat when you're done at your granny's house?"

John's heart beat a little faster.

"Where's that?"

"Parson Cross. You could come and pick me up from Dad's and take me home. Walk to me to my door like a gentleman, then come in for coffee—"

"Tea."

"Way to spoil the moment there, John."

John laughed. He felt oddly young and giddy, like he had with every new guy before Daniel, only oddly more intensely.

"I figure you told me a secret yesterday," Chris continued, "so I'm going to tell you one this evening. And if you're still okay with me being...me, then maybe you could stay the night?"

John swallowed.

"Uh. To sleep, or—*sleep*?"

"To fuck so hard we break my bed."

John choked. "Chris!"

"You asked," came the serene reply.

"No pressure though," John said quickly. "I mean, we don't have to—"

"John. Trust me. Trust *you*. Nothing's going to happen we don't want. If you want to sleep, then we can sleep. If you put your hands down my jogging bottoms after I've told you no, I'll bury the bread knife in your breastbone. Okay?"

It was completely inappropriate how John's brain latched onto the J-word.

"Jogging bottoms?"

"Uh, yes?"

"You're wearing jogging bottoms?"

"Yes?"

"That's—really not fair."

"*Oh*," Chris said, and John could *hear* the smirk in his voice. "In which case, pick me up from Matalan. I'll need to go and buy more."

"I might hate you a tiny bit right now," John complained.

"Mm, don't think so. Call me when you escape your granny's house, and come out to play."

"See you later."

Chris made an exaggerated kissing sound and hung up.

John sank into his granddad's abandoned armchair, turning the phone over and over in his hand and smiling like a drunken idiot.

And then, slowly, the smile slipped away.

Chris hadn't stayed the night at John's. He'd mentioned a doctor, and medication, and a disability that could knock him out.

And suddenly John had an idea of what the secret might be.

Chapter Thirteen

JOHN DIDN'T GET to escape until nearly six—and only then via a convoluted route—dropping off each sister in turn.

He kept quiet about his plans. Thankfully, Nora wanted to go to her boyfriend's rather than straight home, so he managed to get shot of the girls in record time. Once he was alone in the car, he found his phone again.

"Hey, Chris, it's me."

"I know. Caller ID."

"Can you re—"

"It talks to me," Chris said and laughed. "Where are you?"

"Abbeydale Road."

"I'm back at Dad's. Ring me when you're outside, and I'll come out—unless you want to meet my folks?"

"Um. Maybe next time?"

"No problem."

Chris hung up then, and John blew out a shaky breath. Okay. Staying the night. He had an inkling of what Chris was going to tell him, and honestly, if John were right, who *cared*? He wasn't going to bail on someone that gorgeous for that.

So...he dared to hope and stopped by the supermarket to pick up a packet of condoms and some lube.

It was starting to snow again by the time he arrived outside Chris's parents' house. His call was cut off after only two rings, and then a light came on in the porch. Two shadows hovered behind the frosted glass as John got out to open the passenger side door.

Then the front door opened.

John's breath caught at the sight of Chris in an open jacket, tight T-shirt, and baggy black jogging bottoms. His hair was a mess, and the lip ring was black this time. *Oh, hell yes.*

Then his breath wheezed out again in a rush at the squat, fat man who frowned down at the car from behind him. The blue eyes were unmistakeable, even at this distance.

John raised a hand awkwardly to wave at Chris's father and wanted—very, very intensely—to drop dead at that very minute.

Oh, that man did *not* like John.

"Hey," Chris said sunnily, grasping at John's coat sleeve and standing up on his toes in a now familiar pose. John kissed him quickly, hardly daring to take his eyes off the imposing man at the house. "You okay?"

"Yeah. Yeah, sorry, here—"

Chris didn't buy it. The moment John was back in the driver's seat, a hand crept over and found his thigh, squeezing lightly.

"You really okay?"

"Your dad is glaring at me like I'm the spawn of Satan. It's...intimidating."

Chris snorted with laughter. "That's his face."

"He's scowling!"

"Yeah. That's his face."

"Oh, right, he looks at the postman like that, I'm sure..."

"He does. Lauren calls him Gill."

"What?"

"Grumpy gills? Gill. Even I remember my dad scowling. My mum used to say if I pulled faces in the mirror, then I'd get stuck like that, and said that was what happened to Dad."

John laughed. "Really?"

"Uh-huh. I believed her too. So. My place."

A postcode was supplied, slap bang in the middle of the grotty Parson Cross, and John grimaced as he fought through the steadily worsening weather into a steadily worsening estate. He'd done enough jobs in Parson Cross to know the area reasonably well. Some bits were just old widowers and disabled ladies, and they were nice enough. But other bits were stuffed with scrotes, who'd think nothing of mugging a blind lad, and John found himself tensing up as the satnav turned him into a small parking area behind a block of definitely scrote-stuffed flats.

"You live here?"

Chris pulled a face. "It's a council flat. They hardly own mansions, you know."

"I meant more...not exactly nice neighbours round this way."

"Oh, mine are all right, actually."

"Really?"

"Yeah. A mum and her baby across the landing, and Danny in the flat above watches out for anyone giving me shit."

"Mate of yours?"

"Eh. Laundrette friends. He's a bit...he's got a few screws loose. Someone stabbed his brother last year, so Danny burned their house down. But he's nice enough, if you don't cross him. Just overreacts sometimes."

"Reassuring," John said dryly.

"He's fine with me. I think even Danny doesn't go so low as to go after disabled people," Chris said, getting out of the car. "C'mon."

John inched out in the too-small gap between his car and a battered Suzuki Jimny and peered up at the flats. They were little more than a concrete block, ugly and unsightly. But through the grimy windows, he could see traces of homes. Flowers here. Nice curtains there. A set of glittery butterfly stickers on the third floor.

Maybe they were nicer inside.

They were quiet, at least. The faint sounds of TVs accompanied their ascent, but nothing much else. The stairwell was covered in graffiti, smelled faintly of piss, and was freezing from the lack of glass in the windows to the outside world. Chris's front door, flimsy and in need of sanding down and repainting, wasn't exactly inspiring.

And then the door opened, and John stepped into warmth.

"Oh my God."

"Nice, isn't it?"

Even to John's inexpert eye, the flat was kitted out for a blind hedonist. The carpets were ridiculously thick. A sofa that must have cost near enough a thousand pounds was covered in throws and blankets of all different types and textures. A state-of-the-art surround sound system bordered a laughably small TV screen. The kitchenette, just built into the living room, was rammed with odds and ends that John didn't recognise.

"You cook?"

"Yep."

"Is that what these are for?"

"What?"

John toed off his boots and crossed the little room. He picked up a plastic sensor, not unlike a thermometer, and handed it over.

"Oh, those. Yeah."

"What's that one?"

"Tells me when the coffee cup is full."

"Huh," John said. Chris skirted past him to put it back. The lip ring shimmered, and John stared. "Um. So. You wanted to tell me something?"

"Uh-huh. Want some tea?"

John hesitated. Chris seemed oddly nervous.

"Actually," he said. "Can I get the grand tour, and then—"

He trailed off. Chris cocked his head.

"Then?"

"Your lip ring is taunting me."

"I can take it o—"

"Not the solution."

Chris laughed, flushing a little. "You've kissed me when I've had it in before, you know."

"Briefly."

"Oh, I see. You want to tongue-fuck my mouth when I've got it in."

John coughed. "No. I want to—" He blew out his cheeks. "I want to suck on it while opening you up around my fingers again."

Chris coughed.

"Oh," he said weakly.

John shrugged and stuck his hands in his pockets.

"Well, fuck."

Then Chris took it out.

Just peeled it out of his lip and set it on the counter.

"Right," he said, a little breathlessly. "We—we really do need to talk first. And then—then if you're not put off by what I've got to say, then...then maybe I can put it back in and, um. You can do that."

"Then can we skip tea and tour and just talk?" John urged. "Because—I—after everything you said yesterday, and calling me to check I was okay today, and being so damned understanding and *nice* about it all instead of running a mile as you probably *should* have done, and now you're standing there in your jogging bottoms and your lip ring—"

"Minus the lip ring."

"Yeah, only your lip's flushed from you taking it out, and I can see the piercing, so..."

"Right."

"I just...want to make—"

"No!"

John rolled his eyes. "Sleep with you," he amended.

"Well, if you still want to sleep with me in fifteen minutes or so, then I will drop these trousers and bend over," Chris said, which really did not help the dick situation.

Then he sank onto the sofa and tucked his socked feet under him. Chewing on his thumbnail, he looked so suddenly nervous that John's dick softened again from its hopeful semi, and he shucked his jacket and joined him.

The sofa dipped so hard under his weight that Chris almost rolled into him, which earned him a laugh and a hand-on-thigh squeeze again, but then the nail went back into the ring-free mouth, and John bit his lip.

"So..." he prompted.

"So," Chris echoed but said nothing.

John licked his lips and reached out to touch his fingers lightly to the gold chain.

"Is it about this?"

The medical bracelet.

Chris sighed. "Yes."

"Okay," John said. "What do you wear it for?"

"Epilepsy."

That was...

Surprising, but also not. John had actually been guessing at advanced diabetes, given the whole medication at home, gone blind, healthy options at the restaurant, bracelet thing, but it wasn't exactly a shock either. He'd heard of it. Lots of people had it.

"So...you're epileptic."

"Mm."

"Chris?"

Chris sighed and sat back. Finally stopped chewing his nail. "Sorry. I don't really like to talk about it, but...you need to know this, if this is heading into...staying the night sort of territory."

"You have seizures at night?"

"Not usually at night, no, but I have a lot of seizures. Sooner or later, I'm going to have one in front of you."

"And I need to know what to do."

"Mm."

"Okay. Does it...does it help if I say I've seen seizures before?"

"Depends. What type?"

"Uh. Seizure-seizures?"

Chris coughed a small laugh. "There's a lot of different types of seizures, John."

"Well, when I was an apprentice, a guy at work collapsed and had a fit on the floor. And I do first-aid training every year, and they show us videos. So, I know the whole...don't restrain them, wait it out, don't put anything in their mouth stuff."

"The guy at work..."

"Uh-huh?"

"Did he go all stiff, then fall over and start twitching?"

"Yeah."

"Okay. That kind of seizure."

"You have that kind?"

"Yeah. The seizures themselves aren't that severe. I mean, the falling over can be, obviously, but I have a lot of them."

"By a lot, you mean..."

"Two or three a week. And that's when the drugs are working really well."

"Oh, wow."

Chris pulled a face.

"We—we had to call an ambulance for that guy."

"You probably didn't."

"What?"

"My seizures never last more than two or three minutes. And after, I want to sleep. It's exhausting and disorienting, and it can hurt. So—I'm moody, and I want to sleep, but I don't need a doctor."

"You don't?"

"No. It's normal."

"Oh."

"I can feel them coming. I get an aura. So, you know, I won't bite your tongue off and go down in the middle of a shag. But they can happen whenever they want, so...I've ruined dates before. I've ended up fitting and pissing myself in parks and cafés. Dad nearly crashed his car once because I seized in the passenger seat and somehow got hold of the gearstick."

"Christ."

Chris curled his knee a little higher into his chest. "It's humiliating."

"You can't help it."

"That doesn't make it not humiliating to come round on a pub floor and knowing full well your jeans aren't wet because of spilled beer."

"Okay, maybe not, but better than being so drunk you've done it, right?"

Chris looked a little startled.

"I—sort of guessed that there was something else," John said awkwardly. "I didn't think epilepsy, but I'd seen your bracelet. Is that why you're blind?"

"Yeah."

"What happened?"

Chris chewed on his nail again. John dared to reach out and gently tug it away. After a beat, those warm fingers sank between his own, and he squeezed the captured hand.

"I had a seizure. I was six, and I wasn't so good at recognising my aura. So I had this seizure by surprise. And I fell. And I...hurt my head."

"Enough to go blind?"

"Yeah. I don't—it's not something we really talk about much."

Christ, he was probably lucky to be alive.

"I'm better at recognising it now. Haven't hurt myself in years. But...sooner or later, you'll be out somewhere with me, and I'll go. And you'll be left in the middle of the street with everyone staring and taking pictures, and taxis won't take us home if I've pissed myself, and you'll have to wait for Dad or Lauren to come and get us..."

It was an ugly picture. John mentally prodded it and came away...feeling nothing different.

"I also can't take you to rugby practice and taunt you in my shorts," he said. "Still here."

Chris gave him a slightly wobbly smile.

"Is my first-aid stuff...enough?"

Chris shrugged. "Yeah. No. Kind of."

"What else do I need?"

"If I have a seizure," Chris said, "just...leave me alone. I mean, not *alone*, alone. But don't touch me."

"I know that bit. Move stuff out the way so you can't hit it, and wait it out."

"Yeah."

"What about when you're done? Airways, pulse, the usual?"

"Yeah. And I'll usually go to sleep. Like, immediately. I power-nap for about half an hour after every one. And I can be pretty belligerent about getting to do it."

"How belligerent is—"

"I punched a paramedic once."

John snorted and then grinned. "Noted, but—not that worried."

"Hey!"

"You'd have to clout me with a dumbbell to do any damage. I'm not worried."

"Might punch you in the balls."

"Okay, good point. Keep balls away from you. Got it."

Chris finally cracked a proper smile.

"Hey." John shook the captured hand. "I—" *Love you.* "—like you. A hell of a lot. And like I say, I knew from the minute I met you that I couldn't do my usual third-date trick and take you to rugby practice to get you insanely turned on by bending over in my shorts a lot."

"Well, not at practice, no..."

"There's a trade-off, you know."

"What?"

"You touch. All the time. And way better than most guys."

The smile widened a little. "Yeah?"

"Uh-huh. And this isn't big enough to send me out the door."

Chris's hand tightened. "You're sure?"

"Sure."

If he were being completely honest with himself, John found Chris's gender a bigger minefield than he did epilepsy and blindness. There were first-aid certificates and those warnings on films with special effects. He'd seen Braille buttons in lifts, and people out with guide dogs. But he'd never so much as seen a trans man on TV. So, yeah. One was definitely newer than the other, in John's little world.

But he sensed right now—with Chris's thumb damp and the nail chewed—wasn't the time to say it. Chris probably wouldn't take it very well.

"So, still here."

"Yeah," Chris whispered.

"You want to maybe put that lip ring back in?"

Chris laughed, then shook his head.

"I'm...feeling a little bit too raw for all of that right now."

"Okay," John said quickly. "Do you want me to go, or—"

"No. No, I want you to stay. And maybe later, I'll put the ring back. But, um...can we just..."

"Can do whatever."

"You're probably not hungry again yet if you had Sunday dinner, but I do a mean homemade pizza, if you want?"

"You're always hungry when you're this big," John said and dared to lean over enough to kiss Chris's neck. He wriggled, as though ticklish, and John grinned. "Pizza sounds great. And maybe a cuppa?"

"Tea?"

"Tea."

Chapter Fourteen

THEY ENDED UP not having pizza at all after John voiced scepticism that Chris could make quesadillas without burning himself or the food. Chris got enormously offended and demonstrated that John's opinion was, in fact, moronic.

"Okay," John said when Chris took back the empty plate and retreated to the kitchenette to wash up. "I was wrong. You're a master chef."

"Damn right."

"Where the hell did you learn to do that? You could cook for bloody Gordon Ramsay."

"If I wanted to not starve when I was at my mum's, I had to cook. She can only make three meals, and Jack is even worse."

"Jack?"

"My stepdad."

"What do they eat when you're not visiting?"

"I told you, three meals. Steak, chicken casserole, and fish fingers. Over and over again. Mum keeps complaining she's getting fat, but it's not exactly surprising."

"Wouldn't have taken you for a health nut."

"Nut, no. Healthy, yeah."

"Any particular reason?"

Chris shrugged as he wrenched the tap off and began washing the plates. "The epilepsy is worse when I'm not feeling good. And eating right and exercising keeps me feeling good. So...it's not a cure, there *is* no cure, but it keeps it more manageable."

"So, a big binge at the weekend, loads of beer and pizza with the footie on the telly, is out?"

"I didn't say that," Chris said. "It's not *that* delicate. But I couldn't do it for a whole week."

John eyed those jogging bottoms. They were woolly and baggy and left absolutely everything to the imagination.

"Gym goer, then?"

"Um, sort of."

"Sort of?"

"I mainly play football."

John blinked. "How do you s—"

"Bell in the ball? Never seen the adverts?"

"What adverts?"

"A cat with a bell on its collar runs across the pitch during a blind football match and then there's a yowl."

John snorted with laughter.

"Don't tell our Fran that. She loves cats; she'll kill you."

"Can hand on my heart say I've never kicked a cat," Chris said. "On purpose."

John laughed, heaving himself up from the sinfully deep sofa. "So, no gym?"

"I go with Luke, actually."

"Who's Luke?"

"He's a mate. We help each other out. If he comes with me pretending to be my carer or whatever, he gets to use the disabled changing rooms with me."

"Why does he want to do that?"

"Because he's like me. He doesn't want to go into the men's alone, but he sweats like a pig, so he can't not change. So, we go together, he changes with me, and then he helps me with the weights."

John closed the distance, sliding both hands down Chris's exposed arms and nuzzling at his neck.

"He's doing a pretty good job."

Chris wriggled, grinning. "Thanks."

"What gym is it?" John asked, cosying up to that long, lean back and sliding his hands around that flat belly.

"Why?"

"So I know where not to go. Pretty sure seeing you pumping iron would be a bad idea in my gym shorts."

"Oh, look who's talking," Chris said tartly. "Mr I-Could-Benchpress-*You*."

"I could." John kissed the tender spot underneath Chris's jaw and felt the pulse jump. "Happy to demonstrate any time you want."

The plates clanked as he sucked, and John grinned as he let go.

"Bastard."

"Tell me what you want," John whispered into one exposed ear and blew on the shell until the plates clanked again.

"Oh, God..."

"Not quite."

"Feels like it."

John bit down on the earlobe gently. "What do you want?"

"Pin—pin me up against the sink and rub me off. Just like this."

John bit the ear again and pushed one hand into the darkness of Chris's jogging bottoms. With a jolt, he found no underwear. Just hot skin and wiry hair and, behind it, an intense heat. At the very first touch of his fingers, Chris whimpered and gripped onto the lip of the counter with both hands, plates abandoned.

John had never rubbed someone off like this before—neither someone like Chris, nor pressed up against a sink. It wasn't the sort of sensual sex he usually preferred. But there was something so intensely alluring about the way Chris arched back into him as he probed that unfamiliar heat with two fingers. Something gorgeous in the way he moaned when John's index finger grazed his clit. Something sexy as hell in the short bursts of his breathing as John's hand settled in the position that got the best sounds and began to rub.

"*Fuck*. Fuck-fuck-fuck—"

John laughed breathlessly and pressed his mouth to Chris's neck. His other arm was locked around Chris's chest. His dick ached, but he fought the urge to grind. This wasn't for him. This was for Chris.

And, God, did Chris like it. He shuddered and writhed in John's grip, the cursing dissolving into harsh breathing and whines. When John sucked on his neck, the sound Chris made was like a cry, and when John bit—

Oh, *hell*.

Chris *liked* that. He jolted like he was going to tear right out of his own skin, and John's knuckles hit the cupboard door hard as Chris thrust forward. And then he was grinding against John's fingers, faster and faster and—

John found a new patch of skin and tightened his jaw.

"*Fuck!*"

The climax was sudden and sharp. John's fingers were wet. He cupped the heat as Chris shuddered wordlessly, and then, when a slow relaxation swept up that long frame, John neatly tucked a knee between Chris's thighs and began to leisurely rub him from below.

"Oh, Jesus," Chris whimpered. "Jesus, you—you're—"

"Turn around."

Chris did, his whole body shaking.

"Hold onto the sink," John said—and then dropped to his knees, opened Chris's own with his hands, pulled his jogging bottoms down, took that swollen pleasure between his lips—

"Fuck!"

—and sucked.

BY THE TIME Chris came back from his shower, John had explored every inch of the rest of the flat.

The bedroom held nothing but a double bed and a chest of drawers. The main room didn't have any surprises, but he did find Chris's football kit drying on a radiator, along with a tank top that presumably belonged in the same sports bag.

He forgot his discoveries, though, when Chris reappeared from the bathroom in a white T-shirt and...nothing else.

"That's really not helping the whole let's get clean and go to bed idea," John said.

"Yes it does," Chris said. "I'm clean. Now, take me to bed."

"In that state? I'd only get you messy again."

"How terrible. Do it anyway."

John laughed and smoothed back those wet curls to kiss Chris right between the eyes.

"Waste of a shower," he murmured.

"You rubbed me off, then sucked me off," Chris murmured.

"So?"

"Waste of a dick."

John laughed.

"I'm serious. I want that in me."

"That's going to take some working up to."

"And you didn't put anything in me just now to help. So. Take me to bed, and let's make some progress."

John hesitated. Tracked a thumb down Chris's cheek.

Then said: "In the morning."

"Morning sex?"

"Yeah."

Chris cocked his head. "Not that I'm arguing, but...why?"

John took a breath and stepped back. Held Chris out by the hands like they were about to dance.

"Because you look beautiful right now. Really, truly beautiful. And—yeah, you're not the only one who wants inside. But I want to...learn you properly. Take my time about it. So, tonight, I want to cuddle up with you and listen to the way you breathe when you sleep, and then in the morning, I want to kiss you awake and make love to you in a bed that smells of sleep, while you're still warm and drowsy."

Chris took in a sharp breath.

Then he said, "That's not fair."

"What?"

"You just managed to make that stupid phrase sound...kind of romantic."

"It *is* romantic."

"It's tripe. But—fine. If I get a proper goodnight kiss."

John laughed and kissed him lightly.

"Promise."

He let go to duck into the bathroom and tidy himself up—along with a liberal amount of toothpaste for the promised goodnight kiss. He heard Chris moving around the main room faintly before silence fell, and emerged to find the light had been left on, but the bedroom door closed.

John rolled his eyes, switched the light off, and followed.

And—stopped dead, not a foot inside the doorway.

"That's not fair," he breathed.

Chris stared up at him. He was sitting cross-legged in the middle of the mattress, the duvet turned down and the pillows fluffed up. He had a pill in one hand and a glass of orange juice in the other.

"What's not?"

The lip ring flashed when he spoke.

"You know what," John said and closed the bedroom door behind him with a snap.

"I don't, actually," Chris said and downed the pill. The juice followed, before the glass was abandoned on the floor, and he squirmed over to one side, wriggling down until his curls lay like blots of ink on the white pillowcase. "C'mon, then. Hug me."

John did no such thing.

Instead, he crawled over the bed, oozing power and predatory instinct and, poised on all fours over Chris's relaxed form, bent his head to kiss him.

Caught teeth and tongue around that lip ring.

And *sucked.*

Chris whined. Hands scrabbled at John's tense biceps. Squeezed.

And then he sighed.

"Yes."

John didn't touch back, but for his mouth. Rolling. Worrying. Teasing.

And always, always sucking.

The cool metal on his tongue, the whines and whimpers that came from Chris's abused mouth, the hands that scratched and searched every inch of John's upper body—

John was pretty sure he could come from this, and this alone. No sex. No touching. Nothing. Just this.

And he intended to find out.

Chapter Fifteen

A CAR HORN sounded outside.

John blinked sleepily at an unfamiliar ceiling. *Where the hell—*

A heavy weight shifted on his left bicep, and a burst of pins and needles prickled in his hand. He flexed the fingers, rubbery and near-numb, and the weight sighed.

Oh.

John rolled onto his side to cuddle up to the heat. He buried his nose in the back of Chris's curly hair and breathed in a heady scent of sleep and shampoo. Chris's T-shirt had ridden up a little, and John found the warm skin of his waist effortlessly, sliding his free hand over it to settle against the soft hair on his belly.

"Morning," he murmured.

Chris twitched and mumbled something in reply. His legs curled up a little towards his chest. John's followed, determined—now he had created the spoon—not to lose it.

For the longest time, John simply basked like that. And that in itself was unusual—John was a morning person. He usually bounced out of bed at six and went straight for a run. Judging by the grey light outside, it was closer to nine now. And yet, John didn't want to move.

Why would he? Chris lay fast asleep and trusting in his arms. He was so warm that John felt drowsy, almost drugged. His bare skin burned where it touched John's. His pulse was beating, deep and slow, against John's hand on his stomach.

And John could smell him. Sleep. Shampoo. Even the traces of sex, from that rutting orgasm John had given him before they curled together and went to sleep.

John twisted impossibly closer. Sex was one thing. But sleep was somehow far more intimate. To literally sleep with someone was incredible. Waking up beside somebody was one of the best, simplest pleasures in life. Every time a relationship broke down, whether that breakdown had been for the best—Daniel—or, as with the first Chris, completely against his will, John had fiercely missed the company first thing in the morning. He never felt more lonely than when he woke up on his own.

Chris was clearly unused to sleeping with someone else. When John stirred enough to kiss Chris's neck, he was absently swatted, and then Chris's shoulders twisted away from him, hard.

"S'just me," John murmured, and the sudden shock of movement eased.

"Oh. S'rry."

Then Chris turned right over and burrowed into John's chest, bringing the duvet up over his head before stilling again.

"Can I get a morning kiss?" John asked, wrapping both arms around the duvet-covered lump and squeezing.

"No. Sleep," came the muffled response.

"But I'm awake."

"I'm not."

"You sound it."

"Sleeptalking."

"I'm sure," John said sceptically.

"This is all a dream."

"A dream come true, waking up with you."

That got a response. Admittedly, the response was the duvet being pulled down just enough for a hand to emerge and flip him off, but it was still a response. John laughed, caught the wrist, and nipped the middle finger.

"Ow!"

"Mm, sorry." He kissed it better, then took the finger into his mouth up to the second knuckle and sucked on it.

Chris didn't seem to have a thing for finger-sucking, though: he just pulled the hand back with a laugh. But the grumpy front had lifted, and he wriggled up the bed a little to kiss John's cheek.

"Morning," he mumbled and buried his nose into John's throat.

"Can I get a proper kiss?"

"That was proper."

"No, it wasn't."

"Was too."

"Nope." John inched away just far enough to tuck his fingers under Chris's chin and turn his face up for the aforementioned proper kiss. It was soft and sweet, calm and chaste, and Chris hummed, smiling lightly against John's mouth.

"Better?" he murmured when John broke it.

John smiled, stroking the lower lip with his thumb.

"Almost."

The second kiss was longer. More open. Slowly, they wound together. Chris was a lithe length of lax warmth, and John spread his fingers wide over smooth skin and soft hair. Found the gentle rise and fall of ribs. Found a pronounced hip, which disappeared when Chris's leg came up to hook over John's thigh. Found that perfect arse again and squeezed it close and tight with both hands until Chris broke off the lazy kissing to whine and call him unfair.

"Think it's perfectly fair," John objected mildly and rolled his hips gently forward. He was half hard. And neither of them were wearing underwear. "Can I?"

"Uh-huh..."

John began to lightly thrust. He had no designs on anything sophisticated, nor even romantic. His body worked on instinct—there was warmth and heat and the promise of pleasure—and his brain was preoccupied with that gleaming lip ring that pressed cool and careful to his skin. He tugged on it until Chris opened up, both above and below, and turned on him, pressing him down into the mattress, to plunder his mouth. Chris felt a little different here, blurry with sleep and relaxation, than the desperate energy of the hallway floor.

The hand that crept around his cock was not entirely unexpected.

"Ah-ah," John murmured, tugging it away and planting it safely under the pillow. "Let me."

Chris submitted with a gentle sigh as the lip ring was tugged again. Did he have other piercings? John couldn't recall. Nothing down below, and questing fingers found an unmarred bellybutton. But John had never seen him shirtless, and Chris was so reactive—

He smoothed a hand up a slender spine, caught between man and mattress, and found a naked back under the T-shirt. No tight vest.

And—

Faintly, John realised what felt different. The chest pressed against his own was no longer hard and flat, but soft and yielding. He couldn't feel a nipple ring, but perhaps Chris didn't have it in. Was he sensitive?

John had never touched a boob before—never wanted to, didn't like them—but the pull of that possible sensitivity was alluring. What noise would Chris make? Would he yell, or just shiver? Would he squirm like he had when John had fingered him? Would he curse like he did getting a love bite?

John buried his mouth against Chris's neck and sucked at the memory. The whimper was soft. The whisper for another one softer. Legs opened beneath his own, and he slipped between them. Lust, hot and wet, touched the head of his dick.

Oh, God, could he?

John smoothed both hands down slim sides and bit again. Chris thrust up against him. Clutched his hair. Begged in a wordless whine.

They would be sensitive, John was sure of it, and he pushed a hand up under the cotton and found the gentle swell of a heaving breast and the hard arousal of an unseen nipple.

"No!"

John let go like he'd been shot.

"Okay!" he yelled, backing up with his hands out to his sides, even as Chris scrambled up the bed away from him, one hand suddenly clamped over his chest. "Okay! Okay, I'm not touching; I'm off you, I'm off—"

Panic hammered in his throat. No. Oh God, no. That shrill shout of—of what? Fear? Anger? Disgust?

Chris's face was wreathed in an expression John couldn't recognise. Somewhere between upset and angry. His mouth twisted.

"Chris?"

"N-no. No more. I—I need to get dressed."

"What's the—?"

John never got to finish the sentence. In half a beat, Chris was off the bed and out of the bedroom. John heard the clatter of clothes being torn from the drying rack in the main room. And then the bathroom door slammed.

And John was still kneeling on the end of the bed, naked and half hard, and utterly terrified.

He closed his eyes and counted to ten.

No. Chris had—panicked. Or something. But he'd hated that. And John wasn't thick, he knew exactly what he'd done that was wrong. He just had no idea why. And no idea if the look on Chris's face had been fear, or—

"Or," he told himself firmly. "You stopped. You did. You let go."

Immediately. It couldn't be fear. Chris couldn't be scared if John had let go, could he?

Slowly, John levered himself off the bed and found his underwear, figuring that sorting this out naked wasn't the best of ideas. On shuffling into the main room quietly, he found the bathroom door still closed, and an ominous silence.

Shit.

John bit his lip and rapped his knuckles on the bathroom door.

"Babe? You okay?"

"Don't *call* me that!"

John winced.

"I'm sorry. I'll go if you want. Soon as I know you're all right?"

"No."

John hesitated, unsure what the no meant, and then the lock clicked over, and the door opened.

Chris had put his undervest back on, and a pair of grey briefs. They were snug around a soft bulge again. He wriggled the sleep shirt back on and ran both hands through his curls. John itched to touch—a hug, a tweak of wild hair, *something*—but fisted his fingers around his thumbs, and kept his hands resolutely to himself.

"Sorry," Chris said.

"Don't be," John replied. "I should be. I *am*. I didn't know—"

Know what? He wasn't even one hundred percent sure what had happened.

"I didn't mention it before," Chris mumbled through his hands, before sighing and dropping them. "You can't touch my chest."

Oh.

"Ever."

John immediately felt rather stupid. He'd just assumed—

"The minute—the minute you do, the minute anyone does, I get this awful skin-crawling dysphoria. I *hate* it. I absolutely *hate* it, and I know it makes no sense when I love you fingering me or eating me out—"

"Oh, hey, it doesn't need to make sense—"

"—but I can't deal with it. I'm on the waiting list for surgery to get them removed, and I can't wait, but I can't sleep in the binder, and I *forgot*. I thought because you're gay, you'd not be interested in them, and—"

"Chris!"

The tirade stopped. Chris's hands twitched before he wrapped his arms around his stomach, and John grimaced.

"If you don't like me touching your chest," he said, "then I won't."

Chris's lips thinned.

"I'm not particularly interested in them," John said. "Can I get a pass for saying something possibly really dumb?"

"Um. Okay."

"I've been nervous of you taking your shirt off."

Chris frowned. "Why?"

"Because I'm gay," John said. "And while discovering your, uh, original features has been pretty exciting, I didn't know that'd be the case. And I *have* seen women topless before, up close and personal, like—"

"You have?"

"I was working in a builder's yard when I turned eighteen, and the lads took me to a strip joint."

"Oh."

"I spent most of the night texting my boyfriend at the time desperately asking what features I ought to find attractive in a girl so they wouldn't realise I was gay."

Chris smirked, despite the subject.

"My point is, I don't like women. Sexually speaking. And while I—got lucky, I guess, I enjoy making love to you—"

"*Urgh*, John..."

"—I *know* I'm not interested in boobs. So, I was nervous of you...full on stripping and my libido not agreeing with the rest of my brain about how bloody gorgeous you are."

"So...you're okay with...not...?"

"I'm totally fine with not," John said. "I only touched because I figured if you had sensitive nipples, you'd like it."

"I do," Chris admitted, "but I don't like it."

"Then I won't," John said. "I'm really not into boobs. And even if I was, I wouldn't go touching anything you don't like me touching."

"You say 'making love' even though I don't like it."

John hesitated. "I—thought you were kidding. If it's actually upsetting you, of course I—"

"It doesn't. But babe does."

"What?"

"I don't like it when you call me babe. I really don't. That's not— I just think making love sounds stupid. But babe...you don't call men babe."

"I do," John replied. "I've called every guy I've ever been with babe."

"Well, you don't call me babe. Not anymore."

There was a layer of steel in Chris's voice, and John instinctively raised his hands.

"Okay," he said. "Noted. Just...kick me until I get out of the habit."

Chris nodded. He still looked tense as hell, and John wasn't sure what to do. He wanted to offer a hug, but Chris clearly wasn't as completely comfortable being touched as John had thought.

"I'm sorry," John repeated. "It won't happen again. Babe, or boobs."

That earned him a faint smile.

"This is a bit heavy for what I'd hoped would be a slow, sexy start to a morning," John admitted. "How about I take you out for a proper greasy spoon breakfast, just the way electricians like it?"

The smile widened. "Okay. That sounds nice. Lemme get dressed."

John ducked into the bathroom as Chris ducked out of it, and freshened up with a borrowed toothbrush and stolen deodorant in lieu of his own toiletries. Smelling like Chris was weirdly hot, but John thought hard about distinctly unsexy thoughts before stepping back into the main room.

And hesitating.

The bedroom door was ajar, but John didn't know if he was welcome or not. Last night, he'd have just walked in, and if Chris was changing, then what a happy coincidence. Now? Now he wasn't sure.

So he waited until Chris came back out, doing up his belt. To John's pleased surprise, Chris caught him on the way past and kissed his jaw.

"Sorry for freaking you out," Chris murmured, and John smiled, daring to touch his hair lightly.

"Think it should be me making that apology."

"Mm, not this time. You didn't know. If you do it again, though, then you'll have to pull out all the stops. Got it?"

"Got it."

He ducked into the bedroom to retrieve his scattered clothes and get dressed. By the time he re-emerged, Chris had put on his shoes and was waiting with his cane. With a pang, John's suddenly switched-on brain picked out the things he probably wouldn't have noticed otherwise. The shadow of stubble, when every other time he'd seen him, Chris had been clean-shaven. The bulge in tight jeans that hadn't been there last time. The stiff flatness of his chest, when now John knew full well it wasn't by chance.

He looked more masculine than John had ever seen him, and John had the distinct impression it was due to his screw-up.

But to comment on it, John suspected, wouldn't be a good idea.

So, instead, he put on his boots, shrugged on his jacket—and cupped Chris's chin between finger and thumb to kiss him sharply.

"You look gorgeous," he said simply.

Chris's face pinked.

"Now, let's get breakfast, and try starting today over."

Chapter Sixteen

"SO," JOHN SAID as the waitress cleared the empty plates, and Chris asked—of course—for another coffee, "are we okay?"

It was a slightly redundant question. Chris had brightened up after the first shot of caffeine and had flirted outrageously for the last half hour, but John's demons demanded satisfaction, especially with what he was about to ask.

"What? Yes. Why wouldn't we be?"

John rolled his eyes. "Because I freaked you out, and you know my history by now."

Chris cocked his head to the side and smiled.

"Yes," he said softly. "We're okay."

"Sure?"

"Yes. You didn't know, and now you do. And you stopped when I asked you to. So we're fine. Promise."

John blew upwards into his hair. "Okay. So—no pressure, okay? Whatever you pick, I'm totally good with."

"Pick?"

"Christmas is coming."

"And will soon be over, thank fuck."

John raised his eyebrows. "What?"

"I *hate* Christmas carols."

John snorted and shook his head. "All right, Scrooge."

"So what about Christmas?"

"I have this sort of...tradition," John said. "And no pressure, if it's too early for it or you're not interested, then fine—"

"Mind telling me what it is before trying to talk me out of it?" Chris prompted.

John laughed awkwardly. "Sorry. Okay. Uh. I have a thing about the sea. Especially a rough sea, when it's crashing about and you can see the foam on the waves."

"Uh-huh..."

"And during the winter, you can get really good rates at holiday cottages, and I always hate the New Year party scene. I'm not out at work, and the lads always want to go out and get pissed and leer at girls, and I'm not into that. So, I always just...went away. I'd go on Boxing Day, stay a week, and come back when the parties were over. And it turned into this tradition, and I kept it up."

"You want to go away for New Year?"

"Yeah."

"Go...where?"

"The North Sea coast. There's a few nice places. I usually go to Robin Hood's Bay or Whitby, but Aljaz found these great little cottages in Flamborough—"

"And you want to take me?"

John felt a hot flush rising in his face.

"Yeah."

"And do what? I can't exactly watch your foam-tipped waves."

"You can hear it though. And put your feet in it."

"At New Year? You have to be joking."

"I'd warm them up again."

"Not convinced."

"If I go to Robin Hood's Bay," John said hopefully, "I always rent out this tiny little cottage on the cliffs. It's got this big hearth that you can have a real fire in, and rugs everywhere, and the bedroom is up in the eaves of the roof with a huge skylight window. So, you can hear the sea all night, crashing below the cliffs."

Chris was chewing on his lip.

"And the bed is custom-made," John murmured. "It's a huge four-poster job. You could fit a rugby team in there. It's the most comfortable bed I've ever slept in, and I know how amazing you'd look—" He glanced about and lowered his voice. "—sprawled out in the sheets while I make love to you."

Chris groaned.

"What *is* it with you and that phrase?"

John laughed nervously, ducking his head.

"Or, we could go see a band, get chips on the way back to mine, and cuddle in a new calendar?"

Chris toyed with the coffee cup. "I like the sound of this cottage. I like the sea. We always had seaside holidays when I was a kid, and I still like walking barefoot in sand, even though it's bloody hard work with a cane."

"So...?"

"Every Christmas Eve, I have Christmas dinner and drinks with Luke and Gina. I know you're panicky about meeting my family, but we have to start somewhere if this is going to become a long-term thing. I figure Luke and Gina are a good place to start. So, if you come to my Christmas Eve tradition with me, then I'll come to your New Year one with you. Deal?"

Really? John just had to go to dinner with a lesbian he'd already seen once, and the trans guy who worked out with Chris? That was all?

And then he'd get a whole week of this man—*this man*—in a tiny little cottage at the seaside in return?

"Deal," he breathed.

WHEN JOHN GOT home from work, he found himself staring at the closed fridge door.

He and Nora used it like a corkboard, a collection of magnets sticking to-do lists, building maintenance numbers, Mum and Dad's anniversary reminder, and so on, to the white surface.

But it wasn't Mum and Dad's anniversary that caught John's eye.

It was the simple brown card, bordered in white like a fancy chocolate.

Nadia Simmons.

It was just her name and a phone number, and John had never met the woman. Nora had got it for him after the police dropped the investigation, made him promise to think about it, and John had stuck it to the fridge.

He'd never thought about it until today.

Nadia Simmons was a counsellor.

John didn't much go in for that sort of thing. Until Daniel, he'd never felt the need. He knew of people who needed counsellors, sure—Tasha with her anger management sessions, Rhodri's missus with her anti-depressants—but John had never been one of them. Until Daniel, he'd been relatively...

Well, happy seemed a trite way to put it, but...*yeah*.

And then Daniel had happened. Nora told him he ought to think about it, and anyone would have battle scars left over from that fiasco, but John hadn't bothered. He'd be fine, he told himself. Daniel had been a lying c—well, C-word, and none of it was true, and so what if John still had nightmares? He wasn't sleeping with anyone. It was probably just the loneliness.

But the panic attack at seeing Chris's stepmother was undeniable.

And Chris had said—

Well. John had said boyfriend. Chris had said long-term thing. They were heading in the very direction John wanted them to head...and he'd had a meltdown because Chris's stepmother had seen him. At a farm fair. Without even knowing who he was.

"Nora!"

"What?"

"This Nadia woman..."

"Who?"

"Nadia Simmons!"

"Who?"

"Turn the bloody telly off!" he shouted, then gave up and wandered into the living room with the card. Nora scowled up at him, halfway through a marathon of one of the *Real Housewives* series. "Nadia Simmons. Who recommended her?"

Nora stared at the card.

"Oh my God," she said. "Are you seriously thinking of going and seeing her?"

"I don't know. Maybe. How'd you get her card?"

"Gavin at work," Nora said promptly. "He was seeing her after his boyfriend died. Said she was really good, really non-judgemental."

"So, she does...gay people, then?"

"Specialises in LGBT, I think. You could always look her up. Or I could ask Gavin."

"S'fine," John said absently, rubbing the card between finger and thumb.

"What's brought this on?"

John blew out his cheeks. "So…I'm taking Chris to the coast for New Year's. You know. My tradition thing."

"Oh my God!"

"And he said if he came to the coast with me, I had to go to dinner with his mates on Christmas Eve. Apparently, it's their thing."

"So, Nadia because…"

John swallowed. "Because we went to the Whirlow Hall Farm Fair, and his stepmum was there, and I had a panic attack."

"Oh, *John*."

"I mean, she didn't even know who I was, and it was just a coincidence, but I freaked. That's…that's how I ended up telling Chris about Daniel."

She patted the sofa, tucking her feet under to make room. When John sat next to her, he was promptly hugged.

"You think I should go?"

"Yes," she said. "I think if there's nothing to do but wait it out and relax and you'll be fine, then she'll tell you in a couple of sessions, and you can stop going again. Or she might help you with some of the damage, and you can stop worrying so much."

John didn't even bother denying that he was worrying.

"You know, though, if you go off to the coast for New Year, Nan's going to have kittens that she didn't know about this guy."

"Nora…"

"I don't even know him!"

"By sheer luck," he said.

"By sheer not wanting to see my baby brother in the buff," she sniped, hugging her six-foot-eight 'baby brother' tightly. "Can *I* meet him, at least? Just me? Maybe come out with me and Raj sometime?"

"I don't know."

"I *promise* not to breathe a word to the others," she said. "Please? I want to meet this supermodel that's swept you off your feet."

John bit his lip. He wanted to. God, he did. He wanted to show Chris off to them, show them he'd not only gotten over Daniel but caught someone completely and utterly perfect instead. But once he introduced Chris to his family, then he'd *have* to meet Chris's, wouldn't he? It would set a clock ticking, almost. That was how that sort of thing worked.

"Okay," he caved. "But *just* you. And—not long. Just...I don't know...he comes over, and you go out? Nice and quick?"

"Well, not *that* quick..."

"Noz."

Her hated nickname stopped her short.

"I'm scared," John whispered. "I'm scared his family are going to take one look at me and see the thug Daniel lied about. I'm—I can't really explain it, but with Chris— God, with Chris it would be even easier to run with that lie. And I'm scared that's what they'll see, *who* they'll see, and they'll immediately start trying to prise me and Chris apart."

Her face softened. She touched his arm gently.

"If he meets all of you," John said, "then it's only a matter of time before I have to meet his folks, or I'm giving them ammunition to use against me, aren't I? And I need—I need more time."

Nora bit her lip.

"I just need until after New Year," John breathed. "Just—let me keep him until then. And then after New Year, after—after a whole week, me and him, and maybe me getting a session or two lined up with this Nadia woman... maybe then they won't be able to persuade him I'm dangerous."

She squeezed his wrist tightly.

"John."

He glanced at her face.

"If he doesn't already know that," she said, "then he's not the one you're looking for."

Chapter Seventeen

WHEN JOHN AGREED to Christmas Eve dinner, he'd forgotten a crucial point.

It was about a week away.

The run-up to Christmas was busy, as far as work was concerned. Fuses were being blown left, right, and centre as decorations overloaded circuits; idiots fell off ladders hanging lights and brought half the wiring down after them; and—John's personal favourite—an overenthusiastic four-year-old, gift-hunting, managed to topple a wardrobe onto a rotten floor and bring a bedroom tumbling right through into the flat below.

(The four-year-old was fine. The flat was condemned.)

So, as it was, he didn't even see Chris until Christmas Eve itself. By which time, the stupidity of what he'd agreed to had sunk in.

The tradition apparently moved bars every year, and always insisted on nothing Christmassy about it. This year, Gina had picked a Mexican restaurant on London Road, and Chris called telling John to meet them there.

"Luke and I are coming from the gym," he said. "So, if you arrive at about six, that'd be perfect."

So, at ten to, John was sitting in his car, parked around the corner, and sweating bullets.

He'd checked out the restaurant online, and it was a casual joint, so he had no idea how to dress. He'd passed muster with Gina at the farm, but Luke had never seen him.

Would Luke be okay with tattooed muscle everywhere, or would it make him uncomfortable? Even wary? Was he the protective sort of friend, or would he leave Chris to make his own mistakes and to hell with what his new boyfriend looked like? John knew his strengths—love and laughter. Not looks.

In the end, he'd gone for his nicest jeans, a well-fitted, plain white T-shirt with long sleeves to hide most of the ink, and a decent jacket thrown over the top. There was nothing he could do about his neck tattoo, not in a restaurant serving hot food, but at least it was reasonably inoffensive. Just some mountains. Who could get upset by some mountains?

"You look great," Nora had said before shooing him out of the door so she could claim the flat for her and Raj. "You are definitely going back to his place for the night. So, go and knock 'em dead."

John felt more like dropping dead, rather than knocking anybody else dead.

But the car clock hit five to, and he forced himself out.

The restaurant was decently busy, but he caught sight of Chris's curls immediately. He was sitting with two black girls and a white girl with sandy fair hair and wearing a band T-shirt. Swallowing his nerves, John waved away the waiter and strode over—only for Gina, when he got within about twenty feet, to suddenly spot him.

"Oh my God," she said and beamed. "Chris, I thought you were *joking*!"

John coughed awkwardly.

"About what?" Chris asked.

"That your new boyfriend was this guy! Hi." She stuck a hand up to shake his. "I'm Gina. I saw you at Whirlow Hall Farm, didn't I? I thought Chris was kidding that you were a serious thing though!"

John's enormous paw completely enveloped her hand. "John, and, uh, no. He's not kidding."

She beamed as though he'd announced his intention to propose.

"Excuse me. Priorities," Chris said tartly and tapped his cheek.

John laughed, a sliver of relief making itself known, and stooped to kiss him. He went for the mouth, obviously, and caught Chris in a long, slow kiss that gave his usually blank eyes a sexy glazed look.

"Hi."

"Um. Hi," Chris murmured back.

John pulled out the last chair and sat down.

And finally looked at these friends.

Gina looked nothing like the wellie-wearing girl from the farm fair. She was dressed to impress for the occasion: her hair formed a perfect halo around her head in an Afro; her earrings glittered in the bright light. She was enormously pretty, and the transfixed look from the girl at her side distinctly mapped out that relationship. That girl turned out to be Jemma. From the slightly blank introduction, John guessed she was as new to this tradition as he was.

The sandy-haired girl turned out, in fact, to be Luke. John immediately grasped why he and Chris were gym buddies. Luke didn't pass whatsoever, but his handshake was firm, and he instantly homed in on the neck tattoo, showing off a mountainscape in dotwork on his own upper arm. He was friendly enough, and John relaxed a little as Luke asked after bodybuilding tips, and Chris—apparently wholly uninterested in the conversation—casually slid an arm through John's, wound their fingers together, rested his head on John's shoulder, and talked to the girls about a TV show.

This...this was fine.

It was...nice, even. It had been a long time—a *very* long time—since John had gone to dinner with friends and a boyfriend at the same time. But Chris's friends had either been forewarned or genuinely didn't care about this far older, back-end-of-a-bus ugly bloke that their mate had started sleeping with. Luke wanted to talk ink and gyms, and John figured they'd probably get along all right. Jemma was absorbed in her seemingly new girlfriend, so not in the least bit interested, and Gina even seemed to think he was a catch. Her amazement was apparently rooted in her bad gaydar; she'd taken him for closeted and had been insisting it wouldn't last. But his presence at their tradition seemed to have changed her mind, and she gawped at him like it was the first time they'd met.

"Talk about tall," she said, more than once. "Chris, I think it's incredible you can even *walk.*"

John felt himself going red then, which led her to decide he was shy, and therefore sweet.

And it felt—

Good.

Their approval—perhaps not as clear as approval, but their acceptance, or tolerance at the very least—was warming. They hadn't given Chris, or each other, those urgent looks of, *oh my God, is this for real?* that John had come to fear. They hadn't started those awful interrogations of what he did, what he saw in Chris, what his history was. They just smiled, and talked about normal stuff, and acted like he was part of the group. He even dared to filch what Chris didn't want to finish off his plate, and when they made fun of how much he ate, it didn't feel cruel or judgemental. He found himself laughing instead.

It was fine.

Jesus, had it really always been this easy?

Perhaps if Chris's family disapproved, John could use this moment, and these people, to buy himself more time. Maybe if he hung out with Chris's friends more often, then he could lean on their approval a little to help prove to Chris's parents he wasn't—

He choked off the thought.

He *wasn't*.

Christ, what was he trying so desperately to prove? He knew full well he wasn't dangerous. And Chris did too. He'd even inadvertently proved it, by his mistake the other morning.

John told himself to relax and tuned back into the conversation.

They stayed quite late. The girls left first, but Chris and Luke wanted to talk about some idiot personal trainer at the gym who Luke couldn't stand, so it was gone ten o'clock before Luke waved for the bill, and John casually batted Chris's hand away from his jacket pocket.

"I've got this," he said.

"Are you sure?"

"Yep."

Chris's fingers tightened a little on his wrist.

"You can get breakfast on Boxing Day," John said, and the grip relaxed.

It came back, though, when Luke had gone and they were walking to the car, Chris's arm tucked into John's elbow. When the car beeped and unlocked, Chris stopped dead, and his cold fingers rose to find John's face.

The kiss that followed them was sweet from a nonalcoholic cocktail and tingled lightly from the remnants of a spice John didn't know.

"Thank you?"

"See?" Chris murmured, beaming brightly. "Wasn't so bad, was it?"

"It...was actually okay."

"They liked you."

John bit his lip a little, trying to hide the smile. "Good?"

"Wouldn't matter if they didn't."

"No?"

"Nope. I don't think you've figured that part out yet."

"What part?"

"The part where I'm a snotty little shit, and I don't do as I'm told."

John laughed. "Jesus."

"I don't care what other people think you are, John. I care what *I* think you are. And so far, I think you're a sweet, sexy son of a bitch."

John cupped the back of his neck and leaned down to kiss him.

Without Chris stretching up, the kiss was oddly a little more open. The angle made his jaw lax and his lips passive. John nipped once at that lip ring before sinking deeper. Chris sagged against him and simply allowed it. Clutched at the front of his jacket, and submitted. Even when John's hand slid down from neck to the small of Chris's back to pull him closer, Chris made no move to take back control.

And when John broke the kiss, to press his forehead to Chris's and smile, those bright blue eyes were closed. He looked blissfully serene, and John couldn't resist kissing that gleaming lip ring once more.

"Mine's busy," he murmured. "Want to go back to yours?"

"Hotel would be closer," came the reply, along with a hand toying with John's belt buckle.

"Hotel costs money."

"Can't stay at mine for free, you know."

"No?"

"Nope."

"Mm. Okay. How much does half your bed cost?"

"Half?"

"All right, two thirds."

"For the whole night?"

"Yep."

Chris pressed his nose to John's cheek. John felt the wide smile.

"For you? Special rate."

"Yeah?"

"Uh-huh. Only two orgasms per night."

"Yeah? I can do tha—"

"Both mine."

"YOU OWE ME another one."

The whisper was devious. John stretched but couldn't find the warmth. And when he grumbled and rubbed the sleep from his face, the room was full of light.

"Morning."

"Get b'ck here..."

"Can't. It's morning."

"*Can.* Can't pay the room charge if you're not here..."

A laugh. The mattress dipped and the sheets rustled, and then a kiss was being pressed to his cheek, clumsy and off-centre.

John grabbed.

He caught an arm, and Chris came crashing down on top of him with a yell and a laugh. He was wearing a dressing gown, and it made the juncture of his neck and shoulder, when John buried his face there, even warmer than usual.

"Merry Christmas," he mumbled and contracted all four limbs around Chris's wriggling body. "I'm going to stay here for it."

"You can't," Chris said but shivered in a way that completely betrayed him when John gnawed lightly on his neck.

"Still owe you that orgasm though."

"Mhmm, you do."

"And I have a confession to make."

"What's that?"

John kissed the mark he'd left with his teeth. "Been so caught up, I didn't get you a present."

"You got me that leather thing at the fair."

"That's a trinket. That's not a proper present."

"Ooh, bad boyfriending, then."

"Did you get me one?"

"Nope."

"Well, then, we have a situation here."

"Yes," Chris said, hooking a leg over the back of John's thigh. "You're on top of me, but you're not doing anything about paying the room charge. It's serious."

"Oh, yeah?"

"Mm. Might have to call a lawyer."

"Only if he's fit," John bargained and propped himself up on his elbows, resting them either side of Chris's shoulders. "What d'you want for Christmas, then, beautiful?"

"You know exactly what I want."

"Which is?"

"You. Inside. Me."

John laughed and shook his head against Chris's. "Nope. Too much hurt."

Chris whined, and John bit the sound away.

"Tell you what though," he murmured. "Got a whole week at the coast to build up to it."

"Mm, okay."

"So, what do you want for Christmas?"

Fingers knitted together behind his head, dragging him in for a kiss. A hungry, aggressive, plundering kiss that had John struggling to keep his weight from dropping, all twenty stone of it, onto Chris's slender frame.

"I know," Chris whispered against John's lips, "that you want to worship my arse."

John's dick, despite the early hour, twitched.

"Maybe."

"So, get one of my vibrators out of my top drawer," Chris murmured, rocking his hips up again. "And fuck me with it while you're paying homage. Sound good?"

John didn't even bother to remove the dressing gown. Just untangled himself, turned Chris over, and bunched it up above his waist.

"Top drawer?"

"Mm."

John pressed a kiss to the small of his back and got up off the bed.

"When d'you have to go to your parents' for Christmas dinner?" Chris murmured.

John turned back from the drawer, the largest vibrator in hand, and swallowed.

Just—Chris.

Stretched out. Naked from the waist down. Eyes closed peacefully. Arms folded around the pillow, his dark curls spilling across it in a tangle.

Gorgeous.

Absolutely bloody gorgeous.

"Not for ages," John said and switched the vibrator on. "Got any lube?"

Chapter Eighteen

HE WAS LATE to Christmas dinner.

So late that when he finally texted Nora, saying he was on his way, he was tartly told that Raj wasn't as useless as him and had given them all a lift.

Lucky you, John replied. *Is Mum needling him about God again?*

I didn't say he was stupid enough to stay, Nora replied snottily.

Nora's boyfriend, Raj, was a source of controversy in the family. John had never thought much of Nora's ex-husband, Greg, so hadn't been exactly put out when Nora ran off with Raj. Greg was a pompous arse whose every second sentence started with, "When I worked for the Prime Minister..."

Raj worked in his mum's sandwich shop. And he thought football was for nancies. John liked him much better.

Mum, though, had been appalled. In theory, it was the Christian in her—whatever would she tell the vicar, it would be the talk of the village—but in reality, Mrs Halliday wasn't so moralistic as all that. The Christian in her wasn't the least bit perturbed by the gay son or the suspiciously short six-month gap between her own marriage and her eldest daughter being born. No, John's mum's God wasn't *that* fussy. Mum was a pragmatic woman rather than a Bible-thumper, and everyone knew full well what the real problem was.

Greg had been raking in over seventy grand a year. Raj was lucky to make seventeen.

That was the problem.

And John sympathised to a tiny degree. He wasn't the big dreamer that Fran was. He'd trained because he needed to find work, and he saved religiously to weather out the dry spells between jobs. But he'd rather have to count his pennies and take his holidays in drafty cottages on the British coast than put up with a stuffy, suit-wearing bore like Greg for the rest of his life.

Usually, Mum's disapproval wasn't really visible. She and Dad had gone off to France the split second Tasha left school, and they only came to visit at Christmas. Ignoring a frown and curt phone calls was easy if one simply didn't answer the phone. But at Christmas, their opinions—or rather, Mum's opinions—became inescapable.

For Nora. Sounded like Raj was smarter than that.

Sure enough, once John had wrestled the van round the icy, tight roads of Hathersage, he found the driveway empty. He lurched the van up into it and stamped his boots off on the mat before letting himself in through the kitchen door to the smells of roast potatoes, fir trees, and woodsmoke.

"There you are!"

The little cottage was packed. Two newspapers were held aloft in front of armchairs, John's father and grandfather indistinguishable from behind their paper shields. Mum caught him inside the door before he could even take his boots off.

"Let me look at you!" she trilled.

John's Mum didn't look entirely unlike his grandmother, despite the lack of blood relation. She was similarly short and round, though her hair was still firmly blonde and cut practically short. A former nurse, she still walked everywhere in that rapid shuffle that wasn't quite a run, left over from years of scurrying about hospital wards without sprinting and making the patients panic. She always smelled of the same perfume, and if the family joke was that John had been left on the doorstep due to his towering size, he'd at least inherited enough of her fair colouring to know it was a lie.

"Sorry I'm late," he said. "Got a bit sidetracked."

"Hm. Doing what?"

He coloured. "Uh."

"Oh, I see," she said, putting her hands on her hips. "So, Nora wasn't telling fibs."

"Um. Depends what she said?"

"Said you have a new squeeze. And spent the night with him."

"Urgh, *Mum*."

"Did you?"

"My new *boyfriend*. And yeah."

"So?"

"...So?" John asked.

"Well! Where is he?"

"I don't know. Probably *his* parents."

"So, you didn't bring him to meet us?"

"On Christmas Day?"

"It's as good as any other," she retorted.

"No, Mum. It's not that serious yet." He forked over the lie that usually pacified her.

Instead, she snorted. "Spending Christmas morning with him is serious enough. You'll bring him over tomorrow. Your Dad and I don't fly home until the day after."

"Uh, if I can," he hedged, immediately deciding they would have to set off for the coast first thing. It would have snowed on the moors by now. They'd have to go the long way around.

He was allowed to escape into the dining room to join the rest of his family. Nora was looking very mumsy in a fluffy jumper and her hair hanging down. Fran looked more like an elf had exploded on her, her blue hair done up in a bizarre basket-weaving project with a jaunty paper crown askew on the very top. Tasha, as always, was texting furiously. At her elbow, Daisy gurgled in her highchair and threw a plastic spoon at her mother with a wail when gurgling failed to get a response. Nan was flitting about with crockery and cutlery, scolding Mum when she tried to help. They must have been waiting for John, as he heard the creak of chairs, and Dad and Granddad shuffled in—a young fat version of the old thin version entering as though in procession.

"Were you with your boyfriend?" Fran sang.

"Yes. Shut up."

"No. Didn't you bring him?"

"No."

"Why?"

"Because it's not much of a Christmas present, exposing him to you lot," John sniped and got kicked under the table for it. "Ow!"

"Deserved it."

"Did not!"

"Honestly," Nan said, bustling in with the first of the plates. "Francesca, you are twenty-four years old. And John, you ought to set an example."

"She's twenty-four; she doesn't need an example."

"I'm your ickle baby sister and you *luuuuurv* me!" Fran said obnoxiously.

"You're a pain in the arse, and Granddad said I could drown you in the duck pond last week, so watch yourself."

"Did not."

"Did too."

"Children!"

It was like being a kid again. Home was good like that. John wasn't thirty-six and still scraping his life back together after Daniel, not here. He was a big brother with bratty little sisters, and he could throw things at them without people getting touchy about it.

So he did, lobbing a spoon at her before Nan whacked him around the back of the head with a wooden spatula, and put a plate the size of a dustbin lid in front of him.

For a little while, peace descended in the form of food. Nan was a Yorkshire nan: if you loved someone, you fed them. Even Granddad would put down the newspaper in deference to a meal being served, though the minute he cleared his plate, that gnarled face disappeared behind *The Daily Telegraph* again. Conversation revolved around the church service that morning—"Such a shame none of you could make it in time."—and Daisy teething—"The poor dear."—and some announcement in the local paper last week that one of Nora's ex-boyfriends was getting married.

"Good for him," Nora said firmly, "and good luck to his new wife."

"He was lovely, though, dear..."

"He was a prick."

"Eleanor!"

"Come off it, Daisy's not old enough to understand. And I bet Tash says worse."

Tasha smirked over the top of her phone but didn't rise to it.

"There's no need for it," Mum said primly. "What about you, Francesca, dear? Anyone on the horizon?"

"What, a boyfriend?"

"Yes."

"Nope. I don't do relationships," she announced, and John smirked.

"You mean since Marc turned out to have a girlfriend and not be as liberal as you thought."

"Well, he wasn't. Monogamy is a damaging social construct, and—"

"Yes, dear, I'm sure," Mum interrupted. "How about you, Natasha?"

A shrug.

So it came right back around to—

"John?"

John sighed. "I told you. It's new."

"Yes, and you told us very little, you know."

"Um, well..."

Largely because the kinds of things Mum wanted to know, John didn't. He knew Chris's clothing sizes and what he sounded like when he came. He knew he liked oranges, and he used flowery shower gels for the smell. Knew what he had under his clothes and the way he smiled when he was kissed right.

Didn't have a bleeding clue what his last name was though.

"You *will* bring him over tomorrow, won't you?"

"Thing is, Mum..."

"John..."

"I want to take this slow and steady," John said. "I don't want to go rushing in like I always do."

Like he always did, because John did this thing where he fell in love practically at once and pinned everything on each new boyfriend the moment he came along. And he'd done it again—knew perfectly well he'd done it again, and, as far as his heart was concerned, it was far too late. But last time he'd done it, just rushed in without listening to his head and checking out the warning signs, he'd nearly been destroyed.

"I don't want to throw everything at this for it not to work," John said. "And I think—I think it *is* working, but I want to be sure first. After...last time."

There was a tense pause.

They didn't discuss Daniel. It was the one thing Mum never asked after. The one thing Nan and Granddad blithely pretended hadn't happened. The one thing John couldn't talk about.

"Last time," she echoed faintly and nodded. "Yes. Well. Last time. That's very sensible of you, dear."

"Did you tell him about last time?" Fran asked.

John grimaced. "Yes."

"Yes?"

"Yeah, I did, okay?"

"What did he s—"

"Said it sounded like Daniel was an arse, and he didn't believe a word of Daniel's version of events," John said, unable to keep himself from throwing a dirty look Tasha's way.

"Good," Mum said. "He sounds lovely. I still say you should bring him round tomorrow."

"Sure. If I can."

"No ifs, darling. Do it."

"Okay." *Not.*

"He won't," Nora chimed in.

"Noz!"

"John."

"He hasn't even brought Chris to the flat when I'm home."

"That's coincidence," John said.

"Don't believe you," came the reply.

"You don't have to. It's still the truth. Anyway, he *was* at the flat same time as you. You just went out again."

"Uh, yeah, because I didn't want to listen to my brother getting it on!"

"Eleanor!"

Fran crowed with laughter; John felt a savage heat rising in his face.

"I *hate* you," he whined, and Nora rolled her eyes.

"Stop it, both of you," Nan said. "That's no such talk for the table. Eleanor, dear. How is the separation going?"

The talk veered away from John, thank God, and he prodded his half-finished meal and turned over the thoughts that had stirred up in his head. He knew it was inevitable. He'd have to meet Chris's folks someday. He just wanted more time, first. Maybe meet Nadia Simmons, and work on Chris's friends a little bit.

But maybe the longer he put it off, the worse it would be?

Maybe he could return the favour of meeting Chris's friends by introducing him to Nora, at least? Nora would be safe enough. And maybe his tiny hairdresser older sister who bossed him about all the time would be a good addition to the picture Chris had of him, and the picture he could hand to Chris's family?

He prodded the cooling roast potatoes and resumed eating.

Maybe when they came back from the coast, they could spend one more evening together at the flat.

Maybe.

Chapter Nineteen

IT DIDN'T WORK out like that.

John had just arrived at the flats and pressed the bell for Chris's on the intercom, when Nora texted him.

You forgot your wallet.

John's hand flew to his pocket. *Shit!*

"Hello?"

Oh, like hell he'd forgotten it. He always kept it zipped into the inside pocket. She'd poached it, the thieving little—

"Hello?"

Crap.

"Hey, it's me."

"Oh." The door released. "You want to come up for a cup of tea, or...?"

"Um, no, best—best get going, I reckon."

"Okay. Be right down."

The intercom clicked off, and John stood back, quietly seething. The conniving little—just for this, *just* for this, he'd leave Chris in the car while he ran back up into the flat to get it. What *was* it with his family and trying to squeeze their way into this? Jesus, couldn't he have one—

The communal door opened, and John's thoughts jangled to a halt.

"That's—not fair."

"What?"

"You *know* what."

"I don't!"

"Christ…"

That bloody lip ring was back. And to add insult to injury, Chris's hair had curled long enough for him to tuck it behind one ear. And in the midst of those wild curls, a new bit of metal had appeared. A silver bar, punched through the shell of his ear.

And judging by the lack of reddening or swelling, it wasn't new. He just hadn't bothered to show it off before.

"I have no idea what you're talking about," Chris said loftily and skittered the cane lightly over the paving stones until it hit John's boot. "So? We going?"

John's answer was to lean over and suck one of the silver balls holding the bar in place into his mouth.

"Fuck."

Chris shuddered. Grasped at his shoulder. Rocked entirely into him when John slid a palm around that slim arse and pulled him close.

And whined when John let go.

"Not fair," he whispered.

"You put it there," John accused and let go. "Come on. Nora's filched my wallet, so we have to stop by the flat and get it. Then we can hit the road."

"Can't we stop at your flat for a shag first?"

"No."

Chris pulled a face before very deliberately biting his lip so the ring glimmered in the weak sun.

"Sure?"

"Yes, or we'll never get there, you looking like sex on legs in that silver."

"It's titanium."

"Whatever."

With all the insistence of a class A prima donna, Chris pouted all the way into the passenger seat and demanded a kiss before they set off, but settled benignly after and played with the radio to find a station he liked.

"How long is it to your holiday cottage?"

"Depends how bad the roads are. We might have to go the long way 'round."

"Okay." A pause. "You, um. You do realise at some point this week, you're going to see me have a seizure."

"I know."

"You...ready for that?"

"No," John said. "It's going to scare the shit out of me, I'll handle you like glass after, and you'll snap at me to make me get over myself. But, you know. Not going to take off on you."

"Sure?"

"Promise. Though you might take off on me in a minute."

"Why?"

"Mum was nagging about me taking you up to Hathersage to meet my folks today."

"We're not, are we?"

"No. But Nora's obviously pinched my wallet, so we have to go back to the flat."

"Oh."

"You could stay in the car, if you want," John said. "You don't have to meet her. She's being sly."

"Do you want me to meet her?"

"Honestly?"

"Yeah."

"Um. I don't really know."

"What do you mean?"

John sighed as he wrestled the car round an icy junction, heading towards the city centre. "Part of me wants you to, so—so I can show you off, and make a bit of progress past the crap Daniel's left me with. And part of me wants you to say no, because I don't want to worry about what you think of them and vice versa, and I don't want to have to deal with any more nerves this week."

"So—"

"So...it's up to you. It really is."

"Then I'm going to stay in the car."

John was quietly surprised. Chris had pushed the issue with his friends and didn't seem to want to tolerate being a secret. John said as much.

"Oh, that's not it."

"No?"

"No. You came and met Luke and Gina fine. So, I'm not getting those dirty little secret vibes anymore."

John grimaced. "You're not—"

"I know. Now. I'm not worried about that, so I'm not fussed about meeting your family sooner rather than later."

"So, no, because..."

"Because I meet people when I want, not when they steal their brother's wallets and try and force it."

John laughed. "Christ."

"Could you park around the corner and leave me with the radio, so she can't even look out the window?"

"Sure," John said, warming to the idea. "It won't take half a second. There's a café round the corner that sells your posh coffee. You could grab something there?"

That earned approval, of course, so John parked outside one of the many organic-gluten-lactose-free-vegan-fair trade coffee houses (never cafés) and took Chris to the door before walking around to the flats.

And found Nora waiting for him on the landing, looking suitably disappointed.

"I thought you'd already picked him up!"

"I did," John said, plucking his wallet back from her. "He didn't fancy walking up here just to get a wallet."

"I'll come down and say hi, then—"

"Can't stop," John said and laughed at her pout. "He didn't fancy getting coerced into meeting anybody."

"It's not coercion!"

"It *is*. I never forget my wallet."

"Well, you did."

"What, it magically unzipped my pocket and jumped out?"

"Yes," she said. "All right, fine, but you can't blame me for trying. Maybe bring him up after your trip?"

"Maybe," John allowed.

To his surprise, she stretched up and hugged him.

"Have fun," she mumbled into his jacket. "Don't overthink things. Just—*be*. Okay? Just be you, and enjoy yourself."

"Thanks, Nora..."

"And Happy New Year."

"You too."

On the walk back down and around the corner, John prodded at his feelings on the matter and made himself a promise. If the week went well, then he'd take the plunge. If they saw in the new year with some romantic beach kiss— or, knowing Chris, making love to him on the stroke of midnight buried so deep it was impossible to tell where John ended and Chris began—then John would suck up the courage and meet Chris's family.

But he was still going to leave introducing Chris to his own in those pale, sensitive hands.

THE WEATHER WAS foul.

The moors were passable, but barely. All the traffic had converged onto the one major road, and when the heater, overtaxed from the long journey, began to make suspicious noises near Pickering, John gave up and offered a pub lunch.

"It'll give the car time to recover, and I'm bloody hungry anyway."

"Could always eat me."

"You don't offer up enough protein for my diet."

"You're not eating me right, then."

"You sure about that?" John asked, ducking across the car to nip Chris's neck.

"Mmph. Okay. Maybe you are."

John had stopped in the little pub on the outskirts of Pickering before and knew they made a mean pie. They settled in a corner booth, pies ordered and Chris—to John's surprise—nursing a large pint of Guinness.

"You can drink?"

"Can. Don't usually."

"Doesn't it mess with your drugs?"

"Not at this amount," Chris said. "Can't get *drunk*, drunk, but a few units doesn't do any harm."

"Huh."

"What about you? Obviously not when you're driving, but..."

John swallowed. "I, uh. I don't drink."

"No?"

"No."

Chris's voice lowered. "Is that something I shouldn't ask about?"

John chewed on the corner of his lip. "I wasn't in a great place, after Daniel. And I'm...big."

"I noticed."

"I've never been aggressive, not a day in my life, even the lads at rugby rib me for being too nice to the other team."

"But after Daniel, that changed?"

"A little bit," John admitted. "When I drank, I'd get—I don't know. Brusque. Not quite aggressive, but I'd be an arsehole. We had a game in Huddersfield, won, came back and got hammered, and it was after I got into a slanging match with one of the hookers—"

"Excuse me?"

"The *position*, Chris."

"Oh, that's much better..."

"The rugby player," John said, exasperated. "Good God."

"You can't blame me for running with *that* one, come on..."

Strangely, the levity helped, and John chuckled. "Guess not."

"So you had a row with the whore—"

"Hooker."

"Then give me a name!"

"His name won't help."

"Oh my God. What is it?"

John groaned. "Slaggern."

"Slaggern?"

"Yeah."

"Holy hell. A hooker named Slag. That's perfect."

"Oh, we know," John said significantly.

"You call him Slag on the pitch, don't you?"

"Yes."

"What do they call you?"

John rolled his eyes. "Shrek."

"Shrek?"

"Yeah. Big and ugly. And they painted me green for the Christmas do, first year I made the team."

"Aw, you're not ugly."

John raised his eyebrows. Broken teeth, broken nose, ruddy complexion, and cauliflower ears that could be used for satellite transmissions? "Oh, I am. And I'm okay with that. Guns like these, you don't need a pretty face."

"*Very* true. But you have a beautiful voice."

"Not what people mean when they say ugly, Chris."

"Those people are stupid. Beauty isn't a looks thing."

"How would you know?"

"Excuse me, best qualified to know! You people are too obsessed with the things you can see."

"Yeah?"

"Yeah. Like everyone else in here—" A hand landed on John's knee and squeezed. "—probably sees that big ugly thug you keep warning me about. But I know better, because I know you're stunning. And they can't see it."

A warm balloon—not the anxiety balloon, but something a lot more like shy love—expanded in John's chest and made him cough.

"So." The hand didn't move, but the conversation did. "You got mean with Slag?"

"Yeah. And they're good lads, them I play with. Couple of the others split us up before it got nasty, and Steve, er, Slag, rang me up the next day and apologised for his part in it, but he said they were worried about me, that I'd been off for a bit, and it wasn't like me to get so out of hand, even three sheets to the wind like that."

"And knowing you, that got you scared," Chris said softly.

"Well. Yeah."

"Scared you were turning into some violent thug?"

"Yeah. And scared I'd turn into my granddad."

"Your granddad?"

"Mum's dad. He was like me. Massive bloke, absolutely enormous, and he used to work in the steel factories, so he was all muscle, too. Only he *was* hard. Always drinking. He died when I was a teenager. I don't remember him all that well, to be honest, but I do remember we were frightened of him."

"He hit you?"

"Nah, Mum would've killed him, but he would shout loud enough the plaster would flake off the ceiling. Used to tell my dad to hit us more often. You know, that spare the rod mentality. And I don't totally fall out with the idea, you know, in theory, but when you're my size—his size—it's not a smack on the bum and a deserved telling-off, is it? It's bloody scary. He didn't need to hit to scare us."

"And let me guess, he was a proper old Yorkshire bloke and liked his pint and pies."

"Yep. Especially the former."

"And when he was drunk..."

"One and only time I ever saw my old man angry," John said, "was one Christmas when I was about eleven. Me and Nora were messing about, and we knocked over a vase of flowers. Got water on Granddad's slippers, didn't even break the vase because it landed on the rug. And he was drunk, too much beer at dinner, and took off his belt and was wanting to hit us with it. My dad went bananas and clocked him one instead and took us home. He wouldn't leave us unsupervised with him again."

"Christ."

"He died probably a couple of years after that. Looking back, he was an old git, he couldn't have really done any damage, but it was scary."

"And you figured..."

"Yeah. After Slag and a couple of the other lads gave me a talking-to, I figured I didn't want to turn into my granddad. So, I don't drink anymore."

"Teetotal?"

"Yeah. The lads are pretty decent; they don't give me too much shit."

"If it's easier for you if I don't drink..."

"No," John said. "I was never a boozer, never had a problem with it like that. And part of me thinks it was because I was so miserable after Daniel, and maybe if I had a pint or two with you tonight, I'd be the same happy, handsy guy I used to be. But it's not worth the risk. Not to me."

Chris hummed thoughtfully but said nothing to that.

"What about you?" John asked as the pies landed. "Tell me about your family."

"What about it?"

"Well, like for like, I guess. Tell me about your grandparents."

Chris groped for his fork, finding it on the third attempt, and attacked the pie with vigour. "Nothing to say on Dad's side; they died before I was born. My step-parents arrived too late to give me grandparents *really*, though I know Jack's parents, and we exchange cards at birthdays and Christmases."

"Your mum, then?"

"Never met my granddad. Nana's dad—my great-grandpa—was a captain in the navy, and Nana apparently used to like flirting with the sailors. Said herself she didn't know who it was, apparently."

"Bloody hell."

"And then my mum shacked up with a Marine," Chris said, shrugging. "Must run in the family, some thing for big, powerful men."

He grinned, and John coughed.

"I, uh. I'm hoping this is a bit more long-term than...knocking you up and then sailing off out to sea."

Chris laughed. "Mm, I'd not be too impressed if you did that."

John frowned. Wait. "Er. Could I?"

"What? No. I said—"

"No, I mean...physically. Could I, er..."

Chris paused.

His fork slowly lowered.

"Yes," he said shortly. "In theory."

"Oh."

"It's not something I'm okay talking about," came the sharp reply.

"Okay," John said, reaching over to squeeze his wrist. "I'll—use protection. It's fine."

"And it's an off-limits topic."

"Okay. Won't raise it again unless I have to."

"Define have to," Chris snapped.

"Uh, you put on a load of weight and start demanding pickles smeared in peanut butter?"

Chris blinked, thrown. "Wait, what?"

"My sister had the weirdest cravings."

"You're an uncle?"

"Yeah. Daisy. She's about six months old now."

"Gross."

John laughed. "Not a baby fan?"

"Not an anything-under-eighteen fan. And even then, sparingly."

"So no kids in our future?"

"Definitely not."

John grinned and hooked his ankle around Chris's under the table.

"Plenty of the stuff you have to do to *get* kids though," Chris added cheerfully, the bump of, well, bumps, apparently forgotten.

"Okay, okay, I get the hint..."

It was starting to lightly snow outside, the pies were getting cold, and the pub was filling up too much to flirt.

Yet John had never felt so contented.

Chapter Twenty

THEY ARRIVED AFTER nightfall.

The cottage that John had booked was a red-brick, two-storey construction crushed into a tiny cobbled street that was barely ten feet wide. The car couldn't be parked there; it had to be left around the corner, and Chris waited in it while John popped into the local pub to collect the keys from the owners.

The sea and cliffs had sheltered the village from the snow, but the thunder of a raging tide said a storm was brewing, and it was bitterly cold. Salt and rain were in the air. The cobbles were slippery; Chris skidded as he got out of the car, and clung to John's jacket with a yelp.

"Sorry. This might be a bit of a delicate job."

"No kidding."

It was. John had to help Chris down the little lane and into the tiny shelter of the door as carefully as he would have helped his old nan, and then dive back into the weather for their bags. By the time he returned, he was soaked to the bone and frozen.

"This had better be worth it!" Chris shouted over the wind.

"Trust me!" John shouted back and rammed the key into the lock.

The door groaned, shuddered—and popped open with a bang.

And they stepped into warmth.

It was like getting off a plane in a tropical climate. They walked into a wall of pure heat. The little door led right into the main room, a low-ceilinged, rug-adorned place with a fire flickering red and hot behind the little door in the hearth.

Beside the hearth, dark stairs rose in a spiral into the roof space, where John knew the only bedroom to be. On the other side of the fire lay the only two doors: one to the surprisingly modern bathroom, and the other to a rustic kitchen that John had never used, preferring the pub and the local chippie whenever he'd come here. The kitchen backed onto a tiny terraced garden with spectacular views of the sea, but there would be nothing to be seen tonight.

And outside, all the while, they could hear the thunder and boom of a raging ocean.

"Welcome to Shell Cottage," John said.

"Is the door closed?"

"Yes."

"And we're alone?"

"Uh, yes."

Chris dropped his trousers.

John laughed, but Chris didn't stop there. He stripped entirely, until his naked skin glowed white in the gloom, and then shuffled across the carpet towards the fire until his bare toes hit the sheepskin rug laid out before the hearth. There, he sank to his knees, and then even farther, stretching out on the wool as naked as the day he was born.

And, by God, if John had thought Chris was attractive before…

The firelight flickering across his skin recast him in gold. The gentle lines of his back and hips were thrown into shadow; the gentle shadows of body hair, by contrast, were obliterated. The long lines of muscle in those never-ending legs, and the subtle arc of his neck, stretching between slender shoulder and soft curls, called out to John as loudly as any literal voice.

He was struck dumb.

"This is amazing," Chris murmured.

John had to agree.

"If," he croaked, "you don't put something back on, we're not going to make it to bed."

Chris's languid stretch stilled.

Then he turned, slowly, from his side to his front. Tucked his arms under himself. Turned his face to the firelight.

And quite deliberately spread his legs.

"On a rug in front of the fire," he whispered. "This is about the one and only time I'd let you call it making love."

John's throat dried up completely.

He stripped. Left his clothes where they fell. Crossed the room in four long strides and sank to the sheepskin rug.

And paused.

What to do?

How best to love the body stretched out before him? How best to worship? To pleasure? Somehow, John wanted more. Wanted something deeper, something higher, than he'd done before. And he knew what Chris wanted him to do, ultimately, but...

But.

He bit his lip and stroked a heavy hand from the back of Chris's knee to the small of his spine.

He could open Chris up, here. Prepare him. Bring him so much pleasure that he would still be languid and lax when John took him upstairs. And then—

Then, maybe?

John stretched out on the rug beside him—over him, in part—and bent his head to smooth skin. Neck. Back. Hip. Cheek. Leg. Each place was kissed in turn, and then he began to follow the trail back north again with light bites, smoothing the pinch away with the rough, hard strokes of his calloused palms. A massage, of sorts. He found knots in shoulders, cricks in ribs, and gnawed, pressed, until they popped and eased with cracks and breathy sighs.

Until that alluring body appeared to have been poured upon the rug, rather than placed there.

And when that relaxation had spread, from neck to knees, John set about undoing it again. The next set of marks were harder. Deeper. Darker. The neck earned him a shudder and a breathless plea. Another sweet spot lay shy of the right armpit. The spine created a valley to be filled with his tongue, and John held Chris down by the shoulders and did so until Chris was reduced to begging.

And then John reached that longed-for destination.

He pressed a reverent kiss to each cheek and took one in each palm to massage it. Chris groaned at the firmer touch, and John began to knead. Only when his handprints came up, pink and blurred from the motion, did he bend his neck again. The first bite earned a strangled yelp. The second, a curse. The third and fourth, high whines. After those, John glanced up in time to see Chris shove his fist against his mouth, and as the ninth—or perhaps tenth—bite was sunk into that godlike flesh, Chris began to grind against the rug with shameless abandon.

John kissed the bites, one by one, and tracked lower still. Spread the cheeks with both hands to expose Chris utterly.

And licked.

"Fuck!"

John chuckled and did it again. Then he buried his face against Chris's hot skin and began to work at that inner tightness with his tongue. He could taste arousal. Want. Lust. And all of them overlaid by the taste of Chris's skin itself, to form an addictive combination. John could have stayed all night and memorised that taste. He could have lain here forever, opening Chris up around his tongue, and died a happy man.

Chris had other ideas.

The whines turned into soft breaths as he pushed a hand under himself and began to jack off to John's rhythm. John allowed it. Concentrated his efforts, instead, on probing every inch of skin with his tongue and, as he felt Chris's shaking beginning to peak, burying his teeth into the swell where arse left leg and biting.

Hard.

Chris came with a shuddering sigh.

Quiet.

Perfect.

John kissed the bite mark he'd left behind and returned to the sweet taste of pleasure. Chris whimpered, too sensitive, but he had powers other men didn't, and John soon rediscovered the soft sighs of want brewing all over again.

Then he moved north, to kiss the small of Chris's back, and began to use his fingers instead.

It was easy, both to get his fingers slick and to get Chris begging again. Short strokes, from back to front and back again. Shallow probes. Fingertip massages around the entrance, until Chris was pushing back against him and breathlessly demanding more.

"Patience," John chided—and slowly pressed a finger inside.

Oh, *God.*

The tightness. The smoothness. The burning heat. The vice-like grip as John pulled out, and the welcoming tug as he pushed back in. He crooked his finger a little and felt the hitch of Chris's breathing in the palm of his hand.

He wrung lust out, dragging wet arousal out to spread it with fingers and tongue as far as possible, before pushing back inside to find more. Chris lay entirely still but for the whimpers and caught breaths. There was a fine layer of sweat on his back, and John licked it away as he screwed another finger into that intoxicating warmth.

"*Fuck.* Oh, fuck."

"Nope," John said, turning his joined fingers over inside like a key. Opening. Unlocking. He stretched them, deeper and wider, and met resistance. "Okay?"

"More. More than. *More.*"

"Come for me."

"W-what?"

"Come for me."

"Y-you do it. Make me."

John laughed softly, working a hand under Chris's hip and leg. He found wet demand and stroked it softly with his thumb. Chris shuddered. Flexed, both inside and outside, and John pushed a little deeper. He stretched his hand again. The resistance was still there, but less firm.

After this one. After this, he could...

Chris wriggled. Fingers came down to cover John's. The gentle massage became faster. Rougher. Harder. John could feel the warning signs. The shake of muscles forming a rhythm. A tightening pressure. A rush of wet want. Christ, how would that feel around his cock instead of his fingers?

John drew his exploring fingers back far enough to slide the ring finger alongside its fellows, and then push the three back where they belonged.

And—

Not quite hard. But firm. Pushing through the hesitant rejection of a body not used to this. Crooking and working them, following the lines of Chris's own physique, until he was sunk to the knuckles.

And then bent the top knuckles, all three, to brush at the rhythm inside.

Chris groaned. Tightened. From head to toe, and everything between. Shook violently—and came.

Came.

John's fingers were caught in a hot vice. Climax tore at his nails and knuckles, demanding its satisfaction. The tightness was almost enough to bruise, and tried to pull him deeper. The resistance gave way entirely in the rush. John was struck with the wild thought that he could probably have managed his whole fist if he had only timed it right.

And then it was over. Chris sagged into the rug, gasping. John kissed the small of his back as he withdrew, and had his wrist clumsily grasped for.

"Hey, gorgeous," he murmured and tugged himself free to brush Chris's curls aside and kiss his ear. "Okay?"

"Mm."

"What does that mean?"

"Means take me t'bed and f'ck me."

John laughed at the slurred words. "I dunno. You seem pretty wrung out..."

"Get a man with hands like yours to suck you off then finger-fuck you and see how *you* react," Chris mumbled, then caught John's wrist again. "Bed. Please."

John backed up, depositing one last kiss on that bruised arse. "Okay. Get yourself up there while I find my supplies."

"Supplies?"

"Gonna take more than a bit of sucking to make that good for you, ba—beautiful."

Chris pushed himself up on sluggish, shaking limbs. John glanced away as a breast hung free for a moment and turned to the bags. Over his shoulder, he heard the rustle of cotton, and then the shuffle of feet. The now familiar brush of palms on surfaces.

Only when Chris had started up the spiral stairs did John wrap a hand around his cock.

There was no way he'd get inside Chris without this first. He tipped his head back as he stroked. Picturing that body and the way it moved; recalling the tugging and the tightness as he'd come. Christ, that would be around his dick. It would milk him for every last bit of—

It took less than a minute before John grunted and shot off into his palm. He took a moment to breathe, before finding Chris's discarded jeans and wiping the mess off. Then he fished out his toiletries bag and headed upstairs.

Tucked under the roof, the bedroom was an expanse of dark woods and soft red furnishings. A window overlooked the cliffs and the roaring sea when it was light; now, it merely shimmered under a thick layer of rainwater, which sent tiny patterns dancing across the boards. The bed dominated the room—an enormous four-poster that could have been a small room unto itself. Chris, now wearing his T-shirt but still otherwise naked, looked almost frail in the vast expanse. The mattress was near enough two feet deep, and when John crawled up onto the dark red sheets, it dipped like a boat on a surging ocean.

"Oh my God," Chris laughed, as he was tipped into John's hold. "Mm, hello."

John chuckled and kissed his neck. "Hello."

"This bed is amazing."

"Yep."

"It feels like a waterbed."

"Little bit," John agreed, putting the bag on the side table before settling back down into the soft warmth and gathering Chris into him.

"One day," Chris murmured against his mouth, "you're going to fuck me in a waterbed."

John's dick twitched at that. All right. So perhaps this little bit of foreplay wasn't going to be too long after all.

"Speaking of fuck," Chris whispered, hand cupping John's balls. "What happened here?"

"Had to have a quick one off the wrist," John said, catching an ear between his teeth and sucking on it for a moment.

"W-why?"

"No way I was going to last trying to get that inside like you want."

"Mm." A finger stroked the underside. "How long until it's interested again?"

"Oh, it's interested, trust me."

"Okay, how long until you can do something about it?"

"We can't all have multiple orgasms," John sniped. "Anyway, you're jumping ahead. I could stick it in a lot of people but *this*—" He ran both hands down Chris's spine, from the tops of his shoulders right over his arse to his thighs. "—is the why I want it to go here."

"My back?"

"*You*, you berk."

"Oh, charming..."

John kissed him, and that worked. Chris melted into it, a hand coming up to catch at John's hair. Despite their states—Chris half-naked, and John entirely so—it was an oddly chaste kiss. Sweet. Affirming. The feel of Chris's breathing against his own and the brush of soft skin against his chest hair was somehow more erotic to John than any amount of cunnilingus. The play of Chris's fingers over his bicep, tracing the muscle and squeezing it, was strangely affectionate and alluring at the same time. The leg that hooked over his hip and drew them closer together was not so much about sex as it was about a snuggle—not, John imagined, that Chris would like that word any more than he liked 'making love.'

Even after John's dick recovered—Chris's proximity bringing it to a soft but full state within minutes, and then about a quarter of an hour later achieving full hardness when Chris finally tired of the cuddle category of foreplay and fought his way into John's mouth with tongue and teeth—John felt little urgency to act. They were at the cottage, by the coast, for a week. He had all the time in the world.

So, he took his time and loved.

Simply loved. Stroked the skin he'd bruised downstairs. Kissed the sweet spots on neck and shoulder, rather than bit them. Smoothed the juncture of leg and arse over and over, until he had the very hairs themselves memorised. Lost himself in the touch of Chris's lips and hands.

Lost himself so thoroughly that he jolted in surprise when Chris laughed and pushed his shoulder.

"You're too heavy for that," came the breathless protest, and John realised he'd turned them so that his full weight had come to rest on Chris's chest.

"Sorry," he said, levering an arm under himself and propping his frame up over that mesmerising body. He kissed the hollow below Chris's throat and stroked a spread hand up his thigh and hip to rest on his waist. "You still want to—?"

"God, yes."

John nuzzled his ear. "Promise to tell me if it hurts."

"It's bound to hurt a bit."

"It could be uncomfortable," John allowed, "but it shouldn't be much more than that."

"Okay." Chris didn't sound convinced.

John reached for the bag and unzipped it to find the condoms and the lube. For the first time since he was a teenager, his hands fumbled clumsily with the bottle and the wrappers. He nudged his knee up between Chris's thighs and felt him flinch a little at the tear of the packet.

At least he wasn't the only one who was nervous.

Rolling the condom on with the sight of Chris half-naked and waiting below him, was one of the hardest things John had ever had to deal with. Pun half intended. He had to squeeze the base of his cock a little and take a deep breath once the latex was in place, and only when the imminent danger had passed did he open his eyes again.

He shifted his leg, and Chris opened his knees a little wider. Reached up to clutch at the pillow above his head.

Tense.

"Hey." John stroked a hand down his arm. "It'll be easier if you turn over."

"No."

John raised his eyebrows.

"I want to be able to touch you."

John dropped down, elbows either side of Chris's shoulders, and kissed him. Lightly. Almost teasing. When he drew back, Chris followed for a moment, before catching those long fingers over John's taut arms and squeezing.

"Yeah," Chris murmured, like it had been an answer. "Like that."

John chuckled, burying his mouth against Chris's neck and sucking lightly until he felt the tell-tale shiver of arousal. Until he dropped his weight a fraction, to rock their bodies lightly together, and felt an answering relaxation. Until

Chris yielded with a breathy sigh and stretched his head to the side for more.

And out of nowhere, the words spilled out.

"I love you."

Chris gave him a little laugh in reply, and John grinned.

"I do!"

"Mhmm..."

"Love you," John repeated, buoyed both by the warm reception and the streak of disbelief. He kissed the abused neck, the hard angle of jaw, the warm ear, and then began to track downwards again. He left one arm high, the victim of Chris's searching fingers, and smoothed his path with the other, skipping past the T-shirt and the places Chris didn't want him to see as easily as though they weren't there at all.

And then he found himself right back at the beginning.

A gentle exploration with his dry fingers found Chris as open as John had hoped for, and a return with the lube opened him up further with a surprised noise and then a groan that could almost have been a purr. There was an edge of exhaustion in his grip, and John exploited it ruthlessly. It would be easier if he were loose. It would be better if his pleasure didn't have to compete with any pain.

"Let me," Chris mumbled, reaching a hand down.

"Let you what?"

"I want to touch you. Get your dick all primed for me."

"It's primed enough," John complained, but drew a circle of lubricant into the palm of Chris's hand with the bottle, and then drew that hand to clasp about his cock.

And—God. Grit his teeth and fight the urge to come on the spot.

"Don't move," he grunted, and Chris stilled. "Oh God. God."

"You okay?"

"*Yeah*," he groaned heavily, and Chris laughed. The sound was high and giddy. "Jesus."

"I've jacked you before."

"Not like that."

Not naked and lubed-up and half a foot from—from—

Chris's fingers wrapped slowly about his length and began to pump.

John groaned and dropped his head to rest on Chris's chest as he was...primed, as Chris put it. And it felt like it too. It wasn't a loving or shy touch. It was brisk and almost businesslike. John was being readied, not revered. This was a necessary act, not a sex act in itself, not right now. He was pumped like a tool, a toy.

Ordinarily, John might have felt a little cheapened by the gesture. Yet something about Chris's determination was in itself dizzying.

He wanted this as bad as John did, and suddenly, the phrase 'knowledge is power' made a whole lot more sense.

John took a deep breath and removed Chris's hand by the wrist.

Okay.

Now.

"Ready?"

"Uh-huh."

John kissed the inside of one knee. Drew Chris closer by the hips. Lined himself up, until the sheathed head pressed against Chris's wet heat.

"Bear down on me," he coached.

"O-okay."

He heard the nerves.

Very carefully, so as not to shift the position of his prick, John leaned forward and found collarbone with mouth. Wrapped his teeth around the soft spot above the ridge. Licked it until Chris whimpered.

Then bit.

And pushed.

"Fu—oh!"

The cry broke off into a high keen. John groaned. He thrust into unbelievable tightness. Searing heat. A grip like a vice. A pulse pounding all about him. Muscle and flesh and *body*, a physicality he'd never imagined. His hands had no idea. His hands had no bloody, blind idea.

Resistance. A depth his fingers couldn't get to. A soft whimper. He bit again, harder, and felt the yield. Sank deeper—and bottomed out. Christ, he'd bottomed out. He was sunk to the base, completely sheathed. Gulping for air, like his lungs were in his captured cock. He panted harshly against Chris's neck and gathered himself.

God. Christ. This was—this was—

"Move. Please. Please move."

He could feel a tightness in the body underneath him. A discomfort. There was a fine sweat on the skin beneath his fingers, and it was nothing to do with pleasure.

John pulled back, a bare inch and no more, and worked his fingers between them.

"Just relax," he whispered and began to rub.

Chris whined and arched under him. The pressure tightened impossibly. Black spots danced at the corners of John's vision. His lungs caught again—and he forced it back. Not yet. Not *yet*. *Focus*. He refocused. On the heaving chest. On the writhing form. Bent his head to taste sweetness and salt on Chris's jaw. Played him like an instrument, until he felt fingers tightening on his arms, and—

Now.

The first ripple of climax tugged at his dick, and John followed.

A shallow thrust. Barely an inch of movement. And yet—

Chris groaned, more sensation than sound. The second wave was harder, and John followed that too. And they found a rhythm, begun in the crashing tide of Chris's climax and continued even after exhaustion rushed after it, and he lay lax and welcoming, the only grip left in his hands as they dug bruises into John's arms.

As he clung to John's body and rode him as surely as if their positions had been reversed.

John wanted—desperately wanted—to pull back and thrust deep. To plunder and pillage. To get as deep as possible, as hard as possible, and rock the bed with their lovemaking.

One day. In Chris's waterbed, perhaps.

But the blanked-out look of bliss, the soft whimpers emerging from Chris's throat, the sweet little *yes-yes-yes* that escaped when John dropped his weight enough to mould them together and carry Chris's form through the thrusts...

It didn't last long.

It could never have lasted long.

John came too soon, and it shattered him. Broke him apart. His vision went white. His mind collapsed. He felt skin and heat and those clutching hands, and nothing more. The room, the world, his very name, was ripped away. His soul lay bare, basking in primal ecstasy, and only those hands kept it clutched tight and safe. He was—broken. Truly broken. He was the sea, and Chris the cliff-face that tore him apart.

And yet if John ever reformed, he would come right back and do it all again.

He could do this for the rest of his days and not regret a moment.

The world inched back in around the edges. Chris's chest heaved under John's ear. Pulses thundered. John couldn't tell one from the other.

He didn't care to try either.

"I love you," he breathed.

A soft, shattered laugh. Fingers combing through his hair.

He needed to—get up. Take the condom off. Get them under the blankets. Check it had been good. He should.

"I love you," he said again and did none of it.

Just—breathed.

But beneath him, Chris just breathed too, and John figured that maybe, just this once, just breathing was all that was needed.

Chapter Twenty-One

WHEN JOHN WOKE up, he was alone.

Sunlight was streaming through the window, thin and watery. The sheets had been thrown back on Chris's side of the bed. And John felt—

Gross, actually.

He frowned fuzzily at the bed canopy and tried to work out why. The burn of some seriously good sex was lingering in his muscles. His brain itched for a workout, like it usually did after a couple of days away from the gym. He was vaguely hungry.

Yet he felt inexplicably disgusting.

"What the hell—" he murmured and went to sit up.

Oh.

Well, that explained a few things.

Grimly, he pulled the sheets back, took a deep breath, and peeled the sodden condom off his limp dick. It bloody hurt too. Christ. He must have blacked out last night.

Problem resolved, condom tied off and dumped on the side table for the bin later, the good feelings were allowed their air, and John headed naked for the stairs to find his escapee partner.

It wasn't that hard. Small cottage aside, Chris wasn't exactly trying to hide. John found him stretched out on the sofa in jogging bottoms and a tank top, hair wet from the shower. He was listening to something on his phone, earphones gleaming white under his curls, and nursing a mug of—to John's surprise—tea.

"Seriously?" he asked, stooping to kiss the top of his head. "Tea?"

"There's only shit coffee."

"There's some instant in the cupboard."

"Like I said. Shit."

John laughed and perched on the edge of the sofa to take a sip of tea and a kiss.

"Mm, morning."

Chris laughed. "Hello."

"You okay?"

The smile widened. "Think we can stretch to *very* good."

"Yeah?"

"Uh-huh."

"So last night—"

"Oh, I'm sorry, does your ego need stroking as well as your cock?"

John burst out laughing.

"Let's see," Chris said, mock-thoughtfully. "You ate me out to make me come, then finger-fucked me into another one, *then* you beat yourself off because you wanted to do me proper instead of a shove it in and shoot off—"

John's stomach hurt. He had to bend over and wheeze at his knees, cackling.

"And then you took me upstairs and finally, *finally*, fucked me. And make me come on your cock because—actually, I don't even know why. But you did. So yeah, I came three times last night because, apparently, my orgasms are your life energy or something."

"Close enough," John choked. When he finally straightened, he was still grinning like a loon.

"Trust me," Chris said smugly. "I am *very* good."

"Hmm, that's not perfect. What would perfect look like?"

"Decent coffee and a massive breakfast."

"Give me twenty minutes to shower, and we'll go out. There's a café right down by the water that does an amazing fry-up."

"What about their coffee?"

"No idea. But they *have* coffee," John said, levering himself up on groaning knees.

"Instant isn't coffee!" Chris shouted after him, and John laughed as he headed into the bathroom.

And—sod it. Left the door open.

God, his mood couldn't get any higher. It was post-coital, sure—John might romanticise the act and think of sex with no strings attached as pointless and meaningless, but his body didn't agree and was thoroughly enjoying the endorphin shot of getting its rocks off—but it was deeper too. Chris's easy demeanour. The smell of his shampoo. The fact that...

Jesus, the simple fact that he'd smiled and been pleased that John was awake.

Okay, so John would have preferred a good long cuddle in bed the morning after, but it was gone nine, and Chris probably had had to take his medication or something.

He showered, enjoying the stretch of slightly stiff muscles and working the twinge out of his back—being so bloody big caused havoc with his lower back—before stealing a handful of Chris's shampoo and raking it through his far shorter hair. The scent was becoming familiar, though John chuckled at the thought of turning up to rugby practice with hair that smelled like jasmine.

Knuckles rapped on the open door.

"Can I come in and do my teeth again?"

"Sure," John said and cracked open the shower door to watch. "You could always come in here with me."

"Already showered."

"So? Shower again."

Chris laughed. "Mm, waste of water."

"How about I make you dirty again, and then you'll have to."

"Trust me," Chris said. "Attempting to have shower sex with me is a bad call."

He shoved the toothbrush in his mouth, and John spied an opportunity.

"I didn't say anything about sex," he protested. "You've got a dirty mind."

A mumbled argument was his reply, but he couldn't understand it.

"Honestly. I wanted a nice, sweet snuggle under—"

"*Whmph?*"

"Snuggle," John repeated. "Wonderful things, snuggles, you should try them. In fact, tomorrow morning, I'll snuggle you so hard you *can't* sneak out of bed like that."

Chris flipped him—or rather, the towel rail—off, and John laughed. He shut the water off and scrubbed down with a towel before wrapping it around his waist and stepping out.

And, the minute Chris was done with his teeth, stepped up and slid his arms around that slim waist.

"This," he murmured, tightening his arms, "is a snuggle."

"We need to work on your vocabulary," came the snotty reply.

John kissed his neck. "Sure?"

"Well, maybe later."

John grinned and squeezed tighter for a minute.

"I meant it," he said.

"What?"

"What I said last night."

"You said a lot of things last night, most of which I don't remember."

"You don't?"

"I was a bit distracted."

John laughed. "Well, how about the bit where I said I love you?"

"Oh, aye?"

"It's true."

"Most people are in love when they're balls-deep in someone else's body."

John shook his head, rubbing his stubble against Chris's neck. "Nope. Meant it. I know it's a bit soon, and this is still all new and everything, but I know what I feel. And I love you."

Chris turned in his arms and reached up on tiptoes to kiss his chin.

"I don't believe in love this soon," he murmured, "but thank you."

"You don't?"

"No."

"What do you believe in, then?"

"Passion. This is passion. I believe that—I feel that, too—but it's not love."

"So when does love kick in?" John asked.

"When passion stops."

John frowned. "What do you mean?"

"This is the...the honeymoon period, I guess. That exciting bit, when you have someone new. And then it fizzles out and stops. And after it stops, either there's not anything to hold it all together and you drift apart, or love's snuck in and you don't."

"Well," John said, squeezing again. "You believe your thing, and I'll believe mine."

"What's yours?"

"That love at first sight is real, and I caught it when I saw you."

"Caught it? Excuse me, I'm not infectious."

"You bloody are."

Chris laughed and hit him. John trapped his arms to his sides and attacked his ear until Chris yelled and fought him off, cackling with laughter.

"See? Love."

"Passion!"

"Whatever," John said, catching Chris's head in both hands and kissing him flush on the lips. "Come on. Let's get you some coffee and both of us a decent breakfast."

The world outside, when they finally emerged, was quiet and chilly, but the sun was bright and the sea, though loud, not as violent as the night before. Chris tucked his hand into the crook of John's elbow comfortably enough, and John was surprised by the indulgent smiles of a couple of elderly ladies outside a shop. He'd held hands with Aljaz here once, and they'd earned a number of dirty looks.

The café was down another narrow passage, dark and gloomy, but the interior was bright from the large windows facing the glittering sea. John led Chris to a table in prime sea-staring position, before doubling back to order the world-class fry-ups and squint at the coffee prices.

"What's not instant?" he asked eventually, and the waitress blinked before glancing past him to Chris.

"Ah!" she said. "For your friend, I take it?"

"Yeah. I'm not a coffee drinker; all I know is that instant is apparently swill."

"Extra fifty pence," she said genially, "and I'll bring out some ground for him, eh?"

"You're a gem," John told her. She tittered, despite being probably the same age as his mother, and noticeably didn't charge him the extra fifty pence.

"It's lovely," she said, nodding at Chris and lowering her voice. "Too many folks can't get out and about these days."

John stared.

"Sorry?"

"You know." Her voice dropped in volume a second time. "Disabled people."

"Oh."

John wasn't sure what to make of it and retreated with his change. Once she was occupied, chattering away to an elderly local, he leaned across the table and asked Chris for an explanation.

To his surprise, Chris rolled his eyes.

"They think you're my carer."

"I—sorry, what?"

"Gina gets it a lot too. Isn't it lovely she's out with me, blah, blah, blah." Chris pulled a face. "Hell, Luke gets it every single time we're at the gym. I don't have friends or boyfriends, just carers."

"That's fu—bloody stupid."

Chris shrugged. "You should have heard them when I wanted to transition. What did it matter? Not like I was going to be having sex or relationships. Not like I could see myself to have dysphoria. Who cared?"

"*What?*"

"Not in so many words, but that was the gist of it."

John stared, jaw slack. "That's—that's—"

Chris smirked. "Very exploitable, is what it is."

"How do you mean?"

"I mean, short of actually kissing me, you could get very handsy, and they'd keep desperately passing it off as helping me out."

The old ladies who'd smiled, John realised. It wasn't, oh, look at that lovely couple. It was, oh, look at that nice man helping that poor blind dear.

Part of him seethed.

And the other part heard Chris's devious tone and realised its potential.

"I could hold your arse all day, and I'd just be helping you round," John said.

"Bingo."

"Doesn't it—make you mad?"

"'Course," Chris said. "But twenty-odd years of it, you tend to get tired rather than mad. And they mean well. They're just...dumb."

"No kidding," John said.

"You're my first boyfriend, you know."

John's brain stalled. "Seriously?"

"Mm."

"Um. So. Girlfriends?"

"Nope."

"Friend with benefits?"

Chris laughed. "Yes."

John blew upwards into his hair. "Thank God. It would have been a tragedy if someone who looks like you hit twenty-four without getting it. I mean, Jesus. There should be a line of guys waiting at your door with flowers."

"Meh, flowers."

"Coffee tins, then."

"Yeah, okay."

"Why aren't there?"

"Trans *and* disabled? Good luck. Most people don't want to touch that with a barge pole, and try meeting the ones who don't mind when you're stuck inside most of the time and your best friends are a lesbian and a very, very straight man."

John frowned. "Stuck inside?"

Chris bit his lip.

"What do you mean by stuck?"

"It's...been difficult."

"What has?"

Chris sighed. "My...my dog died last year."

"Oh, God, I'm sorry."

"He was getting on a little bit, but it was still a shock. He had cancer. The vet said he was in pain, so I let him go, but...it was hard. I loved him to bits, and he was my assistance dog, so it had a double-whammy effect. It's harder to get out and do things on my own."

"Aren't you—sorry, this is probably really insensitive..."

"Go for it."

"Aren't you getting another?" John asked awkwardly.

"Yeah. But I need one that's trained for blind people *and* epilepsy. Which is hard. And Sam died so suddenly that they hadn't started to prepare for me to have a different dog, so there wasn't one ready." Chris's face brightened and he fumbled for his phone. "They have a puppy in training for me though. I won't be able to have her for at least a year yet, but that's something at least. Look, Gina took a picture for me."

The phone chirped up, saying the names of pictures aloud, and when it said "Poppy puppy," Chris handed it over. John squinted in the sunlight and then laughed. The photo was of Chris and a tall, slim woman who, judging by the dark curls, was probably his mother. They were sitting on the grass in a field, and Chris was grinning down at a young dog—too large for true puppyhood, but too small to be full-grown—squirming in his arms. A yellow dog, either a Lab or a Retriever, that looked lethal. In the sense that it was trying to lick him to death.

"She's cute."

"She's gorgeous. It'll be great to have a dog again. It gets lonely at home, and they don't—Sam didn't..."

When Chris trailed off, John carefully reached over to touch his wrist.

"They don't care if you're having a bad day, or if you can't go to the gig because you've had four seizures, or if you're being a moody, self-indulgent shit. They just—they don't care. You're...you're their whole world, and they love you no matter what you are or what you have or who you've become. And they're always going to love you."

There was something bruised behind his voice, and John tightened his grip gently.

"I was depressed," Chris blurted out. "I'd just come out. As Chris. And my mum split up with her boyfriend about it after he said it was down to my brain damage—"

"What a fu—uh. Tosser."

"Fucking knobhead," Chris corrected primly, and John laughed.

"Yeah. That."

"Yeah, he said obviously the fall had damaged more than my vision. Mum went nuts and threw him out on the spot, but she was upset too—they'd been engaged—so I felt guilty for it, even though I was glad she'd done it..."

John stroked his thumb over the back of Chris's hand.

"And Dad was struggling. He didn't know what to do or what would help, and the doctor was being such a dick about referring me to the clinic to get treatment. And I was just...depressed. It was like the final straw. I was blind *and* epileptic, and now I was trans as well? It was all too much, you know? How was I supposed to build something good out of that mess?"

"This better be your thought process then, and not now," John chided.

Chris laughed. "Yeah. I was a teenager. I didn't have anyone to tell me different except my family, and you know how you sometimes think, *yeah, well you're my mum; you're supposed to tell me that*, sometimes?"

"Christ, tell me about it..."

"I got Sam around the same time. I was growing up, and I wanted to be more independent. And you need to be able to walk them and play with them—they're still dogs, even if they're working dogs—and I was finally approaching that position, so I got Sam."

"And that changed things?"

"No. But it helped me ride it out until I could start unpicking that crap," Chris said. "If I wanted to hide in my room and have a good cry, Sam would come and shove his nose in my armpit and let me. And I learned I could take him into doctor's appointments and everything with me, so he sort of turned into this...I don't know, security blanket?"

"That's kind of what a dog is for, in my opinion," John said.

"You have one?"

"God no, never allowed," John said, pulling a face. Chris seemed to brighten at his tone, so John ran with the story. "Been living in a flat ever since I left home, and when I was a kid, Mum was always so particular. Won't have a mess in the house, and animals are filthy."

"Excuse me, my dog was the picture of perfection."

"He had *hair*."

"So do you, fuzzy."

"I don't leave my hair on the carpet."

"Pretty sure you did last night..."

John choked and cackled into his fist. The lady, who had just arrived with their breakfasts and steaming cups, gave him an odd look, but then chattered blithely about the weather, recommending a little cove down the road if they wanted to see some—ooh, sorry dear, *hear*, hear—some choice waves.

Then she was gone, and John recovered himself enough to rearrange the mugs to the right places. Chris wrapped his hands around the coffee mug and took a long, deep swallow.

"*Fuck*, that's better."

His face looked orgasmic, and John had to concentrate very hard on not spilling his tea.

"So. No dog?"

"Nope. To be fair, Mum had four kids who all wanted pets, and she couldn't have had them all. Dad's allergic to cats, for one, and Nora always wanted a kitten. I wanted a puppy—I think Fran did too, but, to be honest, she wanted a whole zoo—and Tasha's one and only soft spot is for rabbits."

"Oh, we had a rabbit when I was little," Chris said brightly. "Grenade."

"Sorry?"

"It was about the same size, and Dad used to threaten to throw it like one if it didn't stop chewing through the hutch wire."

"That's tiny!"

"Netherland Dwarf. My first pet. I was only four. It went to live with my auntie in Australia when I was seven because rabbits like Australia."

"That sounds suspiciously like how our goldfish went to keep old Mr Peters next door company when he moved to France," John said, and Chris laughed.

"Exactly the same. Bunny heaven is in Australia, don't you know."

"And goldfish heaven in France. Go figure."

"Pretty sure they'd have tried to sell me the same story about Sam if I wasn't the one who'd taken him to the vet in the first place," Chris said, and John snorted.

"Think your twenties is maybe a bit old for the retiring pet story."

"Think so. So. If you're still about in a year or eighteen months, want to come walk my dog with me?"

John smiled and stroked Chris's fingertips where they rested lightly against the warm ceramic of the coffee cup.

"Yep," he said and then tapped the plate. "C'mon. Eat up. Got to take you to the beach and see how gorgeous you look all windswept and covered in sand."

"I am *not* getting sand in unmentionable places."

"Nah, too cold for that. But you'll still look gorgeous. And then, if the heater in my car doesn't complain too hard, we can find ourselves a lay-by and indulge."

"In what?"

"Use your imagination."

Chris's smile widened, and John bit his lip. Christ. Passion indeed.

But then—

The soft way Chris had spoken, the spike of sympathy in John's chest at the obvious wound that Sam had left behind, the painful and raw desire to smooth it over and help—

Sure, there was passion.

But whatever Chris said about love, John knew his own feelings.

Chris might feel passion-then-love.

But John definitely had a dose of both at once.

Chapter Twenty-Two

CHRIS—AND NORA, and Mum, and just about everyone in the world, actually—would call John an over-the-top, exaggerating romantic, but sod the lot of them.

It was the best week of John's life. That was his story, and he was sticking to it.

Sleeping every night cuddled up to Chris's back? Having coffee and breakfast by the sea every morning? Seeing the beauty of Chris's laughter on a windy beach, ankle-deep in a freezing surf, yet his face lit up with so much life that it hurt John's heart? Making love three times—once on the rug in front of the roaring fire—and only three because Chris's body still wasn't used to it and complained about the fact the next morning? And that was only making love the traditional way. If John included any time they started with cuddling and ended with climaxes, then the count hit eight before the week was over.

Yes, it was the best week of John's life, without question.

He felt guilty for thinking it, but...Chris's epilepsy had even—cooperated. Almost as though it somehow knew the week was special. Chris had had two seizures, and John had witnessed neither. He'd been in the shower for the first one and knew nothing at all until he came upstairs and found Chris on the bedroom floor. And the second time, he'd been out for a run and come back to find Chris asleep on the sofa. Only later had Chris told him what happened.

John felt guilty as sin, but—

But also a tiny, *tiny* bit relieved.

It was horrible of him—he was here for all of it, he *was*. John didn't want Chris to think for a minute that he thought less of him because of the seizures, but John also wanted the week to go without any hiccups. No worries, no insecurities, no fussing on his part, and no prickliness on Chris's. So, for the seizures to strike when John was out, and Chris handling them entirely as he always had, was a sick kind of relief.

Chris just laughed at him when he'd explained and said, "I get it. I'm a little bit glad too, to be honest. It's stressful to seize in front of people who don't have a clue."

"I have a *bit* of a clue."

"Until I tell you to go fuck yourself and try punching you when you're trying to put a blanket over me for a kip, you don't."

"Uh—"

"Trust me. You'll see one soon enough. But I'm sort of glad you haven't yet."

John never wanted to leave.

All right, so Chris had seriously cold feet and liked to tuck them up into John's balls during the night. Okay, his taste in food was questionable. And yes, his hair got *everywhere*—the shower drain, the bedsheets, between John's teeth...

Worth it. Even the downsides felt like little pieces John could slot into his new world, like completing a puzzle. When he found himself simply massaging those toes in one hand in the middle of the night, to rub some warmth into them and relieve the discomfort on his own bollocks without even waking Chris up, John knew he was done for. And he didn't care.

The week went by too quickly, and New Year's Eve was on them before John knew what had happened. The day started out like any other—making love in the tangled sheets, getting his hair pulled for calling it that, going out for breakfast and a bucket of coffee for the caffeine addict he'd fallen in love with. At lunchtime, they drove over to Whitby, and when Chris confessed to having never been sailing, John paid for a little jaunt out round the bay in a boat. The spray was ice-cold and the wind harsh, but Chris clung to the railing and laughed like a kid, fascinated by the deafening screech and wail of the birds that perpetually lived in the cliffs just shy of the town. John bracketed him in, really to prevent any accidents, but that close and with Chris that beautiful, it ended up being a hug against the slippery metal anyway.

When they were back on dry—well, moist—land, John snuck a kiss in a narrow street on a trip to find a good café in which to shelter from the misty rain, and Chris's lips tasted like salt.

"Love you," John whispered before he let go.

"Passion you."

John rolled his eyes.

As the night grew in and midnight approached, John rumbled up a torch from his toolkit in the boot of the car, and they walked down the long harbour wall. The sea crashed and bellowed against its stone walls, the spray leaping up to slap them, and as the first fireworks began to rise, little sparkles and crackles of light to prepare for the imminent New Year, John caught Chris's waist in both hands and dragged him close.

"I want to start next year off right."

"Oh, aye?"

"Uh-huh. I'm going to kiss you at midnight. Then I'll spend the next twelve months kissing you."

"No, thanks, might need to breathe."

John laughed. Chris stretched up on his toes and kissed his chin.

"Are the fireworks near us?"

"Not really."

"Good. I don't like the noise."

"Is the sea helping?"

"Yeah. But you could help too."

"How?"

"Hands over my ears."

John obeyed, cupping that narrow face in the dark, feeling the soft shells of his ears and the wild, damp curls around them crumpling under his palms. He felt Chris's smile.

"Best start," Chris breathed. "Just in case their clock is wrong."

John laughed and dipped his head.

His watch beeped as their lips touched. A church bell boomed, somewhere back in the bay. Fireworks exploded.

John didn't care. There were gloved fingers fisted in his coat. Cool lips and cooler metal against his mouth. A body leaning precariously against him, held only by their hands. It was raining. The sea was freezing. The coffee Chris had had before they came out was revolting.

And nothing had ever been more perfect.

THEY HAD TO go home the next day.

John didn't even care about the long drive. He was euphoric from their seafront kiss at midnight and the idiotic, almost giggly attempts at warming up in the car not twenty minutes later, stopped only from full-on back-seat sex by the stern look of a policeman as his patrol car trundled by.

So it was their last day—so what? John had woken tangled up around the most amazing person in the universe, knowing he'd get to do it back home too.

Even the drive home was incredible, Chris having finally found a radio station he liked and singing along to rock songs at the top of his lungs the whole way. And it was a long way, as snow had shut down the moors, and the New Year traffic was in full swing. He was a terrible singer, truly awful, yet so damn stunning, caterwauling without a touch of self-consciousness, so bold and bright and bloody *brilliant* that John enjoyed every second of ear-bleeding noise anyway. Even when they stopped for petrol, he criticised the band playing, and Chris wound the window down and screeched the whole song to him so loudly he was audible from inside the kiosk.

"Good New Year?" the cashier asked with a knowing smirk, and John blushed hard enough to set his hat on fire.

It was perfect. Damn Chris's opinion: John was in love. Certainly in love enough to shut the singing up for thirty seconds by kissing him, before peeling out of the petrol station and the screeching starting up again.

The only downside to the entire week was the bit where John pulled up in front of Chris's flat.

"Home sweet home," he said and put the handbrake on. "I don't want it to end."

"You have work tomorrow."

"Mm."

"And I have to go and visit my mum."

"Yeah..."

"And no doubt your sisters are going to want to interrogate you."

"Christ, yeah."

"But for what it's worth, I don't want it to end either." Chris leaned across to kiss him sweetly. "Come over tomorrow night when you're done with work?"

John smiled. "Love to."

"I could make cannelloni. I'm good at cannelloni."

"It's a date."

Chris grinned and reached for the door.

"Um, hang on."

"What?"

John took a deep breath. "Um. I made myself a promise."

"What's that?"

"That after this week, I would meet your family."

Chris blinked.

His hand left the door release, and the other groped for John's and found it, still resting on the handbrake.

"You sure?"

"Yeah." John took a deep breath. "I—this is going to sound stupid."

"Try me."

"I figured if your friends didn't hate me, and if you spent a whole week alone with me in a place you didn't know, then—then maybe even if your family thought I was this—I was a—what Daniel said...maybe even they said it, you'd not...believe it."

Chris sighed and squeezed his wrist.

"'Course I don't believe it," he whispered.

"And maybe they'd not be able to change your mind."

There was the crux of it. John knew how easy it was to twist a mind. To change it. John knew the truth about what he and Daniel had had, yet Daniel's persistence in his lies got even John questioning it. Chris might know what he was, but families, loved ones, held enormous power. And they could make him question things, just as Daniel had made John.

Chris chuckled. "See, there definitely speaks a man who hasn't met them. And still doesn't know me too well yet. This mind isn't for the changing."

John laughed weakly.

"You sure?" Chris prompted.

"Yeah. Bloody terrified, but sure."

"Going to be totally honest, John. My mum's probably not going to be too keen," Chris said. "She's...protective. My dad's more...whatever, I'm an adult now. So, do you maybe want to start with Dad?"

"Isn't he the Marine?"

"Yeah..."

"How is the Marine better than your mum?"

"From what you've said about *your* parents, I don't see why this is the surprising way around."

John coughed a laugh. "Good point."

"Do you want to come over, or go out somewhere neutral, or—"

"Neutral. Um. Dinner out somewhere, maybe?" It would be more formal, but he could dress up a bit, hide the worst of the tattoos, and escape once the meal was over rather than being trapped in their house.

"I'll sort something out." Chris's fingers tightened. "You sound edgy."

"Yeah, well, I feel it."

"Don't. It'll be fine. Promise."

"Promise?"

"Absolutely promise. If it goes really wrong, you'll get to see me explode in a temper, and I've got the feeling you might find that sexy."

John found a smile and darted it Chris's way. "Really?"

"Oh, yeah. You seem the type."

"Dunno," John said. "Might be a bit vanilla for that."

"The fact you know what vanilla means says you're not."

John laughed.

"Anyway, I'm always sexy, so you probably will."

"That's true."

"C'mon. Give me a kiss, then go away. Gina's coming over this evening to get the tell part of kiss and tell, and I need to clean up before she gets here, or she'll rearrange all my stuff in her tidying up."

John laughed for real then and leaned over. The taste of coffee was becoming familiar.

"Thank you," he said.

"For what?"

"Everything."

NORA WASN'T HOME, so John found the business card and shut himself in his room with his phone. He would have to meet them. And despite Chris's assurances, he was bricking it.

Part of him was terrified that, in spite of all Chris's reassurances and all the perfectly logical, rational reasons why they couldn't possibly think he was a ra—a thug, he would still freak out and have a panic attack.

John knew what he looked like in a panic attack. Clenched fists. Wide eyes. Scowl. Heavy breathing. Every muscle tense and bulging.

Scared.

Scary.

"Psalter Clinic."

He swallowed. "Uh, hi. Is this—" *Obviously it was the Psalter Clinic, idiot.* "—Nadia Simmons?"

"This is their secretary."

"I'd—I'd like to make an appointment."

"All right." A keyboard clattered in the background. "Are you a current client?"

"N-no. No."

"All right," she said again. "You'll have to book an initial consultation. That's forty-five minutes, at which Mx Simmons will go over what it is you're seeking help with, and recommend a course of action. That consultation is free, any sessions after that are priced as on the website."

John nodded, then rolled his eyes at himself.

"Sir?"

"Yeah. Sorry, yeah. Let's book that."

Keys clattered away for a long minute.

"The next available appointment is the seventh of February at two o'clock in the afternoon."

John almost said: *Well, it wouldn't be two o'clock in the morning, would it?* But he caught himself just in time. Bloody hell, Chris was catching.

Then—

"The seventh of *February*?"

"Mx Simmons is very busy."

No shit. "Okay. Okay, fine. That's fine."

"You want me to book that for you?"

"Yeah."

So much for seeing her before meeting Chris's parents.

"What's your name, sir?"

"John. Halliday."

She rattled through a few other boring details, and then John was finally allowed to hang up. He wrote *7 Feb* on the business card and went back into the kitchen to stick it to the fridge.

A month. Five weeks.

Okay. Five weeks was not that bad. He could cope with five weeks. Maybe Chris's family would be too busy to meet anyway, so soon after New Year.

And if not...

Well, screw it. If not, John would just have to start practising breathing exercises. And not looking homicidal in the middle of a meltdown.

It would be *fine*.

Chapter Twenty-Three

JOHN'S PLAN WAS to try putting the dinner off until after he could at least have the consultation with Nadia Simmons, and then have it on neutral ground, armed with some coping mechanisms if he had another panic attack, and promising himself a nice evening with Chris after, no matter how it went.

The plan did not happen.

At all.

Work hit hard and heavy—New Year's and taking down Christmas decorations caused as many electrical nightmares as putting them up in the first place. So John didn't get to see Chris for a week, being too exhausted to stay over and Chris's epilepsy putting paid to the weekend. It wasn't until the following Tuesday before John got a cancellation and was able to lock up the van at four fifteen, free as a bird.

He ought to go and see Mum and tell her about his trip. He ought to pop down the supermarket and refill the fridge. He *really* needed to get his hair cut, and more antifreeze for the car.

Instead, he called Chris.

"Hello?"

"Hey, ba—beautiful. You free?"

"Uh. Well. Yeah."

John frowned. "That didn't sound convinced."

"I'm free. Not feeling very well."

"Oh." John's frown deepened. "You got a bug, or—?"

"Seizures."

"Oh, Christ. Had any?"

"One this morning. Not sure if I'm going to have another."

John bit his lip. After the run of the luck on the week away, part of him wanted to ride it out and not go round. And the other part told himself to man up—that if he wasn't prepared to handle this part of Chris's world, then he could sod right off and let Chris find a better man.

John squared his shoulders and his jaw.

"How about I bring some pasta and meatballs from that little Italian place you mentioned in Jordanthorpe, and a bottle of massage oil, and come over armed with food and a foot massage?"

"You sure?" Chris sounded uncertain.

"Sure. I want to see you, and if you're not feeling well, maybe I can help you feel a little bit better."

He could almost hear the smile in Chris's voice. "That'd be nice. Thank you. But no pasta—makes me feel sick if I seize. How about Chinese?"

"No problem. Any favourite dish?"

"Anything with duck. And all the spring rolls, forever."

"I know a place in Ecclesall that does duck spring rolls."

"Bring me every single one in the place."

"Got it. See you in half an hour, yeah? Love you."

That earned him a spluttered laugh and another thank you, and despite the news, John found himself grinning as he heaved the van into gear and set off. He was in Jordanthorpe already—a quick jaunt into Ecclesall to get the Chinese, and then back up to Parson Cross. No problem.

The Chinese had only just opened, so everything was fresh out of the fryers, and John splashed out for extra portions of all the sides, wondering if, for seizures, bite-sized would be the way to go rather than real meal food. Was Chris sick during seizures? All the first-aid courses warned about it, but Chris had mentioned losing bladder control rather than vomiting, and he hadn't been sick at the cottage that John knew of.

The sky was threatening more snow as John headed out for Parson Cross, but it held off, barely. It was a bruised brown colour when he finally pulled up, tucking the van carefully between the same Suzuki Jimny as last time, and a Peugeot with a pair of fluffy nipples hanging from the rear-view mirror. He juggled the Chinese cartons and was pondering how to get a hand free for the buzzer when a tall, skinny man with short, dark dreadlocks came out and held the door for him.

"Fuck me, mate," the man said, grinning manically. "You got a thing, you 'ave."

"Uh-huh," John said, but the man decided not to hang about, and headed off. Apparently, he was the Suzuki driver. It screeched out of its space, barely avoiding taking John's wing mirror with it, and set off down the hill. "All right, then," John muttered to himself and headed up the stairs.

He kicked Chris's door rather than knocked on it, and a couple of minutes later, it cracked open. The security chain was still on, Chris frowning around the edge of the wooden frame, and John rustled the bags.

"I bring food."

"Oh," Chris said and smiled. "Thanks, leave it there, and I'll pick it up."

"Charming."

The chain fell free, and the door opened wider. "There's an entry fee."

"Oh yeah?"

"One kiss per food carton."

"Oh, Christ. Right. Stretch up, then."

Chris rose on his toes, precise as a ballet dancer, and John leaned down to pepper cheeks, lips, jaw, and chin with little kisses. When he was done, Chris laughed.

"How much did you *bring*?"

"A lot."

Chris finally let him in and took the bags to let John take his shoes off. In socks and coat-free, John locked the door again and turned to squint at Chris a moment.

He looked tired. Stiff. He was moving slowly and almost delicately, and John frowned.

"In pain?"

"Little bit. Back aches."

"Had another one?"

"Not since you called."

"Going to have one?"

Chris sighed and braced his arms on the counter. Dropped his head. Lowered his voice.

"Yeah. Think so."

"Okay. You wanna go sit down and let me—"

"No, I bloody don't!"

The snap was sudden and vicious, and John flinched back. But just as sudden as the anger had sparked, it died again, and Chris ground a hand into his face with a groan.

"I'm sorry. Sorry. I—I just—it gets to me. People go into this awful mother-hen mode, and if I sat and let everyone do everything for me every time I thought I might have a seizure, I'd never stand up again."

John licked his lips.

"You said you have tonic-clonic seizures."

"Yeah."

"So...the go stiff and fall over kind?"

"Yeah."

"I don't want you cracking your head on the tiles," John said. "I'll sort food. You sort something on the telly."

The angry line of Chris's shoulders eased a little. "All right. What do you want to watch?"

"Nothing I have to have seen the first eight seasons of." John deftly took over plates and forks and opening cartons. Chris's kitchenette was so small it didn't take much searching for anything, and soon he'd cleared off the coffee table and began to decorate it with cartons.

"Duck spring rolls," Chris commanded, holding out a hand. John deposited the plate of them there, and two immediately vanished.

"Holy hell."

Chris swallowed with an unholy wrenching sound. "Hey, I like them."

"No kidding."

Two more disappeared before Chris put the plate aside to pick a DVD case up from the TV stand. "Do you mind audio descriptive?" he asked as he fitted the disc into the player.

"No."

"Good. You've probably seen it anyway."

The first Hobbit film. He hadn't. And he made the mistake of saying so.

"Ex*cuse* me?"

"What! I haven't!"

"You're a sick, sick man, Mr Halliday."

John laughed, settling at the other end of the sofa and drawing Chris's bare feet into his lap. He started up a gentle, dry foot massage as they ate. The audio descriptive was a little odd, but he got used to it quickly enough. After a few false starts—where John commented on the appearance of the actors, then flushed deeply and stammered apologies—Chris started to demand more of the hilarious descriptions.

They'd reached a part where a lot of short, fat men with beards were dancing and throwing blatantly plastic crockery around—despite Martin Freeman's insistence it was his mother's best china—when the first twitch happened.

John let go and eyed Chris warily.

"Chris?"

"Sorry." Chris's voice was a little vague. "Think—think I'm gonna go."

John hastily removed the plate balanced on Chris's stomach. "That's all right." He carefully extracted himself from under Chris's feet. "If you have to go, just go. It's fine."

His heart was beating a tattoo in his throat. This was it. This was it.

Only—it wasn't.

At least, for a little while. Chris was ignoring the film. When John tentatively uttered a few more absurd descriptions—especially about the homeless-looking gay wizard—they earned very vague smiles, and when he touched Chris's hand, the fingers squeezed back.

And then Chris said, "Oh."

It slipped out maybe eight or nine minutes after that heavy twitch. He made that single sound, and then his eyes rolled up in his head.

And he froze.

It wasn't quite a stiffening, at such, though the way his feet jerked and his neck tensed, he would certainly have fallen over if he'd even been sitting up. For maybe twenty seconds, he stayed perfectly still like that, even his ribcage still. John stared. Counted. Held his breath alongside him.

And then the chest relaxed. The whole body relaxed. And—

Jerked.

The first shudder was powerful, seemed to almost rock the sofa, and a series of smaller twitches followed, radiating outwards from his spine. A hand caught the edge of the coffee table before John could block it, and he carefully shifted the table farther away. Chris's feet scraped and scuffed against the arm of the sofa; his head rocked at the other, his long frame barely fitting. Thank Christ it was a three-seater. His mouth foamed; his throat made a horrible choking sound, and John tensed up in a panic. But the vomit never came. There was no pink tinge to the spit. And his chest rose and fell—in jerky, harsh breaths, yes, but it did anyway.

It seemed to happen in little waves—a set of shivers would almost die away, John would lean forward expecting it to be over, and then the next wave would strike, and it would almost begin again. But for the uneven breathing and the rolled whites of his eyes, John would have thought it multiple seizures, instead of one.

John fought to stay still, quiet, and out of the way. He eyed his watch, counting the terrible seconds. Chris had said three to four minutes at most, and only two minutes had ticked by. He hadn't—yet—lost bladder control. He hadn't—yet—been sick. But could he, would he, do those during the seizure, or after it? He'd been eating. Did how long he'd kept the food down before the seizure matter? When was the last time he'd been to the bathroom? Did—

A great sigh.

A rolling relaxation.

And then it passed. Almost like a shadow ghosting past Chris's face, the seizure vanished, and he sank into the cushions, sweat-soaked and shivering. John hesitated, hands touching his arms and shoulders in fleeting strokes, before checking his pulse and breathing—rapid, and steady, in that order—and calling his name softly.

"Can you hear me, babe?"

The loathed nickname slipped out but got no reaction. Carefully, John ran his palm firmly down Chris's neck and back, so perfectly memorised under such different circumstances, and found nothing wrong. He felt down each limb and around his head. Nothing. No strange shifts, no breaks or dislocations.

Very carefully, he turned Chris onto his side, into the recovery position, and used a napkin to wipe his mouth clear of the foam.

His pulse was calming down. His breathing was regular and reaching into the lower lobes of his lungs, by the gentle push of his stomach.

He was fine.

Right?

John's first-aid training said yes. Even the information Chris had given him said yes. He'd said he slept after, didn't he? And when John pressed the beds of his nails with a key, the hand was jerked away from him. There was some level of consciousness going on. He wasn't—

He was *fine*.

But this wasn't first aid and a café conversation; this was a real, live seizure, right in front of him, and happening to someone he loved. John's heart and head warred with one another, the former terrified and demanding an ambulance, the latter insisting Chris was absolutely fine and didn't need one.

But John sort of needed one.

Or...

Maybe someone who knew what they were doing? Maybe—

He looked around and saw Chris's phone on the kitchen counter, charging. Maybe he could call Gina and ask her to come over? Yes, he'd do that. Get someone else to come and just...check for him. Make sure he'd done the right things. Make sure Chris was fine.

Gina didn't pick up. He couldn't tell which Luke—Luke L, or Luke J—was the right Luke. And suddenly, John was faced with the next most obvious choice, and one he really, really didn't like.

Dad.

Second top contact, right under *Caroline*. And the same number, listed elsewhere as *ICE*.

In Case of Emergency.

John swallowed and glanced at Chris, still and silent, on the sofa.

He hit call.

The phone rang only four times before a deep voice grumbled, "This had better be good, kiddo."

"Um. Is this—Chris's dad?"

The voice cooled. "Who is this."

It was flat, not voiced as a question at all.

"Uh. Hi. My—my name's—"

"I don't care what your damned name is," came the brusque reply, tinged with a faint undertone of a Scottish accent. "What are you doing with my son's phone?"

"I'm at his flat. I'm—a friend. And he's had a seizure, and he seems fine, but I've never really dealt with a seizure before, so...could someone...come and check on him?"

The harshness eased a fraction. "You ever done any first aid?"

"Yes. He's breathing, clear airway, his pulse is fine." John crossed back to sit by the sofa. "He's out though."

"Asleep?"

"I'm not sure."

"Probably asleep. All right. I'll come over. Just keep an eye on his pulse or breathing. When did the seizure stop?"

"Maybe five minutes ago?"

"How long was it?" John could hear metal jangling in the background.

"About two and a half minutes."

"Not too bad. Keep an eye on him. I'll be about fifteen, twenty minutes."

And with that, the man hung up.

John, hoping that he'd done the right thing, settled in to wait.

Chapter Twenty-Four

IT WAS ABOUT half an hour before anyone arrived. Chris didn't move, but John grew increasingly convinced he was asleep. The hand John had tucked under Chris's face to support his airway had slowly curled into a fist. The other, hanging limp from the wrist over the edge of the sofa, twitched occasionally when John carefully stroked the fingers. And when the film—which John still hadn't turned off—bellowed an orchestral crescendo, one leg shifted a little higher in a motion John recognised from a full week of spooning that body in bed every morning.

Then John heard footsteps outside on the landing.

"Let me go and let your dad in, bab—beautiful," he murmured.

The jerk of the front door and the violent catch of the security chain did what John's petting hadn't though: Chris twitched violently and then half sat up with a loud shout.

"Fuck off!"

"Whoa!" John said.

"What the—"

"Just me," he said quickly. "It's just me."

"The *door*!"

"That's—"

A voice boomed. "Chris?"

"Dad?"

John jumped for the door and unhooked the chain. And froze.

Just froze solid at the thunderous look he was given by the man on the threshold. And then that man was shoving past him and into the flat, and John was simply...

Stuck.

Stuck by the socks. Shaking. The look, that *look*, that angry and aggressive stare—

John's lungs weren't working. His fingers were shaking. He hadn't done anything. He hadn't, he hadn't, he *hadn't*—

"What're you doing here?"

"Your mate called—"

"Well, you can go. I had a seizure; I'm fine—"

"Who's he?"

"You know who he is..."

John bent at the waist, raking in air. Gulping at it. He hadn't done anything. He'd just—watched, and called Chris's dad, and—and why the look, why did the man look at him like that, why—

"I'm not sure that's a good idea."

"What the hell's that supposed to mean?"

"Leaving you alone with—"

"With *what*?"

With you, John's brain supplied. *With you, with you, with you*—

He pushed his feet into his shoes, numb. He had to get out. Had to go. Chris's dad was right. It would be a bad idea. Leaving an unconscious person along with a bloody great thug like—

"That's *John*, you moron." The sofa creaked. "I just spent a whole week alone with him!"

John walked out. Down the stairs. Out through the communal door. There was a Land Rover where the Suzuki had been. It had had snow on the roof, last time John had seen it. Outside number sixteen. In Greenhill.

He slammed into his van, shoved the keys into the ignition, and drove.

Just drove.

Not a good idea. Leaving Chris alone with him. God, that *look* at the door. That scowl. It was—it was—it was like that copper who'd arrested him. That defence lawyer who'd come to give him advice. *Tasha.*

That man believed John to be a—to be a—

No, no, no, no—

The anxiety balloon swelled so far that it cut off his air. The next breath was thin and reedy. Black spots danced around the edges of his vision. His fingers—his fingers—

Numb.

John swallowed and scrambled for some sense.

Indicator. Lay-by. A car horn beeping. The van shuddered to a halt.

He leaned his head on the steering wheel and took a deep breath.

Another.

One more.

The spots receded slowly. Air came back. Awareness followed it. The indicator was clacking loudly in the otherwise silent van. He wasn't wearing a seatbelt. The heater was off, and he was freezing.

He needed to go home.

"Go home," he told himself croakily. "Call by in the morning before work."

He'd have nightmares again. Knew it, sure as he knew his own name. He'd barely sleep. Hit the gym early to try to work out some of the panic. Probably do his shoulder in again. Have to take painkillers, and then be groggy at work. Make mistakes. Get annoyed with himself, cancel a few jobs, go home to sleep, and—have nightmares all over.

"Why are you so *fu—*"

His phone started ringing.

John finally lifted his head from the steering wheel and arched his hips to squirm it out of his pocket. It was Chris. John swallowed. He wanted to not answer, have his freak-out in private, pretend it hadn't happened.

But Chris had had a seizure.

And the last time John had melted down all over him, he'd been so good.

The tiny part of John's brain not quite fizzled out from the panic piped up with the other thing.

He'd called his dad a moron.

John answered.

"John?"

"Hey."

John's voice sounded terrible, even to his own ears.

"You okay?"

"No."

"Where are you?"

"In—in my van."

"It's not outside. Dad said so."

"I'm—no. Some road. Not sure."

"Can you come back?"

John hesitated.

"John?"

"I—"

Chris's voice dropped into something very low. Soothing. John closed his eyes and drank the sound in.

"Are you having another panic attack?"

"Y-yes."

"Oh, sweetheart."

"I just—I just—"

"Was it Dad?"

"Y-yeah."

"Talk to me."

There was a note of soft sympathy. There was a note of crisp command. John swallowed, and something about the combination unlocked his throat.

"The way he looked at me," he breathed. "And he said—said it would be a bad idea."

"Said what would be a bad idea?"

"To leave you alone with me."

Chris snorted. "Yes. John? He finished that sentence off after I called him a berk."

"Moron."

"What?"

"You said moron."

"Well, he's both. I can have both. Ssh."

John sshed.

"He *meant* because you've never dealt with a seizure before."

Something very tight in John's chest creaked.

"Really?" His voice sounded high. Childish. Weak.

"Yes. Really. Sometimes I have another one quite quickly. And you *did* call him in a bit of a tizz."

John found a smile warping his face. "A bit of a tizz?"

"Oh shut up, my mum says it."

John sniffed, taking a deep breath. Chris was okay. Chris was calling him. Chris—

"Come back?"

—wanted him to come back?

"What?"

"Come back? There's still Chinese. And the movie. And you were giving me this lovely foot massage before my epilepsy fucked things up."

John stared blindly out of the windscreen.

"Is—is that a good idea?"

There was a long pause.

"John?"

"W-what?"

"I know—I know right now you're having one of your ex-related freak-outs, and...and if you really need to go away and calm down on your own, then you do that, okay? You do what you need to do to feel better. But...but, firstly, I think maybe you don't need to do that—that you'll try and wrap what Dad said around what your ex said and make it worse. And, secondly, you know that thing you were talking about when you *know* something to be true, factually, but your emotions aren't listening to you, and you feel something else?"

"Yeah?"

"I have a bit of that right now. I *know* you've done a runner because Dad stomped all over your issues with your dickhead ex. But...right now, my emotions are all like, I had a seizure and you took off."

John took a sharp breath.

"No."

"I know that's not why. But I don't *feel* like that's why. So, if you need to take a breather and regroup and come back tomorrow, then you do that, okay, I don't want you to—"

John took a deep breath. "Is—is your dad still there?"

"No."

No?

"Really? He's just—gone?"

"You hearing me okay? I'm fine. I had a nap. Usually happens."

"Are you—are you feeling okay?"

"As okay as you would feel, waking up after a seizure to your dad and your boyfriend having a paddy with each other."

John snorted and choked on a sob.

"Oh, *hey*, no. No-no-no. Come on, John, come back here. There's a sofa and Chinese food and we both need a good hug, don't we?"

"Sorry. Sorry, Jesus—"

"Ssh, don't be. Hey. *Hey*. You wanna exploit the chink in my armour? I'd totally let you get away with a snuggle right now."

John coughed a feeble laugh and scrubbed his wrist over his eyes. "Okay. Okay. I'll—yeah. You sure?"

"Yep. Come on. We'll both feel better if you stay the night, I think."

"Okay."

"How far away are you?"

"I don't know. Ten minutes?"

"I'll reheat the food and reset the film. You get yourself back on my sofa, okay?"

"'Kay. Chris?"

"Mm?"

"Love you."

A short pause.

"Passion you."

John laughed and hung up. He blew his nose on a scrap of tissue from the glovebox, only to discover it was a receipt, and tossed it out of the window before turning the indicator to the other side and doing a very illegal U-turn. The phone glowed brightly on the seat. Rain had started up again, and John squinted against the streetlights. He had a headache. His body wanted to go home, have a shower, and go to bed.

But his mind wanted Chris.

It couldn't have been more than half an hour, but the Land Rover had gone, the Suzuki had returned, and the fluffy-nippled Peugeot was being de-iced by a man not much smaller than John. They grunted hellos, and John hunched his shoulders as he paced to the communal door, bitterly regretting leaving his coat behind.

No answer to the buzzer, but the door clicked open.

John took the stairs slowly, wondering what to say, or if Chris would even need anything to be said. A sense of shame was creeping over him. One scowl, and he'd fallen apart. He'd not even listened to Chris's dad's reasoning before freaking out and running off. And Chris was right. His boyfriend had had a seizure, and John had done a runner. Jesus, what was *wrong* with him?

Chris met him at the door and simply lifted his arms. John stooped into the hug and sighed with the power of it.

"Hey." Chris's voice was a soft whisper against his shoulder. "You okay?"

"No. Are you?"

"Nope. C'mon. Let's get ourselves back to okay."

The Chinese had been reheated. The sofa cushions had been refluffed, and a blue blanket had been rustled up from somewhere. John perched carefully on the end of the sofa, and Chris—rather than sit beside him, as John had expected—sat right down into his lap, brought his feet up onto the sofa cushions, and relaxed into John's neck and chest like he owned them.

John twisted his face to bury it in Chris's curly hair and breathed. Stroked a hand up a cotton-clad thigh. Looped the other around his back.

And relaxed.

"Better?" Chris murmured.

"Little bit."

Chris nuzzled into his shoulder a little.

"So," he said, "Dad meant he didn't think leaving me with someone who hadn't dealt with seizures before was a good idea."

John swallowed and nodded.

"I told him to naff off because, clearly, you'd done fine, and that would have happened at the coast anyway if our timing hadn't been so weird."

"Yeah," John croaked. "And—and it was—I just wanted to make sure, you know? You...you weren't waking up, and I wanted someone to tell me I was doing okay. I tried Gina first but she didn't answer, and then I didn't know if Luke was Luke L or Luke J—"

"J."

"Okay."

"So you wanted Dad to double-check?"

"Yeah. That was all. I was planning on staying anyway. I...the way he looked at me when he got here, and then what he said, I—*freaked.*"

"Like with Lauren?"

"Yeah. Like with Lauren."

Chris stroked his fingers idly up and down John's chest.

"You can't keep doing that," he said softly.

"No. I know."

"Lauren didn't even think twice about you. And you know what Dad's single comment on you was?"

"What?"

"That you better not be the driver of that weird little Peugeot with the tits on the mirror."

John choked a wet laugh.

"*Are* you?"

"Christ, no."

"See? Fine."

"I—I rang a counsellor the other day," John mumbled. "I'm going to get some help, see if I can't get rid of what Daniel's left behind. But I can't even get an assessment until the seventh of February."

Chris's fingers hooked in the neck of John's T-shirt.

"You want to put off dinner until after that?"

"No point. She won't be able to do anything in that session."

"Okay," Chris said. "Do you maybe want to try dinner here instead of out somewhere? And maybe break them up a bit?"

"What d'you mean?"

"Well, maybe if I get Lauren to come over? Just Lauren? Or—"

"That'll make them even warier. They'll think there's some horrible reason you won't introduce me to them all at once, and—"

"There is. You have a real bastard of an ex."

"You can't tell them that."

"No?"

"God, no. Come on, Chris." John shifted a little. "Who'd believe he was lying? Doesn't it sound like a convenient excuse to you? I got arrested for ra—for *that*, but it's okay, the guy was lying. Even I wouldn't believe it if my sisters brought home boyfriends saying that."

"Mm, good point..."

A soft silence fell. John returned his nose to the mess of curls and simply breathed.

Then: "Mum."

"What?"

"We'll start with Mum instead."

"What? Why?"

"Because she'll not be too keen, but there's only one of her. Jack won't care. And you can talk rugby with Jack; he's a huge fan."

"League or union?"

"What's the difference?"

"Oh, God," John groaned.

"All right, all right," came the snotty reply, and a kiss landed on John's cheek, clumsy and off-centre as usual. "Hey. No more planning tonight, yeah? Let's cudd—"

"Snuggle."

"*Fine.* Let's snuggle up, watch the film, eat the Chinese, and then go to bed. Yeah?"

"Yeah," John said, wiping his face one last time and taking a ragged breath. "What hurts?"

"What?"

"After your seizure. What hurts?"

"Shoulders ache."

"Okay, shuffle 'round, and I'll give you a shoulder rub."

"Ohh, okay."

John pressed a kiss to the nape of the presented neck and felt the anxiety balloon slowly deflating inside his chest. This was—this was fine. They were both a bit shook up in the head, but it was okay. They'd talked. They were being honest. They could do this.

Chris's deep groan at the first roll of John's thumbs down his knotted spine was louder than his just-came groan, and John found a smile flickering into place.

"Chris?"

"Yeah?"

"Thanks."

"For wha—*ohh*, yes, that's it."

John rubbed the released knot until it faded away. "For listening to me."

"Only way we're going to make this work. You with your screwed up ex and me with my health crap."

John kissed the back of his head.

"John?"

"Mm?"

"We *can* make it work, you know."

Oddly—despite the nasty turn of the evening, despite the scowl at the door, despite the ache in John's chest and the lingering burn in his eyes—

"Yeah. I think you're right."

Chapter Twenty-Five

"JOHN!"

John tossed the steak and shouted, "What?" as he narrowly avoided oil burns.

"Your phone's ringing!"

"So?"

"So it's bloody annoying; come and get it!"

John eyeing the smoking steak. "Bit busy here, Noz!"

"Jesus, *fine*, you useless—ooh!"

He did not like that noise.

"*Hello*, Chris!"

"Shit!" John yelped. He switched the burner off and lunged for the living room. Nora was perched on the arm of the sofa, his phone to her ear and grinning widely.

"He's just comi—hey!"

"Tart," John snapped at her, before slamming back into the kitchen with the rescued phone. "Hi. Sorry. Sorry."

"Something I should know?" Chris laughed.

"My older sister is an annoying, conniving tart, and I obviously didn't bully her enough as a kid?"

"Oh, I gathered that. So that was...Nora?"

"Yeah. Soon to be my late sister."

"Aw, she seemed nice."

"You've not met her," John said pointedly.

"Yeah, but I'm sure she's—"

The phone beeped. John lifted it from his ear and frowned at the private caller icon flashing.

"Sorry, Chris, hang on. I have another call coming in."

"Customer?"

"Maybe."

"All right. Ring me back, just going to get dressed."

John ruthlessly squashed the mental image of Chris naked and hung up before answering the incoming call.

"Hello?"

"Mr Halliday?"

"Speaking."

"This is Mx Simmons's office. We have a cancellation next Monday at ten o'clock, if you'd like to move your assessment forward."

John's throat went dry.

Move it forward? That would be—

"Yes. Please."

His stomach clenched as she rattled away, and talked to him about parking, about arriving on time, about bringing notes if it would help him remember everything he wanted to discuss. Monday. It was already Wednesday. That was less than a week. In less than a week, he could maybe start—

Start what—treatment? Was counselling really treatment? It wasn't like drugs or physio or anything, so it wasn't really. Was it? If it could stop him having panic attacks because his boyfriend's stepmother waved from across the street, it *was* treatment.

Whatever, he decided. Start whatever. Start sorting it out.

So when the secretary finally hung up, John shut the kitchen door on Nora's blatantly eavesdropping ears and picked Chris out of the recently called list.

"Hey!"

"Hey, ba—beautiful."

"I heard that."

"I didn't say it!"

"You *nearly* said it."

"So I *nearly* get punished, but not actually, right?"

Chris snorted. "Sure. So? Customer?"

"Er. No. Counsellor."

"Your counsellor?"

"Well, her office. I managed to get my appointment with the counsellor moved to Monday."

"As in, next week?"

"Yeah."

"That's great!" Chris enthused. "I'm free Monday night if you want to come over after, you know."

"Um. Maybe. See how I feel." His stomach squirmed, and the idea spilled out. "So—so I thought, seeing as how it's going to be sooner rather than later, um..."

"Um?" Chris echoed.

John blew upwards into his hair. "Do you, er. Do you want to come to Sunday dinner?"

"This weekend?"

"Yeah."

"As in...meet your family?"

"Yeah." His throat was getting scratchy and awkward. "I just—I know I'm going to completely brick it meeting yours, but there's no reason you shouldn't meet mine, and I—I don't want you to feel like you're some dirty little secret, or I'm keeping you away from them, or—"

"I get it." Chris's voice was very gentle. "But I can't this weekend. I'm really sorry, but I'm away. My cousin's getting married."

"Oh."

There was a sharp pause, and then John glanced at the closed door.

"Are you free now?"

"Er. Yes?"

"You could come over for dinner. Meet Nora. I'm sure Fran would be round like a shot if she heard you were coming."

"Oh, *that* kind of visit—"

The sobriety broke. John groaned, and Chris cackled in his ear.

"Oh, trust *you*."

"You do!" Followed by a kissing noise.

"Do you want to though?"

"If I can stay the night."

John bit his lip to avoid the grin. "Always."

"Okay. Are you going to come and pick me up?"

"Can do. Give me half an hour. No, forty minutes," he decided, glancing at the clock. "Traffic won't be great, because of the football. Forty minutes."

"Okay. See you."

"Love you," John said, almost automatically, before hanging up and taking the steak off the heat. He could chop it up into a salad or a wrap or something for lunch tomorrow. "Nora!"

"What?"

"You're a tart!"

"I'm a queen amongst women, and you know it!"

"Whatever," John said, opening the door again. "Chris is coming over."

She pulled a face at him. "I just did my toes!"

John pulled a face right back. Nothing like an older sister to turn someone into a five-year-old again. "And he's coming over so he can meet you."

Her face went white under the mud mask. "Are you *kidding* me? I just did my toes, John!"

And the rest of her. She was wearing mud on her face, something weird holding all her toes out, and polish on every nail. Her hair was wrapped in a towel that smelled like a mummified body. And because apparently it was a beauty night in, bras were banned, and baby brothers could see everything they never wanted to, as she was wearing nothing but a massive pair of granny knickers.

"Oh my God, you *suck*!" she shouted and launched off the sofa to waddle awkwardly into her room. "Don't you *dare* open that front door for an hour!"

"You have forty minutes," John lied, fishing his car keys out of the pocket of his discarded jacket. She swore at him as he closed the front door behind him, and loped leisurely down the stairs. He texted Fran as he got into the car—nothing about Chris, simply *fancy beer and curry night at ours? Can pick you up in 45*—before shifting the beast into gear and peeling out of the parking area.

The city was intolerable—the match had just started—but John cruised out to Parson Cross. He felt...calm. Surprisingly. His sisters were reasonably good with boyfriends, despite their teasing. It was just Mum and Nan that would immediately start demanding bank statements and opinions on marriage. The girls would be more interested in his opinions on food and football. And he had a feeling Chris would get on well with Fran. They had a similar sort of humour. Hell, they'd probably gang up on him.

And next week...

Next week, after he saw Nadia, John had decided he was going to meet at least one set of Chris's parents. He was going to take the plunge. He was determined not to let Daniel ruin the best thing he'd ever had. Even if it was just meeting Chris's mum for a cup of tea and a chat in some coffee shop somewhere, he was going to do *something*.

It was raining when he pulled up to the flats. A couple of teenagers were smoking by the communal door, and eyed him. One grunt and a tightened bicep, and they shifted aside. John hit the button, heard the door catch release, and bashed through into the hall like he owned the joint. It'd make them think twice about touching his car, that was for sure.

The flat door was on the latch, and John let himself in to find Chris putting on his shoes. His hair was damp, his skin hot from the shower, and John cupped the back of his neck and kissed him, catching the surprised noise against his lips.

"Hello," John said and grinned. "Ready?"

"Just about. Is this okay?" Chris tugged at the neck of his T-shirt as he stood up from the sofa. "I didn't know—I mean—"

"You look great," John said, sliding a propriety hand around Chris's arse. "It's nothing formal. Just a few drinks and a takeaway with the girls."

Chris stretched up on his toes, kissing John's chin and looping both arms around his neck.

"And then later, you'll peel me back out of these jeans, right?"

John squeezed the caught cheek. "Yup. Got your overnight bag?"

"By the door."

John kissed his ear and let go. He hefted the bag over one shoulder, waiting patiently while Chris unfolded the cane and locked up the flat, then paced a few steps ahead the whole way down the stairs. He didn't fancy letting those shitty kids know a gay guy lived round here.

Then he felt a little guilty as one of them held the door and said, "Evening, Chris," like Chris played darts down the pub with them every night.

"Evening, Craig," Chris said genially. The cane tapped lightly on the paving stones, and John took his arm to guide him to the car.

"I thought they looked right dodgy," John muttered as he opened the passenger door and shielded the lip of the roof with his hand.

"They are," Chris said as he sat and folded up the cane again. "But Craig is Luke's little brother. And Luke's a right vicious git if Craig starts getting shitty with his mates."

"Ah."

Fran had texted back—a couple of emojis that John translated as she'd like to join them and could he possibly come and collect her from her flat.

"I might not have told Fran you're coming," he confessed, phone poised to correct the error, but Chris smiled.

"Okay. We'll surprise her. Will she hate me?"

"To be honest, I think she might adopt you."

"Oh?"

"You're her type."

"Do I need a gay badge to ward her off?"

"Won't work. She'll like you even more if you tell her you're gay." John cocked his head. "Are you?"

"Gay?"

"Yeah."

"Dunno."

The casual ease of it was surprising. John said as much.

"I tend to say I'm queer more than anything," Chris said, shrugging. "I don't really know yet. It's all tangled up with how I feel about me."

"How d'you mean?"

"Well...I like girl's voices a lot more now mine's dropped. Before, I hated them."

"Oh, I see."

"I think maybe after surgery, things will shift a bit. I like girls enough I'm not gay, but not enough that I'm comfortable saying I'm bi. And I have no idea how other trans people fit into that, whether I'm attracted to them or not. So I'm queer."

"Not bi?"

"Well, I've never liked a girl more than in theory."

"In theory?"

"Dad's a massive *Stargate* fan, and I've had a crush on Amanda Tapping since the dawn of time," Chris confessed. "I literally remember what blonde hair looks like because of hers."

John made a mental note to binge-watch *Stargate* and find out who Amanda Tapping was.

"But I've never met a real-life girl I like."

"So you're...theoretically bisexual?"

"I'm queer," Chris repeated.

"Huh," John said. "Queer was still, you know, stop being such a faggot—that kind of territory—when I was a kid. And I don't think I've ever had a bisexual bloke. Just other gayer-than-gay lads."

"Yeah, well, you're old."

"Hey!"

Chris grinned as John shoved his knee.

"Old man!"

"Naff off, we can't all look like nineteen-year-old supermodels."

"That's the hormones."

"Bollocks it is. I've been doped up on testosterone since I was twelve, and I look forty."

"And the rest..."

"Oi!"

Chris quieted a little as John slowed down and took the turning into Fran's road.

"I am queer though. If you don't like that—"

John winced. "Oh, hey, no, I didn't mean that. I was just a bit surprised. Just not heard someone use it before."

Chris hummed.

John reached over to squeeze his knee. "Okay?"

"Yeah. Sorry. I get prickly."

"Don't be. I'm kind of crap at this. It was just—you know, bisexual was barely a word when I came out. Well. When Mum told me I was gay."

Chris snorted with laughter.

"She did," John whined as he pulled over into a free space. He hit the horn and sat back. "Now to wait for the hurricane to arrive."

"Fran?"

"Yeah."

"Is she like you?"

"How d'you mean?"

"Big and sweet."

John coughed a little. "Uh. No. Tiny and demonic."

"Tiny?"

"All my sisters are tiny."

"What are you, the milkman's boy?"

John laughed.

"Or did your mum plant you in a tub of soil and water you with Miracle-Gro?"

"The latter, I reckon," John admitted.

A door banged. The hair was green this week, and the car dipped as Fran launched herself into the back seat, seized John's head and headrest in a hug—and stopped dead.

"Hello!"

Chris grinned, turning vaguely to wave in her direction. "Hi."

"Who're you, then?" came the blunt, blank question. And then she squealed. "Oh my God! Are you Chris?"

"Yes."

"Oh my *God*, hello!" she shrieked. She let go of John only to shove her entire upper body into the front and squash Chris up in a tight, awkward hug. "John's been keeping you a secret! I'm Fran; I'm his little sister."

Chris managed to extract himself. "Yeah, he said."

"At least he told you *something*! He told us nothing! So, so, so, how did you meet? Is he a total great clumsy berk? Are you coming to Sunday dinner this weekend? Have you done the nasty yet—he keeps saying he's classy, but I bet he's not, I bet you shagged on the first date, *did* you?"

"Fran," John said in a measured voice, "if you don't shut up, sit down, and put your seatbelt on, I'm going to tow you instead."

"Oh, what*ever*."

"Watch me!"

"You're cute when you try to be manly," Fran said, but she did sit back and belt up. "So, Chris—stories, tell me all the stories."

"He spilled my coffee on me, so I asked him out," Chris said, and John knew he was screwed.

"Please don't gang up on me with my sister," he implored.

"Why not?"

"I'll lose!"

"You lose anyway," Fran said. "So, what are you into, what do you do—*oh*, do you like Chinese, there's an amazing Chinese place that's opening next month in town that I want to try. Come with me, and I'll tell you all about John—"

She talked a mile a minute all the way back to Kelham Island, barely pausing to breathe, never mind letting Chris actually answer her. John was horrified. But amidst the horror was a slice of relief, for Chris kept laughing into his hand and seemed weirdly charmed by the energy.

And Fran, for all she was a hurricane and had the social grace of a herd of rampaging elephants, wasn't a total dunce. She bounced out of the car the moment John pulled up outside the flats, seized Chris's door, and had him halfway towards the block, arm in arm and without a word about why.

John paused to be grateful for her unexpected tact, then returned resolutely to mortification.

He caught up to them in the lift and whined when Fran hugged Chris's arm, telling John to get his own.

"I *did*. You've stolen him."

Chris shrugged. "I'm sorry, but she promised me fudge cake."

"You'd leave me for fudge cake?"

"I'd leave *anyone* for fudge cake."

"Fine," John said. "I'll get you bigger fudge cake."

Laughing, Chris extracted his arm from Fran's death grip, swapped the cane over, and tucked his other hand into John's elbow.

"Traitor," Fran sulked.

John rolled his eyes as he fumbled for keys. The lift spat them out, and Fran retook her new favourite as John wrestled with the front door. He heard her whispering invitations to various gigs and galleries, and Chris's fight not to start laughing again.

Then the door popped open, and Nora was right there.

Hand out, ready to shake Chris's. Dressed up, but also down, in a deliberately well-fitted pair of jeans and a fluffy jumper. Her hair artfully mussed. The purposeful look of having done nothing special, but probably took her an age to achieve.

And completely still.

"Nora, Chris. Chris, my other sister, Nora."

Silence.

Chapter Twenty-Six

"YOU SHOULD HAVE said," Nora whispered the moment John turned the tap on.

It had been a nice evening. But it would have been better if Nora hadn't been silent and staring for most of it.

Luckily, Chris didn't seem to have noticed. Fran kept him busy, talking nineteen-to-the-dozen over their Thai food, and then they discovered a shared loathing of some book series and spent a good hour comparing the author to various parts of animals. John had, for the most part, simply sat on the sofa, one arm around Chris, and watched.

But when he'd offered to wash up and get some ice cream out of the freezer, Nora followed, shutting the kitchen door behind her.

"Said what?" John asked.

"That he was—you know."

"What?"

John genuinely wasn't sure. He *thought* she meant blind, but Chris was wearing a sports bra under the T-shirt—John had felt it when Chris wriggled under his arm for a hug earlier—and he'd shaved. So maybe she could tell? John was kind of used to how Chris looked, and he wasn't very good at when other people were about to say 'pal' or 'darling.'

"You *know*," Nora whispered, throwing a furtive look at the door. "The—" She waved a hand in front of her face.

"Blind?" John guessed.

"Yes!"

"But...why?"

She blinked. "Are you kidding?"

"Um. No?"

Why would he have said anything? It was dinner. Not like he'd wanted them all to go rock climbing or something.

"John! The flat's a mess, there's stuff all over the floor, and what about the bathroom? We don't have an accessible bathroom!"

"He...doesn't need one," John said uncertainly. "He goes to the gents when we're out somewhere, like anyone else."

She folded her arms and hunched her shoulders. "I—is this really a good idea, John?"

"What do you mean?"

"After Daniel? After what he did? Is—is Chris a good idea?"

John stared.

Did she—?

"Why?" he whispered.

"He got inside your head and made you believe some of what he said," Nora whispered back. "Is Chris really going to help with that?"

"He *is* helping with tha—"

"You've gone from someone who didn't say no to someone who *can't*, John."

His mouth stopped working.

The unfinished protest hung in the air between them, and John found himself staring dumbly. *Can't?* There—there was no can't. Chris could say whatever he wanted. *Did* say whatever he wanted.

Didn't he?

The treacherous whisper crept in around the edges, and John throttled it ruthlessly. *Yes. He did. He had.* John had touched his boob, and Chris had nearly slapped him. He'd said no.

"Of course he can say no." John turned his back on her and opened the freezer. "Just because he's different," he told the ice cream tubs, "doesn't mean he's bloody incapable, Nora."

"I'm worried about what other people are going to see. That they'll say things, and fuel your—"

"That's why I'm going to see a counsellor."

"You—what?"

"I have an appointment with Nadia Simmons next week."

"That's—that's good, John, that's really good, but—"

John banged the tubs down on the counter and closed his eyes.

"So, you believe I did it."

"*What*? No!"

"Then why would Chris be a bad idea?"

"Because *you* believe you did it."

John hesitated.

"You do. You're afraid of yourself," Nora said softly. "And Chris is—God, I know you like him—"

Love him.

"—but he's vulnerable, John. People *are* going to look twice. People *are* going to think the worst of you. And I don't think you're in a place where you can handle that."

John tightened his jaw and opened his eyes again. Rummaged for spoons and bowls, all without looking at her.

"John."

"People," he snapped as he dished out scoops, "can think what they bloody well like. That's what Nadia's going to help me with. She's going to help me undo some of that, so I don't freak out thinking about what people think. I never did before Daniel, so why should I do it now?"

"Chris won't help with that."

"How the fu—heck would you know?" John gathered up the bowls and walked out. He was seething. Nora was supposed to be on his side. She was supposed to stick up for him! She'd liked everything about Chris, everything about a new boyfriend, right up until she'd seen the cane. Christ, what would she think if she knew he was epileptic as well? Had she figured out he was trans?

"Finally!" Fran proclaimed dramatically.

"It's best half-melted," Chris opined, shuffling casually back to lie against John's chest. John dipped his head to kiss the curls almost automatically. "Okay?"

"Mm."

"The angry whispering says otherwise."

"Oh, Christ, you heard that?"

"Oh, we listened in," Fran said. "And Nora, stop being like Mum!" she added in a shout.

Chris simply smirked but didn't say anything. John slid his hand down to rest on a warm stomach, tucking his fingers tidily under the T-shirt.

"So," he said, going for normal but probably failing. "What are we watching?"

FRAN DISAPPEARED AT nine and Nora soon afterwards into her room. John watched the news while Chris texted Luke with the ease of access voiceover—which was, incidentally, incredibly annoying. And then John put the phone aside and kissed Chris sideways until that lithe body turned over in his arms, distracting them both.

"Can I still stay the night?" Chris murmured softly, and John nudged their noses together.

"Be offended if you didn't."

"Good. I wanna hold your—"

"Oh, God."

"—snake."

"What?"

"You said you had a corn snake!"

"I...did?"

"On our second date. When I touched your tattooed version."

"Oh. *Oh.* Uh, yeah. Sure. I keep her in my room."

"The pet, John, not your—"

"*Yes*, the pet! Christ."

Chris grinned and bounced up off the sofa eagerly.

John's bedroom was fairly large, and he kept the vivarium tucked away in the furthest corner—mostly so if Lucy escaped, he'd probably find her before Nora did. Which was a must, because Nora would not think twice about killing a snake, pet or no pet.

"Just sit on the bed, and I'll pop her in your hands," John said, closing the bedroom door behind them.

"Is there a special way to hold her?"

"Cup your palms together and keep your hands low to your lap. She shouldn't fall off, but just in case she makes a dash for it."

A hesitant note crept into Chris's voice. "Does she bite?"

"Nah, she's pretty placid." John popped the lid up and reached in to warm his hand. "C'mon, girl."

"What's her name?"

"Lucy."

"Lucy?"

John flushed a little as twelve inches of solid, muscular body wound around his fingers, a tongue tickling his skin hopefully. "Um. Well. Yes."

"Why?"

"After Nora's ex-mother-in-law."

Chris snorted with laughter.

"Okay," John said, fetching her out. "Here you go."

He unceremoniously plonked Lucy straight into the bowl formed by Chris's fingers. Chris jumped, then laughed breathlessly. Lucy slithered between his right thumb and the side of his hand and hissed grumpily at John before beginning to explore the new perch.

"Bloody hell." Chris gingerly ran his index finger over her. Lucy was only a baby, maybe a foot long, and she wound around hand like a trap, tongue flickering over his skin in sharp bursts, a spiral of pale orange and white on lightly freckled skin. She curled her tail around his index finger, squeezed momentarily, then set off towards his elbow. Chris smiled widely, so brilliantly that John's heart hiccuped wetly in his chest for a second, and said, "She feels like warm leather."

"Yeah, people expect her to be slimy," John said.

"What's she doing? Something tickles."

"Her tongue. She smells with her tongue," John said. "She's kind of licking you."

Chris extended his arm, still grinning, as Lucy powered up the inside of his forearm. "Where you going?" he murmured, trying to pull her off, but she simply switched hands, latching onto his left instead of his right, and started up the other arm instead.

"She's seeking out your body heat," John explained, shifting to catch her. She hissed again and then suddenly shot away up Chris's sleeve. "Bugger."

"Shit!" Chris yelped, his arm twitching madly for a moment, then he laughed. "Oh shit. Oh my God, that feels weird. *Jesus.*"

"It's all right, she won't bite," John said. "Um, sorry about this, I swear I'm not trying to touch." He unceremoniously pulled the front of Chris's T-shirt forward and slid his hand up that hot chest, looking for Lucy.

"Oh, so *that* was your plan," Chris said, and John laughed, feeling oddly embarrassed. Trust his luck. Trust *Lucy*. John swore she was in cahoots with Nora sometimes, or maybe Fran. "Oh my God, she *really* tickles. Left shoulder. *My* left."

"Come out of there," John muttered, seizing her around the middle and whipping her out of Chris's shirt before she decided to hang on. With her fangs. "Sorry. Um, I'll just...I'll put her back; she's obviously a bit lively. Sorry."

"Don't be," Chris said and laughed. He still sounded surprised, his voice a fraction higher than usual, but he was also still smiling, and when John locked the vivarium lid down and returned to the bed, Chris reached out with both hands.

"What?" John asked, catching them—and was promptly pulled back down onto the mattress. Chris seized his wrist and returned John's right hand to his waist.

Under the T-shirt.

John rubbed it around to the small of Chris's back. His skin was very warm, as though he was flushed. John toyed with Chris's belt for a minute before brushing back around to touch the slightest edge of hip, barely visible above his jeans.

"This okay?" John murmured, and Chris answered by kissing him—the cheek, the edge of the mouth, and then properly, cupping his face in those long hands.

"Get rid of this." Chris pulled at John's T-shirt, and when John sat back to obey, Chris's palms slid up his abdomen and stomach, fingers splayed and searching. "Let me see," Chris insisted and sat up, hands creeping around the back of John's neck. John cupped a hand around the back of Chris's head and kissed him, bracing them both against the headboard with his other arm while Chris mapped him out, rubbing those searching fingertips over John's stubbled jaw and powerful neck, finding the top of the tattoo and tracing the whirling lines down to his wrist, squeezing briefly at his bicep before walking those long fingers back up and sliding them down his chest, grazing a nipple with the edge of a nail and pausing to repeat the action when John hissed and shifted his hips over Chris's lap. Chris's hands were maddeningly hot, the touch infuriatingly light, and the way he kissed—alternating a deep, breath-stealing *hunger* with fleeting pinches and catches at the edges of John's lips. Slowly, John pushed them back into the mattress. Chris's hands traced his sides and back as John buried a hand in that soft, dark hair and kneaded in a slow scalp massage. He ran the other down that flat belly, raking his nails lightly against the skin until Chris wriggled and broke the latest kiss to murmur something encouraging, and then caught his fingers in the belt buckle with a soft *clink*.

"Oh, I *see*," Chris murmured softly.

He smiled, and John undid the belt.

The sex was slow, sweet, and almost silent, but for the breathy whimper when Chris came, and the second when John buried his teeth into that perfect neck and followed. It was quietly euphoric, devastatingly peaceful, and John felt the entire world moving with them, a gentle tide ebbing and flowing that would never cease. When they were done, Chris simply kissed him, chaste and soft, and it was better than any desperate tongue-tangle John had ever had.

"Leave it," he murmured when John tried to go get a towel to clean up, and tightened his fingers around John's wrist. "J'st leave it."

Then silence, wrapped around the blissful heat in the bed, almost dragged John under.

So he wasn't best pleased when Chris pinched his wrist and said, "Hey. So. Nora."

John grunted.

"She doesn't like me, does she?"

"Sleep."

"Does she?"

John sighed and kissed a bare shoulder in the dark. "She doesn't not."

"That's a glowing review…"

"She's worried that you won't help with my anxiety issues."

"Why?"

The words stuck in John's throat.

"Because I'm…?"

John swallowed. "Because of your sight."

"Uh-huh."

"I didn't tell her about the other stuff."

"I wouldn't," Chris said, stroking John's wrist where it lay on his stomach. John tightened his grip in a hug, and Chris squirmed.

"She—she's wrong."

"Well."

"She *is*."

Chris made a hushing noise and tapped John's wrist sharply.

"I heard what she said."

"Fu—fudge."

"Fuck. Dear Lord," Chris muttered. "Look. She's wrong about me not being able to say no. You know that, don't you?"

John stroked a thumb over soft hair and softer skin and nodded.

"John."

"I do," he croaked. "'Cause you did."

"What?"

"When—when I touched your...um. Chest."

"Oh, yes, my lady-lumps."

John chuckled hoarsely.

"See? So you and I both know I can say whatever the hell I want. And that you'll listen to me."

John swallowed.

"You did listen."

"I know," he mumbled. "That's what makes this all so bloody stupid. I'm so fu—damn scared of it happening again, even though I know it's not true. I'm scared of *doing* it, even though I know I wouldn't."

"You trust me to tell you if I don't like something?"

"Yeah."

"Honestly?"

John searched the answer. "Yes." He did. He flat out did. Chris was so bright and bloody-minded. He'd reacted so fast to the wrong touch, and—okay, John still felt guilty he'd done it, still figured he ought to have known better, but...

But Chris hadn't put up with it when he had either.

"Then keep trusting me," Chris said, "and go and see this counsellor to help unpick the mess Daniel's left behind, and screw other people."

"What!"

"Not literally."

"I should hope not!"

Chris chuckled, then wriggled over to cuddle into John's chest. John's heart squeezed tight. Secretly, he might love that position even more than the spoons.

"It's your brain being daft," Chris murmured. "We all have those little wounds left over from old battles. Things that don't make sense."

"Do you?" John murmured.

"Sure."

"Like what?"

"Like this." Chris's arm tightened around John's chest. "Like how I know you're crazy about me, and yet I still catch myself wondering what you're up to when you're chatting me up."

"What?"

"I've spent my whole life hearing nobody is ever going to want me," Chris said. "If it's not that nobody wants someone who can't see what they're doing and has seizures several times a week and pisses themselves in public, it's that even if they miraculously were to put up with that, why the heck would they want a mangina anyway?"

John blinked into the dark.

"A—what?"

The sombre bubble burst, and John snorted with laughter. Chris clutched at his chest with a startled sound, then began to laugh.

"*What* did you call it?"

"It is!"

"Never say that again."

"What about original plumbing?"

"Oh my God. No. I'm an electrician, not a plumber."

"Ooh, the plug socket, then."

"No!"

Chris cackled, a leg sliding over John's, and then a weight was straddling his lap in the dark. John's cock woke up from its nap, pleased by this turn of events.

"Insert Tab A into Slot B?"

"Please stop talking," John said, laughing helplessly.

"Aww, why?" A breath washed over John's ears. Hands were splayed on his heaving chest. "Don't you want a guy with the gash?"

John caught at his back and twisted them over. He caught that laughing mouth with his own, the kiss sloppy and askew. Limbs were everywhere, and the bed creaked alarmingly.

"I'll give you bloody gash..."

"Oof, no thank you."

If the sex before had been slow and sweet, this was nothing less than ridiculous, giggling like drunks and spoiling every kiss with more poor jokes, until voices gave way entirely, and Chris gasped and grinned against John's cheek, invisible in the dark but mesmerising all the same. It was over too soon, and John got his ear savagely bitten when they realised, too late, he'd forgotten a condom. They ruined the sheets and lost a pillow.

It was messy, clumsy, stupid.

It was perfect.

Chapter Twenty-Seven

JOHN PULLED UP outside Nadia Simmons' office, five minutes before the appointment was due, and wished he'd given himself ten. Fifteen. An hour.

The anxiety was huge inside his chest, squashing his lungs, and he wanted to leave. He tugged on his ear to try to calm himself, the little shot of pain distracting him from the airless interior of the van. His earlobe was still swollen from Chris's bite.

His dick twitched at the memory of Chris's demand for penance—John eating him out until every bit of evidence of the split condom had been licked away, and so what if it was a bullshit excuse for cunnilingus, John had done it anyway—and the tiny shot of arousal helped, too.

Not that he could think about cunnilingus all the way through this assessment, but whatever worked to get him in the door.

The office was literally that: the first floor of a small building near Hillsborough Stadium. The ground floor was an accountancy firm. The second and third floors belonged to a cleaning company. Either side of the building stood a scrap metal dealer, and a newsagent. John felt simultaneously very out of place, and very in his element.

The waiting room looked a little bit like a dentist's office, and the receptionist was pleasant but featureless. John was given a contact form to fill out, but there was no list of what brand of loony he was, and the only box out of the ordinary from any new-loyalty-card jazz was one asking for details of any medication. He figured the best sex of his life wasn't a medication and left it blank.

There was a clock ticking on the wall.

Chris had offered to come with him, but John said no. Said he'd be fine. Truth was, he didn't want to have another meltdown and end up crying on Chris's shoulder again. And, anyway, Chris had had three seizures last night, and John didn't want to be dragging him anywhere.

"John Halliday?"

He swallowed back against the fear rising up into his throat and stood.

Nadia Simmons was a tall, willowy woman with long fair hair and a thing for black clothes. She was pristinely stylish, wearing an odd mix: the skirt was plainly feminine, by its very existence, but it was topped by a man's shirt and suspenders, and a bow tie proudly displayed the rainbow flag. Her nails were polished, but cut short, and she wore no make-up. She was also, very clearly, trans.

"Hello, John." A hand shook his own, and he was waved to sit in a red chair by the window of the little consultation room. There were three chairs, a coffee table with glasses and a jug of water, and a bookshelf covered in psychology books and pictures of a pretty Indian-looking lady and two young children, both sporting the same long nose as Nadia.

John relaxed slightly. This wasn't some stuffy doctor's office.

"Now, John." She sat opposite him, clipboard on her lap, smile on her face. "This is a casual assessment to get a feel for what you're looking to get out of counselling and whether I'm best placed to help you, or if we're better signposting you to someone more qualified in your particular concerns. So how about we launch right in with an introduction, eh?"

John fidgeted. "Um. I...don't really know what...I mean...you know my name, so..."

"Shall I go first?"

"Please."

"All right. I'm Nadia, I use gender-neutral pronouns, I'm originally from London, and I live in Dronfield with my wife and our two little girls. Currently, I suspect one of my little ladies may in fact be our son, but we're not quite there yet."

John blinked at her totally matter-of-fact tone.

"Sorry, um...what's a gender-neutral pronoun?"

"They or their. So, are you transgender at all?"

"No."

"So if I were to tell my secretary you wanted another appointment, I would say 'he'll be back next Monday' rather than 'she' or 'they'?"

"Oh. Oh, yeah." Then the rest of her words caught up, and John flushed. "Oh, fu—fudge. I'm sorry. I'm so sorry; I've been saying she. About you, I mean. Christ. Um, sorry, I'll try and remember."

She—no, *they*—smiled. "It's quite all right. I'm not upset by she. So, tell me a little about you."

"Um. Well. I'm John. I—I'm from Sheffield, I live in Kelham Island with my sister. I've recently started seeing this guy. And—and I'm having issues." The words unstuck and poured out. "My—my ex-boyfriend was cheating on me and tried to get away with it when he got caught by saying I'd—that he'd been too afraid of me to say no when I made advances, and he—he got me arrested and everything before he gave it up, and now I'm terrified everyone's going to think I'm doing the same to Chris."

The words fell out in a rush and lay in a heap on the office floor.

And Nadia didn't so much as pause. They just said, "All right," and leaned forward a little in their chair.

"I'm not." John's throat felt swollen. "I'm not a—a—*abusive*. I'm *not*."

"John."

"He pushed the issue so long that it got all twisted up in my head, like he kept saying and saying it, and I *wasn't*, but then I started to wonder if maybe I *had*—"

"John. Look at me."

He looked.

There were dark spots dancing around the outside of their face.

Their calm, open, patient face.

"I believe you," they said.

And just like that, the balloon deflated.

Not all the way. It didn't burst. But the pressure eased. His spine creaked as he sagged into the confines of the too-small chair.

"I take it this is the reason you wanted to seek some counselling?"

"Yeah," he mumbled.

Nadia made a quick note. "What exactly were you accused of?"

The word stuck.

"I can't say it."

"Try. Just once."

John's lips and tongue rolled around the first letter. It tasted like vomit.

"Rape."

Silence.

And then Nadia ducked their head to peer at him. "Don't be afraid of the word, John."

"W-what?"

"The more afraid we are of words, the more power they have to hurt us," they said softly. Then they leaned back, pen poised once more. "How long ago did the relationship end?"

"Coming up to a year, now."

"How long have you been seeing your new partner?"

"E-early December." John scrubbed at his eyes with his sleeve. "Um. We met in a café. I knocked his coffee over, bought him another, we talked, and he asked me out."

"Are things going well?"

John found a shaky smile. "Yeah."

"Does he know about your former partner?"

"Yeah."

"And he knows you're here today?"

"Yeah."

"So, is the issue that you're worried what *he* thinks, or what *others* think?"

John took a deep breath.

"Mostly—mostly others. He's, um. Chris is disabled. And trans. And I'm...well." He gestured at himself. "The big ugly builder type. So, it's mostly...you know, people look at us funny in the street, and I get all panicky, thinking that they think I must be some kind of a-abuser. And I ran into his stepmum once, by accident, and had a massive panic attack. And I had to ring his dad to come over when Chris had a seizure, and had another one then."

"And Chris?"

"What?"

"You said it was mostly what others think."

John licked his lips. "I think...initially, yeah, I was terrified of what he'd think too. But lately I'm doing okay there, I think. I did something he didn't like, and he was really firm about it, so I've been doing okay since."

"Do you mind telling me what happened?"

John coloured a little. "Uh."

"I'll have heard it all before," came the wry response.

John coughed. "Well, um. We were...you know."

"Let's pretend that I don't."

"We were making love—well, we were about to. I was, um. Heavy petting, I suppose. And I...well, I didn't know I wasn't supposed to touch his chest. He likes it when I, um...I *can't* explain this."

"Am I to assume," Nadia asked, "that your partner has not had the full range of transitional surgery available?"

"Um, no. I mean, yes. I mean, he hasn't had those."

"So, I'm gathering that what he regards as off limits to you may not appear to be entirely consistent from the cisgender viewpoint?"

"What?"

They chuckled. John flushed.

"Very often, trans people will still tolerate or even like—especially sexually—some of the features of their assigned sex. Would an example help?"

"Um. Yes, please."

"A trans woman may still like penetrating her partner with her penis. Even though most women don't have one, and it's a feature of a trans woman's assigned sex."

"*Oh*," John said, finally grasping it. "Yes. Like that. Um. Is that...common?"

"Perfectly common," came the easy reply, and John found himself unconsciously relaxing.

"Okay. So—yeah. I thought because I could touch other stuff and he really liked it that I could touch his chest too. And turns out I can't. And he proper just...shoved my hand away and got off the bed and said no. And ever since, I've been okay with that part, you know? Like...he told me no, and I stopped at once, and I haven't tried since. So I can't be what Da—my ex said, and Chris can't believe I am, right?"

"So your main challenge is internalising that knowledge and trusting it when other people aren't so convinced?"

That was a lot of long words. "I guess so?"

"Did you have these concerns before your former partner?"

"No."

"Did you have partners before him?"

"Yeah."

"All right, pick one for me. Any one."

"Um. Aljaz."

"You're exceptionally tall, I trust Aljaz wasn't your height?"

"God, no."

"So you're having dinner with Aljaz, and someone is looking at you funny. What would your emotional response have been then?"

"Mostly amused," John said. "I used to think it was funny. People would give us dirty looks—you know, dirty queers and stuff—but I'm so massive I think maybe one guy has ever had the balls to say anything. Ever."

"Whereas now, the same looks are making you upset?"

"Yeah."

Nadia nodded, making a few notes. "Is that always the case?"

"How d'you mean?"

"Does anyone giving you that look cause it, or only certain people? Or is there no effect if you're feeling confident and you're having fun, or Chris is visibly happy?"

"I...I don't know."

"That's okay," Nadia said. "What's the impact on your relationship?"

"I freak out at the idea of meeting his family. I had to force myself to go to dinner with his friends, and I only did that after he said he was getting dirty little secret vibes off me."

"So Chris isn't happy with the situation either?"

"No. I mean, he's patient," John said quickly. "He's been really good when I freak out, and he—he kind of understands, because he obviously has issues, too, but he's...you know, he's made it clear this is going to be a problem, long-term."

"Hence you're here."

"Hence I'm here."

They made a few more notes. "Are you out?"

"Um. Sort of."

"Sort of?"

"To my family. Not to friends."

"Any reason?"

John shrugged. "I work in the building trade. It's not exactly gay-friendly."

"So if you're having relationship problems, who do you tell?"

"Um. Well. Nobody re—"

Ah.

"Nobody."

Nadia waited.

"I just sort of...deal with it myself," John said eventually.

Only, he didn't. He bottled it up. He'd only told the family about Daniel's accusation because he'd been arrested for rape from his flat, right in front of his sister. He'd never told Rhodri what had happened, only that 'Danielle' had been a bitch and he was better off without her. The lads at rugby had never even known 'Danielle' existed, never mind Daniel.

"I don't talk about it."

A final note. Then Nadia set the clipboard aside. Leaned back in their chair. Uncrossed their legs. And said, "There's nothing wrong with you, John."

John held his breath.

"You have had a very nasty experience, which you haven't fully talked out with anyone, and so you haven't moved past it. And that's what's causing these issues."

"So—so what do I do?"

"I would recommend a short course of counselling to begin that moving-on process," Nadia said. "I think you're a very resilient man, mentally speaking. That you're able to function within a romantic and sexual relationship after your experience is testament to that."

"So I can get better?"

"Better, yes. Over it completely, no. We don't ever forget these kinds of wounds, and so we never truly get over them. But certainly, I think you can get to a point where you can find people giving you and your boyfriend dirty looks in public funny again. I think you can get to a point where going to dinner with the in-laws is no more terrible a prospect than it is for the rest of us. And I think you want to be at that point, which is half the battle with our minds."

John nodded, fisting his hands together in his lap.

"I want to not be scared," he said, "that someone's going to persuade Chris that Daniel was right. I *know* Daniel was wrong. I want to *feel* it too."

Nadia nodded.

"I think I can probably help with that."

Chapter Twenty-Eight

HE WAS FIXABLE.

Okay, Nadia had said he'd never truly get over it, but John didn't need that. He needed not to have panic attacks because women in green boots came to say hi. He needed to find people giving them weird looks funny again.

And they said he was fixable, for that. That there was nothing really wrong with him.

He could get better.

The assessment itself was buoying, and John found himself halfway home before turning the car around and heading to Parson Cross instead. The pink-titted Peugeot was still there. An enormous bloke was bending over the bonnet of the Suzuki, and the skinny lad with dark dreadlocks handing him tools beamed toothily at John.

"All right," John said, nodding in greeting, then veered off towards the communal doors. A little old lady shuffling out of the block held the door for him, and he jogged up the stairs. It only occurred to him when he reached Chris's landing that he didn't even know if Chris was home.

Luck was on his side though.

Sort of.

Knocking on the door produced footsteps and the rattle of the security chain, but it was Gina who answered.

"Oh," John said. "Sorry, I—"

"Don't be daft, come in," she said, smiling. "He's in the bathroom. Chris! John's come over!"

A muffled shout came from the tiny bathroom, and John smirked as he closed the door behind him and toed off his shoes. Gina was fine. Gina even liked him.

"If you've got plans—" he started, and Gina scoffed.

"We've just had plans. Been round the park. We were arguing about lunch."

The door cracked open. "Because I have *no* intention of playing third wheel while Jemma gawps at you all afternoon. Just screw her and be done with it."

"I *did* screw her!"

"Oh, God, you made it worse..."

John rolled his eyes and crossed the room for a quick kiss and a cuddle, burying his nose in Chris's hair. It needed a trim soon, or Chris would have to start tying it back.

"Decision made." Chris tucked a hand around John's hip, the fingers curling against the back of his belt. "You go screw Jemma; I'll stay here and screw John."

"Teamwork!" Gina proclaimed dramatically but grinned. "Got it. Text me about Monday."

She bounced over for a hug, gave a bemused John a high five, and then was gone.

And Chris turned right into John's front, tucked both hands into the back pockets of John's jeans, and grinned up at him.

"So."

John coughed a laugh and ducked down to offer another kiss.

"Wanna shag, or wanna shag?"

"Um—"

"Or," Chris said, "want to get something to eat, then eat me out for dessert?"

"Wow."

"There's a song about sweet honey, after all..."

John groaned and silenced the awful jokes with a proper kiss, cupping Chris's face in both hands to keep him still.

It worked. Sort of. Chris stopped talking, but his hands had moved between them by the time John let go and were picking away at his belt buckle.

"Um, later."

The hands stopped.

"I want to try something."

"Ooh, what kind of something?"

John took a deep breath. "I went to see Nadia."

"The counsellor?"

"Yeah."

"Did it go okay?"

"They said—"

The predatory smirk smoothed away. "You don't have to tell me what they said."

"I have to tell you this bit."

"Um, okay..."

"They said there's nothing wrong with me."

"Oh, good, you're not seeing a complete hack..."

"And they said I can fix the things that Daniel left all crumpled up," John continued. "And—and I want to start today."

"Okay. Do we get brain glue at Screwfix, or is that the solution? A good screw fi—"

"You," John said, "are a bloody nightmare."

The grin was wide and wild and lit up Chris's face like lightning.

"But you love me for it."

John couldn't deny it.

"Okay, okay. Serious face. What's your idea?"

"I want to meet your mum and dad."

Chris hesitated. A cautious smile pulled into place. The hands returned to John's back pockets.

"You sure?"

"Yeah."

"Any particular way you want to do this?"

John shook his head. "I—just—whatever works."

Chris slid his arms up around John's waist and squeezed tightly, head tucking against John's breastbone for a long moment before he said, "Mum. As I said, she might not like you much, but my stepdad will."

"I can...I can cope with not liking," John said. "Just not..."

"Oh, she won't think you're dangerous," Chris said. "She just—well. She wants me to find some classy lawyer or something. Wants me to go up in the world. Guess she doesn't realise I'm a whole eight inches taller when I'm riding your co—"

"Chris!"

Chris laughed helplessly. John caught him around the waist, twirled them once, and set him down with a sharp kiss in reprimand.

"You're *awful*."

"And it's in the genes." Chris looped his arms around John's neck and nosed in for another kiss. "I had my injection yesterday."

"Your what?"

"My hormone shot."

"So?"

"*So*, I want you."

John frowned. "How are those rela—"

"Because for a week after every shot, I want to get off at *least* four times a day."

That wasn't fair.

"Oh," John said weakly.

"How about," Chris whispered, barely an inch from John's mouth, "you take me to bed and show me how much you love me? And then we go round Mum's for dinner, like we're totally respectable people."

"O-okay."

THEY DIDN'T LEAVE the flat until nearly six o'clock that evening.

John almost thought Chris had forgotten and was ready to back out of the whole idea in favour of calling for pizza and staying the night, with maybe a bit of a ban on clothes. But when he took a bathroom break from the film they were watching, he returned to Chris finishing a phone call and smiling up at him from the sofa.

"Come on, then. Mum's making steak."

John's gut clenched.

"John?"

"Sorry. Yeah. Uh. Okay."

"You changed your mind?"

"No."

"You sound like you have."

"The nerves are kicking in, that's all."

"Okay." Chris came up off the sofa, and John caught him by the hips. "I want you to do this. But if you can't, I'm okay with that too."

John smoothed both hands down Chris's arms and took a deep breath.

"I can do this," he said. "Right. Where am I driving?"

Chris rose up on tiptoes for a kiss, then pulled away and headed for the door. A jacket was shrugged on. Socked feet vanished into shoes. The cane was pulled down off the hook.

"I need directions," John complained as he followed suit, and Chris shrugged.

"I know the postcode. You have a satnav?"

"Yeah."

"Then we're good. She lives off Ecclesall Road."

"South or normal?"

"I don't know. Near the park."

"There's like three parks off that road..."

"Near the park where they have Pride."

John admitted having never been to a pride event in his life, Chris was horrified and insisted they do the entire circuit in the summer, and—for a little while—the nerves were eased by slightly unwilling laughter at all Chris's terrible jokes about having rainbow sex all over the country.

But they came back, with clammy palms and a tightening stomach, as the time on the satnav ticked down to less than five minutes away, and John was directed off the main stretch into the tight terraced houses off Sharrow Vale Road.

And there it was.

It was a mum sort of house. He recognised its style. The tiny rose bushes by the front gate. The welcome mat. The net curtains glowing yellow from a lamp left on in the front room.

Number fifteen.

John couldn't release his hands from around the steering wheel.

"Hey."

Chris's fingers were soft on the crook of his elbow.

"You okay?"

"Bit shaky," John ground out.

"Trust me," Chris said. "She'll just be mad you're not a doctor."

"Not a chance," John muttered.

"Me neither, I see enough of those without dating one. Hey. I know this is hardly the most romantic time—"

"You're hardly the most romantic type."

"—but I love you."

The nerves jangled, like slammed piano keys. John's chest caught. His tongue fumbled, his lips stuttered.

And then he swallowed and jerked one hand off the wheel to take Chris's fingers in his.

He knew.

He already knew that, yet the quiet words were so simple and so powerful that the fear couldn't hold on. John brought the captured hand up to kiss the knuckles, resting his lips there for a long minute.

Chris loved him.

So what if his mum didn't?

Chris loved him, and that was the only thing that counted.

"Let's do this."

Chris had a key. He fumbled with the set, pinching at them, before he found the right one and jammed it into the lock with excessive force. The door creaked when it opened into a narrow hall, warmly lit and with a fluffy cream carpet. A fluffy cream cat was lounging on the stairs. It hissed and shot away up them to the darkened first floor.

"Mum! Jack!"

"Kitchen, love!" a woman shouted back.

"What's with the cat?" John asked.

"Oh. I've fallen over him a bit too often."

"Ah."

"C'mon."

Chris took John's great paw and tugged him towards the living room. The house was tiny, and John felt more outsized than usual. He was as wide as the hall itself, and if he hadn't shaved his head that morning, his hair would have brushed the overhead lights.

The living room was cosy though. A mantelpiece with a flickering gas fire warmed the squashy sofa wedged against the wall, and a TV set occupied the bay window. A greying man in his fifties was sitting in an armchair, broadsheet up in a pose just like John's dad preferred, and it lowered to show a craggy but gentle face, brown eyes crinkling in a smile.

"Ah, there you are, boy."

Chris smirked. "Yeah, yeah, I know."

"You ought to visit more."

"Well, if I could *drive*..."

"They're called taxis. You know your mother and I would pay for them if you're struggling." The man heaved himself up out of the chair with a creak and hugged Chris like father and son, before extending a hand to John. "Jack Rosenberg."

His hand was weak and shaking in John's grip, but the gentle smile never wavered.

"John Halliday."

"So, you're the mysterious new lad," Jack mused, eyeing him up and down. John shifted uncomfortably. "Tea? Coffee? Something a bit stronger?"

"Oh, I'm driving. Tea would be nice though."

Jack shuffled round him and out of the room, feet barely leaving the floor. His hands shook violently.

"Can he carry tea?" John whispered in Chris's ear as they sat.

"Yeah," Chris said, stroking his knee. "He has Parkinson's. Early stages. The shaking stops when he holds things."

"Oh. So he's your...stepfather, right?"

"Yep. They only got married six months ago, but he's been around for ages."

"Do he and your mum have kids?"

"Nope."

John rubbed the hand on his knee, and Chris smiled.

"You doing okay?"

"Yeah. Yeah, I think so."

There were soft voices in the kitchen. John distinctly caught: "Fine, Ruth, seems a nice lad." He relaxed a little.

"So...tell me about them."

"Ask them yourself." Chris chuckled and ducked in to kiss John's cheek. "Stop worrying."

"What if she tells your dad I'm a thug?"

"She isn't going to be telling Dad anything. They don't speak."

"Oh." John winced. He hesitated, glancing around. The living room was oddly devoid of pictures. "Did you grow up here?"

"No, they moved in last year after I got the flat. Got that bloody cat too. Thing's a menace..."

A kettle whistled, and John raised his eyebrows.

"Was that a proper old metal kettle?"

"Oh, yeah. Mum's got an Aga in there."

"Seriously?"

"Yep. Extension. If you want to get on her good side, compliment her kitchen. She's very proud of it."

The sound of shuffling reached their ears, and Jack reappeared with a tray. True to Chris's word, it was perfectly steady—although the minute it was set down on the coffee table, Jack's hands started to shake again. John wordlessly took the mug of dark coffee, handing it off to Chris, before taking his tea and offering a quiet thank you.

"So what do you do, John?"

Conversation was easy and standard fare. They talked about John's job, about Jack's old job at a factory, about the rugby results. They bonded a little over a shared disinterest in football, and John found himself relaxing further and further into the sofa, toying lightly with the medical bracelet adorning the hand still resting on his knee, and thinking that this was fine. This was okay.

Then the shadow fell in the doorway.

The woman was instantly and very apparently Chris's mother. John recognised her from the picture with the new puppy. Her hair was a tight, neat crop of black curls. She had the same wide cheekbones, narrow chin, and soft mouth. There were crow lines around her eyes, very faint for the lack of a smile, just where Chris's eyes crinkled up in mirth as well. She was tall, slender, and long-limbed, and she even had the same narrow feet, albeit in neat house slippers rather than frayed socks.

But for a long moment, she simply stared.

John shifted uncomfortably and set the half-finished tea down. "Uh. John Halliday, ma'am." He rose to shake her hand.

Chris jumped. "Mum?"

"Ruth." Her voice was high and oddly soft. Her handshake was firm. "Tea's ready. John, was it?"

John nodded, already feeling uneasy. They almost filed into the kitchen—a large space at the back of the tiny house, dominated by the black Aga. The cream cat had spread out on the brown-tiled floor and hissed at Chris again before slinking away into a corner. The air was warm and brimming over with the smell of beef.

Chris sensed something, for his fingers found John's again as they took their seats.

And here it came: "I wasn't quite expecting you, John."

John swallowed as a plate was set in front of him. He barely glanced at the food. "Oh?"

"Yes."

"Uh. How so?"

She shrugged a little. "I suppose I just wasn't."

"Mum," Chris said, in a vaguely warning tone.

"How did you meet?"

John told the café story, blaming the first date entirely on Chris, and although Jack laughed at the reciting of how forward and stubborn Chris had been, Ruth's face didn't change. It was polite, but closed-off. She was working him out, and John felt a sweat breaking out across his back.

"I'd presumed you had mutual friends," she said. "Not that you were strangers."

"Even friends start out as strangers," Chris said philosophically.

"A little risky, though, love."

Chris's face tightened a fraction. "As is going to a café on my own in the first place."

"They know you there."

"Yes, because I keep going on my own."

"John." Jack's voice rose effortlessly over the building tension, as though nothing were happening. "You said you were an electrician."

"Yes..."

"You couldn't take a look at my stairlift, could you? Darned thing keeps cutting out."

And just like that, John was on familiar ground. This had happened with every meet-the-in-laws he'd had since he was an apprentice. Stairlifts, doorbells, changing lightbulbs, the works. And he liked it. All right, so it was a bit presumptuous, but people liked other people who were useful.

"Sure," he said. "What's it doing?"

They discussed the issue, which sounded as simple as a button with some loose wiring, and as Ruth changed out the plates for dessert bowls, John nipped out to the car for the toolkit he always kept in the boot. They talked rugby as he pried the guilty button off and pinned the wire back into its proper place, and prodded the faulty doorbell as Jack tested the repaired lift.

"I could have done it myself, once," he said, raising one of those trembling hands. "Bit past me now though."

"It's no problem," John said. "Just give me a ring if you need anything else. Family rates."

"Which are?"

"Free, except for one of my sisters, because she wrecks things out of sheer stupidity. I'm hoping to train her out of it by charging."

Jack chuckled as they closed the front door on the repaired bell. "Does it work?"

"Six years of trying, I'm going to say no."

"Listen, lad." The sudden sombre tone brought John up short. "Don't you worry about our Ruth. She's just a fusser. Protective sort. Chris is her only child, and after the accident, she's none too keen on releasing the apron strings."

John paused. "Accident?"

"Aye."

"Oh. Accident." He feigned knowledge. "No, it's...fine. Understandable. Just makes me a bit nervous."

Jack chuckled. "Big lad like you?"

"Yeah, well. Takes all sorts."

"Does indeed. I know our Chris. He's got a good ear for people. Just let our Ruth stew on it a bit, and she'll come around."

John mentally crossed his fingers. "Hope so. 'Cause I'm not going anywhere."

Jack smiled and shuffled back into the kitchen to claim his dessert and complain about the stairlift company and their false guarantees.

John hovered in the hall a moment longer, clutching the assurance to his chest.

He wasn't going anywhere. And Ruth would come around.

A deep breath, and the anxiety balloon burst.

She'd come around.

Chapter Twenty-Nine

JOHN STARTED THE car and then hesitated.

"What's up?"

"Wondering where to go."

"Well, my place is empty…"

John took a deep breath. "Um. Maybe a drink?"

"Is…everything okay?"

"Yeah. Just…need to unwind a little bit."

Chris touched his arm. "Hey. How about my place, and we walk round to Al's and get some chips?"

"Al's?"

"It's the chippie round the corner. *Amazing* chips and curry sauce."

"Yeah, okay."

They drove in silence, Chris's hand resting gently on John's thigh, and John turned the evening over and over in his head. The anxiety balloon was back, but small. Jack liked him. Ruth…didn't, but Jack had said she was overprotective. But how overprotective was overprotective? Was it him, or would she have been the same with any new boyfriend? Would she tell Chris's dad? Chris had said no, but…

"You're thinking too loudly," Chris said softly as the car joined the main road.

"Sorry."

"Share?"

John flexed his fingers on the wheel. "Just…trying to figure out how I feel."

"Okay..."

"I mean, it went better than I thought. I think Jack likes me."

"He does. He's never that chatty."

"Your mum doesn't though."

"She doesn't like anyone, first time round."

John licked his lips. "Um. Jack said she's overprotective."

"Mm, yeah, a little bit."

"Because of the accident."

Chris went quiet.

"What accident?" John asked.

Chris groaned. "Right."

"You don't have to tell me if—"

"It's not...I don't remember it. It's no skin off my nose to tell you. But it sorted of...wrecked the family a bit, so we *don't* talk about it."

"How do you mea—"

"My parents divorced after I went blind."

"What?"

Chris pulled a face. "Yeah, everyone does that."

"How could—how—"

"I was six," Chris said, "and I was too young to really understand why I shouldn't do some things. You know, you're a little kid, you don't understand consequences properly. The idea that epilepsy could kill people was unfathomable to me. I used to kick off every time any of my friends at school had a birthday party at a swimming pool and I wasn't allowed to go. I didn't understand drowning. I figured if I had a seizure in the pool, Dad would fish me out, and I'd have to sit on the side in my towel for a bit."

John didn't know whether to laugh or grimace at the mental picture.

"I wasn't really very good at auras either. I think it's because I'm not conscious when I have a seizure, so it doesn't hurt until afterwards, when I've sprained something. So, I'd be feeling unwell, but I wouldn't say anything. I didn't figure it would be a bad thing. So..."

"So you'd just...start having one, and nobody would know it was coming?"

"Yeah."

"Oh." John had a faint idea he knew where this was going.

"So that day, Aunt Kelly had picked me up from school. Dad's sister. She used to come and pick me up, and we'd walk home via the park and through the estate to the house. There was this wall I used to like to run along, maybe five feet off the ground."

Oh, God.

"That day, I'd not been feeling well at school, but I ignored it. And Aunt Kelly came to collect me, and we walked home. And I was standing on the wall waiting for Aunt Kelly to catch up and watch me jump down—I was proud I could jump that far—and the seizure hit."

John clenched his hands around the wheel until his knuckles went white.

"I bashed my head open on the brick wall and then again on the paving slabs when I fell off."

"Jesus."

"I had brain damage. The epilepsy was worse, after. I had to relearn how to speak, and I talked funny well into my teens. I was in a wheelchair for three years because I had to relearn how to use my arms and legs properly, like a baby. Years of physio to get control back. It's why I still walk so slowly, even with the cane and when I had Sam. My brain still can't handle holding things and walking quickly at the same time; my hands just open like they're paralysed. I should have died. It should have killed me."

John's throat closed up, and he wordlessly reached down and held the hand in his lap tightly.

"You okay?"

"Yeah. Sorry. Go—go on."

"Mum blamed Aunt Kelly. Dad didn't. They fought over it like mad—Mum didn't want Aunt Kelly anywhere near me ever again, but Dad said it was a silly accident, and they'd both let me run along the same wall before. And in the end, Mum couldn't forgive her, and Dad couldn't tolerate her blame."

"So they divorced?"

"Yeah."

"Christ. With you in the middle?"

"Oh, no, that part they were very careful with. They don't talk now, but all the time I was growing up, you'd never have guessed they weren't still married."

"What—what about your aunt?"

Chris went very quiet.

"Chris?"

"We don't talk about Aunt Kelly," he said eventually, and John's heart nearly stopped beating. He knew that tone of voice. They used it at home, about his uncle. Dad's brother. Nan and Granddad's younger son. Who'd lost a lot of money at the greyhound tracks one day and shot himself the next.

"Oh," John breathed.

The hand in his rubbed at his knuckles. "Hey. It was a long time ago. So, yeah, she can be a little touchy about new people. But she's not that bad. She'll warm up to you just fine."

"You...you sure?"

"Positive."

John took a shaky breath and exhaled. "Okay. Um. So. Chips? Want me to drive on, or park up and walk?"

"Park up and walk," Chris said. "I want a hand in my back pocket."

The sudden levity was startling.

"You what?"

"I want a hand in my back pocket. I want us to share chips on the way back. And then I want you to take me into my flat, strip us both naked, and cuddle up in bed together. And in the morning, you can shag me."

"Make—"

"No. Shag me."

A tiny smile playing about the corner of his mouth as John pulled into the little parking area and found his now-usual spot beside the fluffy nipples.

"Sleep with—"

"Shag me."

CHRIS WAS AFFECTIONATE, and John felt oddly clingy after the story in the car, so he found himself not going home. He went to work from Chris's flat in the morning and returned in the evening armed with takeaway coffees and kisses.

And he did again the next day.

And the next.

The weekend was the most obvious change. John woke up on Saturday morning without his rugby or gym kit, and having no idea of a running route around the flat. He lay there pondering his options for a good few minutes before rolling over, kissing the back of Chris's neck, and whispering, "Hey. Want to come to rugby practice?"

It took a bit of cajoling and the promise of company before Chris would agree. He rang Luke, and John was shooed out of the door with a vague, "We might stop by, we might not."

Might won—John looked up halfway through practice to see two figures in the stands, clutching cups of coffee, one blond and one dark.

"That your girlfriend?" one of the lads asked.

"Nah," John said.

But—why not explain?

Watching Chris and Luke watch *him*, heads bent together and Luke probably translating the random shouting and colourful language into what was actually happening, John suddenly wondered what the hell he'd been afraid of. This was *rugby*. It wasn't work. It wasn't like he'd lose his job or get kicked out of his flat if the lads knew. Maybe they'd be fine with it, and nothing would change. Maybe they'd be shits, and John could quit and get back to swimming again in the freed up time. He liked swimming but hadn't done it regularly for years.

So, after practice, he waved off the offer of a post-practice pint and jogged up the stands.

"Hey, beautiful!"

Chris beamed. John caught it with his mouth.

"I'm going to be sick," Luke proclaimed loudly.

"Then fuck off," Chris said, and John laughed.

"Enjoy it?"

"Enjoyed Luke's commentary."

Luke grinned. "I made up names for everyone."

"What's mine?" John asked.

"You don't want to know," Chris said and rapped the cane on the ground. "We going?"

"I need to shower and change quickly."

"Yes, you do."

"Charming."

"I love you, John, but right now, you're humming a bit."

John scoffed but peeled away after another quick kiss. Shower, change, then maybe whisk Chris off for lunch somewhere.

"Ey-up, Shrek, thought you said that *wasn't* your girlfriend?" came the shout as he ducked into the changing rooms.

To hell with it.

"Try the other one."

"Eh?"

"The lad with the curly hair," John said, stripping off his kit. "He's my boyfriend."

He ducked into the showers to a short, sharp silence.

Then Slag barked a laugh and shouted, "Fuck me, we got it wrong, lads! Shrek's swinging for the other side!"

"You what? We're not playing 'til next month."

"Fuck off, Baby Spice. *Blokes*, you tit. He's into blokes."

John tipped his head back under the spray, heart hammering. Slag was all right. Slag was on his side. So the other lads—

"A fairy in our midst. Oi, Tinkerbell, no cheeky groping, a'ight?"

—followed.

John grinned. "I'm gay, not sick, Baby Spice!"

And that was it. He was renamed Tinkerbell. A towel got whipped his way when he stepped out. And then Andy 'Twilight' Cullen let rip a stinker of a fart, and everyone ignored the development in favour of throwing water bottles at Twilight until he took his offensive smell somewhere else.

So John was grinning when he left the changing room, sports bag over his shoulder and a spring in his step. Chris and Luke were waiting on the wall by the car park, and John ducked in for another kiss, flipping off a couple of the lads for wolf-whistling.

"What's that all about?" Chris asked, smiling.

"Nothing. Them being twats."

Only it wasn't. He'd come out, really, and it felt right. Just *right*. Like everything was sliding into place.

Life felt like that in general, that week. And the following, when John more or less continued to live at Chris's flat, only popping back to his own for clothes. It felt—domestic.

It was certainly headed that way. Chris refused to let John disturb his space or routine, so John got used to spending the evening in front of the TV, watching Chris cook or do his laundry, and waiting until he could be snagged and cuddled for a bit in front of the evening news. Sometimes, he was even sent out on a shop run, or told to fix something like he lived there.

Like he belonged there.

His toothbrush moved into Chris's bathroom cabinet. A drawer was suddenly his. He was allowed control of the remote if Chris was in the bathroom or making dinner.

Other things started to look long-term, too. His negative test results from the STI clinic came back, with a Braille version as John had asked for, and he was permitted to use rubbers a bit more sparingly. Chris started to sleep without a bra on. John was allowed to take him to the doctor's surgery for his hormone injection.

They were a thing.

And Chris had said I love you.

Just once, but he had. Not passion. Love. John knew it to be true, now. In the way cold feet ended up in his lap on the sofa, and how Chris made pizza the way John liked it best.

Knew it in the way he murmured and soothed, gentle and patient, when Lauren left a message on Chris's phone threatening to invade the flat if he didn't bring his new boyfriend round soon, and John had a panic attack out of nowhere.

Knew it in that he said, "It's okay," and deleted the message without a word. And, for the following week, answered the doorbell instead of releasing the buzzer without checking.

The first session with Nadia came at the end of February. They talked mostly about the visit, and how John had changed how he viewed boyfriends' families from before—when they hadn't mattered, who cared if they liked him—to this fear of not measuring up.

"You're still afraid they could persuade him you're bad news," Nadia surmised, and John resolved to work on it. To absorb the easy way Chris had moulded John into his flat and life, and the way he smiled when John touched him, even something so innocent as a hand in the small of his back. The way he'd said I love you, because it was what John had needed to hear. And the way John didn't quite need it, right now. Then the first of March arrived, and John went to work with a knot in his gut the size of a football.

One year.

One year since he'd heard the words, "I am arresting you on suspicion of rape."

One year since Daniel had brought the world crashing down.

John didn't know what to do that morning. It had snuck up on him so much. It was only on the way to the house that he and Rhodri were doing up that it hit him, and he had to pull over into a layby and pause for a moment.

What the hell was he supposed to do?

It was an anniversary of sorts.

John had never had a bad anniversary before. His heart felt achey. His chest felt tight. The anxiety balloon was absent, but he felt oddly fragile, like his ribs could break at any minute. But why the hell would he feel bad? Daniel had completely screwed him over, and now he was getting help from Nadia, and he had Chris.

He tightened his fingers on the wheel and pulled back out into the traffic.

No.

He wasn't going to let Daniel run things anymore. He was done with that tosser. It had all been lies, every last bit of it, and he was going to go to work, have a good time with Rhodri, then go back to Chris's flat and take him out for dinner. Proper fancy dinner, with dress shirts and everything.

Rhodri was waiting outside, smoking, when John pulled up. He grunted a greeting, and the day began by hefting wood up into the back bedroom to fix the hole in the floor. They worked in relative ease and quiet, exchanging insults occasionally and scathing commentary on last night's match, and the sick feeling began to ease.

And then, out of nowhere, Rhodri said, "So how's yer Chrissie?"

John blinked. "Eh?"

"Yer lass."

John opened his mouth.

"Take it yer still dating? Been bloody hard to get you out fer drinks after work, any'ow."

"Yeah. Yeah, we're still a thing."

"So? She all right?"

She.

It wasn't Daniel, standing in his way.

"He."

"What?"

"He."

Rhodri glanced up from the joists. "Who?"

"Chris."

"What, Chrissie?"

"Yeah. Chris. He."

Rhodri's face screwed up. "You what?"

"I don't have a lass, Rhod," John said carefully. "Chris is a bloke."

There was a long, pregnant pause.

Then: "Yer shagging a bloke?"

"Yeah."

Another pause.

"As in, gay, like?"

"Er. Yeah."

"As in—"

"As in, I've never slept with a woman in my life."

"You bloody 'ave."

"I haven't."

"Yes, you 'ave. Leanne. And Jess. And—"

"Lee. And Jason."

"What?"

John felt himself going red. "They've all been men, mate."

The next silence was even longer. John itched to move. He wanted madly to backtrack and laugh it off as a joke, yet he also wanted to shake Rhodri and tell him if he had a problem working with a faggot, better say it so John could deck him and then they could part ways properly.

"Yer mean to tell me," Rhodri said, "tha' when we was training with old Whittaker, and you used to drive his snot-nosed little shit of a lad up th' wall by bragging you did more birds in a week than he'd managed in his life, you were shagging blokes instead o' birds?"

"Yeah," John said.

Rhodri...laughed. Rolled up onto his heels and started to laugh. A deep belly laugh, shaking the fag end loose from between his teeth and rumbling the belly rolls that swelled over the belt of his trousers.

The tight feeling in John's chest eased.

"Fark me, classic!" Rhodri chortled. "Farking classic!"

John smiled thinly and returned to hammering the planks down.

"So," Rhodri said when he'd recovered. "'Ow's yer Chris, then? Yer bloke?"

The smile widened.

"He's fine," John said. "We're just fine."

Chapter Thirty

"WAIT," CHRIS SAID, "so you've been friends for like a decade, and he didn't know?"

John rolled his eyes.

"Yes," he said. "And trust me, it's not unusual for me. Nobody's ever guessed."

"Your mum did, you said so."

"Okay, yeah, but only her."

"And I took the chance."

"Yeah, but you didn't know."

"I suspected, though."

"But you didn't know. And Rhodri's not exactly your bleeding-heart-liberal type. He wouldn't guess a *Dancing on Ice* judge was gay."

Chris laughed.

"I don't know…"

"You don't see me," John said.

"I see you fine."

"Okay, then you don't see what other people see. You never had that first 'oh shit' impression."

"I did. It was when you splashed scalding coffee on me."

"Please," John said loftily. "You drink it like that, no way that burned you."

Chris laughed, but then his face softened.

"Still," he said. "I'm kind of proud right now."

"Yeah?"

"Yeah. Reward time. What do you want?"

They were in a quiet corner of the café. Chris had been out in town all day, and John had gone to join him for a drink after work. A pint each in a nearby pub and several cups of tea later in the café, and John was still a bit loathe to move.

"I don't know," he said, stroking his fingers over Chris's. "This is kind of nice on its own."

"You did a big thing today. You've earned something special."

"You're something special."

"Oh, that was *bad*."

"Like you can talk, some of the lines you come out with!"

"Those are about sex," Chris defended himself. "That was just pure cheese. Smelly, awful, stinking cheese."

"It was wonderful, and you're blushing. That's proof."

"That's humiliation I'm seen in public with you."

John laughed and squeezed the hand he'd caught on the table.

"If you really want to reward me," he said quietly, "then...well, it's your birthday next week."

"Yeah, so?"

"So, I was hoping maybe you'd let me take you back to the coast?"

Chris's smile was very soft. He propped a hand on his chin.

"That sounds like a reward for me, not you."

"Trust me, New Year's at the coast with you was definitely a reward for me."

"Hmm..."

"Please? It'd make my month."

"Only your month?"

"You already made my year."

"I did? When?"

"When you kissed me on the harbourfront at midnight."

"Oh my God." Chris threw a napkin at him. He missed spectacularly, as usual. "You're really full of it this evening, aren't you?"

"Well, yeah. I realised I'm standing in my own way," John said.

Chris paused.

"Daniel's gone. It's just me that's carrying this around. And I'm done. I love you, more than anything, and this is— I know it's still kind of early, but I love you, I really do, and I think this could really be something, you and me."

"If you dare say—"

"You might be the one."

"Oh, *Gawd*, no. *Noooo*," Chris whined, and John started to laugh helplessly. "My *God*, no, that's nearly as bad as 'lovemaking.' Go away. I take it back. No reward for you."

"You love me."

"I tolerate you."

"You *love* me."

"I *barely* tolerate you!"

John grinned, pushing his chair back. He stood, and his enormous size was enough to lean over the table like it wasn't there and kiss the protesting man on the other side. Who quieted, smiled into it, and curled both hands around John's on the table.

"Fine," he murmured when John pulled back. "Let's walk back to yours..."

"Walk?"

"Yep."

"Okay. And then what?"

"Then maybe—*maybe*—I'll let you do a bit of that lovemaking you're so keen on."

John grinned. "Yeah?"

"Yeah."

John beamed all the way out into the street and decided to throw sense to the wind. He took Chris's hand, rather than his arm, and showed off their entwined fingers. He was six foot eight, for Christ's sake. Let anyone say anything.

They walked slowly, Chris oddly tired that evening, and the crowds were thicker than usual. A tram rumbled along the very end of the high street. A police car nestled in the midst of the shoppers, watching and waiting.

And then Chris stopped dead.

"Oh."

"What's up? Forgotten your wallet?"

"No. I—oh."

John frowned.

"Chris?"

"I need to lie down."

"Oh, *hell*."

"I don't feel right."

"Okay. Okay, here, there's a bench just—"

"No. Now. Here."

Chris went to his knees clumsily but under control. John hastily shucked his coat off. The ground was damp, and it was cold. He rescued his phone and started thumbing through it for taxi firms.

"Okay," he said, trying to keep his voice—and heart rate—under control. "It's fine. You go ahead. I'll ring for a cab."

Chris was already gone. The vacant stare was somehow blanker than usual. The hand John groped for had gone limp.

And then the long body sitting on the pavement went stiff and fell the rest of the way.

John's jacket caught head and shoulders and dulled the impact. There was a nasty sound from the left wrist, though, and then the shaking started. People started to stare. A woman had her phone out, and John suppressed a surge of anger, deliberately shifting around to get in her way.

"It's okay," he murmured, half to Chris and half to himself. "It's fine. It's okay."

He could feel the balloon expanding.

"Sir?"

The deep voice was familiar, even though the speaker was a stranger. It was the way he said it. John knew who he'd be looking at long before he raised his head. Black boots. Black trousers. Kit belt.

Copper.

The balloon exploded. *Police.* His palms were slick. His heart was in his mouth.

"Is everything all right, sir?"

The copper squatted down. He had blue eyes.

Like Chris.

John's mouth unglued. "Yeah. Uh. Yeah. He's—"

"Are you with him?"

"Yes. He's my partner."

The copper nodded. "Do you need an ambulance, sir?"

Chris's vehement insistence jarred the terror.

"No. No. He's epileptic. This is—" Normal? Standard? "This happens a lot."

The copper frowned. The balloon turned into cement, hard and unyielding under John's ribs. His heart was beating like a rabbit's.

"He has a bracelet," John said, pointing to the trembling wrist. A glint of gold showed below the sleeve. "I'm timing him, see." Pointing at his own watch. "I know what I'm doing. I do."

"I'd feel better if you'd let me call an ambulance, pal."

"He doesn't need an ambulance."

The copper was still frowning. His mate had gotten out of that car, too, and was coming over. Coppers. Two coppers. John couldn't get enough damn air.

"He'll be fine," John insisted and licked his lips. "Look, can you just—stop people filming him and stuff? I know—I know what to do. It'll be over in a minute."

Less than. The shaking was beginning to ease.

The copper's mate did just that, turning and beginning to shoo people away. John forced himself to blot the other out and focus on Chris as the shivering slowly leaked away, and he sagged against the jacket, limp and lifel—

No, just limp.

John carefully felt along neck and back before turning him, easing him into the recovery position with gentle hands. The copper turned and barked something to his mate, who jogged back to their car.

"Chris?" John smoothed back the messy curls. "You with me yet, babe?"

The endearment slipped free. Chris twitched and mumbled something incomprehensible. The copper's mate came back, unfolding a foil blanket.

"Here."

John managed a wobbly smile as the coppers tucked it around Chris carefully. He could do this. They were fine. He was fine. Still, he kept his eyes firmly on Chris, stroking his fingers slightly too hard through his curly hair, so the motion dragged a little and made him stir.

"S'just me," he murmured when the mumble turned into a distinct snarl. "S'just me. You ready to go home?"

"F'k off."

John winced and glanced at the coppers. "Chris? You wanna wake up a bit for me?"

Hands curled into fists on the floor. Chris scowled but didn't really stir.

"Chris..."

Chris lashed out. The bracelet flashed. John caught the hand easily and put it back under the blanket.

"Look, pal, I'm going to call a paramedic at the very least..."

John tuned the police out. He already felt like passing out. He didn't even hate cops, not even after the investigation. They'd only been doing their jobs, but he couldn't help but remember. Couldn't help but think all it would take would be one check on their little radio things, and they'd find out he'd been nicked for—for—

Rape, he told himself.

He couldn't be afraid of the word. Nadia said so. He couldn't be afraid of the word. This wasn't him; this was epilepsy. This wasn't him. *It wasn't anything to do with him.*

Chris was just like he'd been in the flat. Out like a light but just sleeping. John coaxed gently, trying to wake him up a bit faster. He rubbed at a shoulder, played with his hair, called his name. He earned a few grumpy scowls and snarls—but it wasn't until blue lights started flashing, and he looked up to see a paramedic car creeping towards them across the pedestrianised zone, that the body under his hand really stirred.

"What's..."

"It's all right," John murmured.

"What's going on?"

His voice was sleepy and slurred, and then the car door slammed, and he jumped violently.

"Hey, it's okay."

"Where the fuck are—"

"High street," John said. "You had a seizure. Attracted a bit of attention from the police, and they've called a paramedic. They just want to make sure you're okay."

The frowning copper looked at ease again. The paramedic—a young woman with blonde hair in a high ponytail—squatted down by John's side, snapping on gloves and firing off questions. At first, John answered and Chris simply lay there, clutching his arm and frowning. And then, slowly, his brain came back online.

"You called an ambulance?"

"I didn't."

Chris scowled. "Right. Well. I don't need an ambulance. I want to go home."

"I just want to check you're—" started the paramedic, but Chris made as if to get up, and she had to back up or be headbutted.

"I'm fine," Chris said shortly, fumbling for the pavement and John's arm to orient himself. "Look, I have a bracelet and everything. This is embarrassing. I want to go home."

"You really ought to get checked over at a hosp—"

"I'm not going to hospital, and you can't make me go," Chris said. He sounded pissed. In both senses of the word. "John? Ring a taxi, let's go. I'm knackered."

John helped him to his feet, bracing Chris's weight entirely until they were completely upright.

"Sir, we just want to make sure—"

"I know my own damned disease!" Chris flared up.

John winced and could see the coppers beginning to frown again. This was going to get ugly.

"Hey—" He caught both of Chris's shoulders in his hands. "Calm down. Come on. Let's go. There's a taxi rank at the bottom of the road. We can get one there. Come on. No," he said to the copper's mate, who reached out as if to stop them. "He's fine; you can see that for yourselves. I appreciate the help, but we just need to go home."

The paramedic fell back almost at once, but the policemen tailed them right down to the taxi rank, and it was only when John shut the door of a black cab on their faces that he felt able to breathe again.

And then he groped for Chris's hand and bent to put his own head between his knees.

"John?"

"M'fine..."

"You sure?"

"In a minute."

Chris's hand rubbed soothingly at his back. It was clumsy and his words were slurred, but it helped all the same. "What's the matter?"

"Cops," John mumbled.

"Oh. *Oh.*"

"Yeah."

"God, I'm sorry."

"Not your fault. Or theirs, really. Just...had a bit of a panic," John admitted.

"How bad?"

"Didn't freak out and start crying or anything. Just...you know. Felt like crap. No air. The usual."

Chris hummed. "Yours."

"What?"

"I want to go to yours."

John straightened. "You need to go home."

316 - | Matthew J. Metzger

"I have two doses still at your flat. And your bed's bigger than mine. I need a nap, and you need a hug."

John couldn't really argue with that. He sighed, then shouted the change of address to the cabbie. Chris leaned against him, sagging bonelessly into his shoulder, and John winced. He forced the worry aside. Now wasn't the time. He slid an arm around Chris's back and pulled him closer.

"You okay?" Chris asked sleepily.

"Yeah," he murmured. "You?"

"Think I've bashed my wrist, but I'm okay."

John buried his face against cool, damp hair.

"John?"

"Mm?"

"Y'handled it."

"What?"

"You handled it."

"So?"

"So, you're getting there."

John lifted his face free again.

"I still wigged out."

"Only on the inside, by what you said. You sounded calm when I came round."

John opened his mouth to argue—and subsided. Yeah. He had, actually. He'd completely bricked it on the inside, but on the outside...

He squeezed tight until Chris wriggled in protest.

He was getting better.

Chapter Thirty-One

"I THINK YOU'RE too hard on yourself."

Nadia's voice was firm. Their gaze was equally so, and John fought to hold it.

"In a single week, you came out to your rugby club, an old friend, and you managed to keep your anxiety under control until you were in a position to deal with it. That's very impressive and would take a toll on anybody."

John fidgeted.

"I—they were trying to help, and I was shi—losing it."

"You didn't sound like you were losing it to me."

"It felt like it."

"Of course it did. That's how anxiety works," they said calmly. "But from the actions you took, I think you handled it excellently. You're still a long way from not having the attacks at all, but that you can keep yourself functioning long enough to ride out the situation is a hugely positive step."

"I guess..."

"After all, you couldn't do that with Chris's stepmother, or his father. Could you?"

John opened his mouth...and slowly closed it again.

No.

He'd wigged out immediately, both times. He'd not had a hope. This time...

And this time had been cops. People primed to think the worst. People who *had*, when Daniel had falsely accused him.

"No."

The timer beeped.

"Well, that's all for today," they said, sitting forward. "Do think about what I've said, John. You have wounds. Perfectly normal, understandable wounds. It's going to take time for those to heal, no matter what relationship you're in now. Don't beat yourself up for needing that time."

John nodded. He shook their hand, and thanked them, and kept his face perfectly impassive, all the way out to the van.

Only then did he crumble. His eyes burned. His lip wobbled dangerously.

And then he sucked the lip in and squared his shoulders. He hadn't fallen apart in the street, when the coppers were scowling and Chris was seizing on the floor between them. So he wasn't going to do it now, when he'd only talked about it.

His phone started ringing in the glovebox, and John scrubbed both hands over his face before reaching for it. Unrecognised number. So, customer.

Deep breath.

Then: "Hi, John Halliday."

"Oh." A woman's voice. "Hello. Is this Reet Breet Electrics?"

"Yep."

"I'd like to get a quote for getting a cable laid out to our summerhouse and some plug sockets put in. Is that something you can do?"

"'Course," John said, maybe a little too flippantly. "I'd need to see the property to quote you though. Price really depends on the cable length and how much earth you'd need to disturb. Might need a landscaper or a builder out as well." Rhodri, ideally, but some people chose their own.

"You'd have to bury it?"

"Yeah, can't leave live cables exposed to the weather or your gardening."

"Oh. Well. All right. When can you come over?"

John glanced at his watch. A quote wouldn't take long. He wasn't meeting Chris until dinner, and the girls were all at work.

"Could do it now, if you're free."

"Really? Oh, that'd be marvellous." John raised his eyebrows at the odd choice of words. "Yes, that'd suit nicely. Have you got a pen for the address?"

It was oddly familiar when John jotted it down—maybe a repeat customer—and he hung up with the sense that he was about to earn a lot of money. Posh women wanting cables laid? He got his best markups on those kinds of jobs.

The address was a way away, and he stopped off for petrol halfway there, but then he found himself winding his way into vaguely familiar streets. The satnav announced his destination at a spot he distinctly remembered, and he hauled on the handbrake with a frown, squinting up at the house.

There wasn't a Land Rover on the drive.

But he could have sworn he'd kissed Chris right here on the pavement, under this streetlight, when it had been snowing.

The voice on the phone hadn't been Lauren's though. She'd spoken with a broad Sheffield accent, not that cultured southern sound. John racked his brains, trying to pull up anything else, any other female relative Chris had mentioned that might live there. Grandparents were all gone, weren't they? And he'd implied his Aunt Kelly was gone too.

Slowly, John pulled the satnav off the windscreen. Scrolled through the recent destinations list.

Yes.

There. Before the first time he'd gone to the flat at Parson Cross.

Same address.

John swallowed tightly and glanced up at the house. Christ. So it had to be Lauren. Because that was Chris's dad's house.

Damn it. Damn-damn-damn-da—

John shook himself and shoved the satnav in the glovebox. No. Time to stop wussing out. And, anyway, maybe they wouldn't remember him. Maybe Chris had never mentioned what he did for a living.

He threw out his chest and threw open the van door.

His fist hammered on the door in time with the hammering of his heart in his throat. He took a good four or five steps back so he wouldn't loom so much. Prayed silently for Lauren, and for Chris's dad not to be home.

And then the door opened, and John's jaw sagged.

This was not Lauren.

A thin woman wearing nothing but a pair of fluffy slippers and a dressing gown stood in front of him. Her hair was long and frizzy, and soaking wet from a recent wash. It was dark like Chris's but obviously dyed. Her wrists were covered in silver bangles and bracelets that clinked musically as she tucked a clump of hair behind her ear and beamed at him.

"Caroline," she said. "Come through, come through..."

John swallowed. Great. Chris's dad was having an affair, and here was John, right in the middle of what could turn into a World War Three scenario in about five seconds.

The house smelled of incense. It was airy and light, wooden floors everywhere, and pictures on every spare inch of wall in the kitchen. He saw several of Chris and had to suppress the urge to pinch one of him as a chubby baby, those big blue eyes still recognisable twenty-four years later. But apart from the pictures, the place was pristinely tidy. Almost like a show home. It had been scrubbed to within an inch of its life, and he could see the tracks of a vacuum cleaner as he was lead through the building to the back. Glass doors opened onto the long garden, and at the end stood a glorified shed.

"There." She threw out her arm, and the dressing gown almost opened. John stared determinedly at the shed.

"So you want a cable laid out to give it power?"

"Yes."

"What are you planning to do with it?"

"It's going to be my meditation space," she proclaimed.

"Right," John said slowly. "So, uh. What kind of electrical items would you use in a meditation space?"

She gave him a look like he was an imbecile. "Lamps. Stereos..."

"What I'm getting at," John said, "is are you running everyday household items, or something big and exhausting that needs a lot of power?"

"It wouldn't be a meditation space if I need a lot of power."

"Uh. No. Guess not."

He paced off down the garden. It was very long and narrow, a white gravel path snaking through a jungle of flowery bushes. A hammock was hidden in the nest of branches and leaves, and bees buzzed harmoniously by as he reached the summerhouse. It really was just a shed with a window knocked through, and he snorted. In truth, he could bury an extensional cable out here and plug it in next to the washing machine.

Still, he said, "Hmm," and feigned seriousness as he poked around, looking for the best way to run the lead into the shed.

"So," Caroline said chirpily. "Do you run your business?"

"Yep."

"John, wasn't it?"

"That's right. John Halliday."

Her beatific smile widened. "That's lovely. So when does my stepson get to meet your father?"

John paused. Turned to tower over her and squinted at that bright, brilliant smile.

"Excuse me?"

It widened. "You heard."

Oh, God.

But—

How?

A door banged. Someone, a very familiar someone, shouted Caroline's name. John heard the grating slide of the glass doors, and then there he was. Chris. In a jacket and jeans, cane-free, one hand on the doorframe, frowning down the garden.

"Caroline!" he shouted again. "You out here?"

Wait—he *knew* about this?

"Summerhouse, darling! I've caught something!"

John had the sudden violent urge to throw himself over the fence and escape via next door's garden.

"What's that?" Chris asked, stepping out a couple of feet into the garden. "Dad wants your help with the shopping. Says I can't be trusted with eggs."

"Well, you can't, darling. Here, you take your boyfriend here inside. I think he might combust."

"My—what?"

John groaned.

"John?"

"Yeah," he called weakly.

"What the—" Chris's face twisted, and then he groaned. "Caroline, what the *hell*?"

"Well, you wouldn't invite him over, so I did."

"How did you even kno—did you hack my phone again?"

"Hack implies you even protected it." She sniffed and sailed up the garden path, a display of regal aloofness that could have been funny, had John not been suffering from an intense heart attack and unable to appreciate it.

And then they were alone, and Chris gingerly took a few more steps.

"John?"

"I have no idea what's going on," John said but stepped into range. He reached out for a hug and found himself leaning heavily onto Chris. "She called wanting a quote for a cable laying..."

"Oh my God, trust her," Chris muttered. "I'm so sorry. I didn't think she'd go and take things into her own hands. She's been sort of impatient to meet you."

"She's—why? Who is she?"

"My stepmum."

"I thought Lauren was your stepmum."

"She is."

John pulled back a little and stared.

"What?"

"They both are," Chris said. "My dad has two girlfriends."

"Oh my God."

"Well, technically, he and Lauren are engaged, but that's never going to actually happen."

"I—what?"

Chris laughed quietly. "Dad's poly. Always has been. He met Lauren after splitting up from my mum, and then she met Caroline at a protest."

John's jaw sagged.

"Is that...too much?"

"I—it's weird," John admitted. "I've never even heard of that. Is your whole family crazy, or what?"

Chris chuckled. "They're not crazy. It's kind of nice, actually. I get five sets of presents for my birthday."

"Why am I here?" John breathed.

"Because she tricked you. If you want to go, I will bawl her out and then come over."

John wanted that. He felt a little cheated, a lot thrown, and very, very scared. This wasn't even on a par with Nora stealing his wallet. This was downright sly.

But then...

He'd known it was Chris's dad's house. He'd made that choice himself, to walk into the wasps' nest. He hadn't been expecting Caroline, that was all. And he felt a little warmed, too. Chris's quick defence of him, Chris's lack of involvement in it, was kind of nice. He hadn't known about it. He hadn't been colluding to get John here.

And maybe—maybe this was a now or never situation. He'd met Chris's very normal, very bland mum and stepdad. Chris *had* said they were the conventional half of his parents. Maybe this kind of explained Chris's piercings and the sex frankness.

"No."

"No, what?"

"I'll—stay and meet them."

"You sure?"

"Yes."

Chris leaned up to kiss him, stretching on his tiptoes. John squeezed him close and straightened until he came right up off the floor.

"And after, you owe me," he mumbled.

Chris laughed. "Yes, I'll owe you whatever you want."

"That trip for your birthday?"

"Okay, okay. That trip for my birthday."

"Yeah?"

"Yeah."

John beamed, shoving the nerves away with determination. Okay. Met three people—all of whom he'd now already met, technically—and then get to whisk Chris off to the seaside again for a private little holiday. He could totally do that. He could totally—

He looked up.

The red-haired man was scowling at him from the kitchen door.

Oh dear God, he couldn't do this.

"Uh."

"What?"

"Your dad."

"Face!"

"What?"

"Just his face, remember," Chris said.

John looked up again, and the man had gone. He'd turned away to the fridge and was packing bags away.

Okay.

"Let's do this," John said and let go.

Strode out for the door.

Stood on the threshold, in his dirty boots and workman's trousers, and stuck out one enormous paw.

"John Halliday."

The man turned.

He was very short, very fat, and very frowny. The red hair was greying in places, and his face ruddy and sagging with age. But he paused not a second before sticking out his own and shaking John's hand like he was trying to fling water off it.

"Ted Bannerman."

"I, uh, didn't realise I was coming here, or I'd have dressed better..."

Ted snorted. "Like I care. What pretence did she use?"

"Cable-laying out to your shed."

"Bollocks to that," came the flat reply. "Not having my deckchairs moved out for some meditation nonsense. Caroline! That's my damn shed!"

"Oh, hang your deckchairs!" came the breezy reply from the hall, and the front door closed. She shuffled back in, a bag in each hand and breasts on full display through the opened dressing gown. John choked. "Ah, John, dear. Would you prefer dinner here, or shall we all eat out?"

John averted his eyes to the table, squashed into the kitchen that really had no room for it. Then Chris slipped back inside and closed the glass doors, and a hand worked its way into his own.

"Out," Chris said. "I want Italian."

"Demanding shit," Ted grunted.

"Ted! Company! Out's fine, darling. I'll need to get ready, though. Ted, put the kettle on. John?"

"Uh—"

"Cup of tea?"

Chapter Thirty-Two

IN THE END, they all ended up going out for dinner. Lauren came home half an hour later, in those lime green wellies, and then Caroline swanned back down the stairs in a floaty blue dress and corralled Ted into changing his trousers.

"There's *holes*, dear!"

"Like anyone cares, woman!"

Chris smiled, holding John's hand on the table, a mug of coffee in the other.

"They're bonkers," he said. "Ignore them."

It was actually a nice chance to get to figure them out a little bit. Lauren seemed fairly normal, and John relaxed quickly when she admired his neck tattoo and jealously said she'd be covered herself, if not for a crippling fear of needles. Ted seemed a fairly typical grumpy old man. Caroline was mad as a box of frogs, but actually seemed kind of harmless. And she certainly bossed Ted around just like John's mum and dad.

John watched, utterly fascinated.

He'd never really met too many alternative types up close before. Mum and Dad were very traditional. His mates down the yard were very traditional. The rugby lads were the definition of traditional. Even Chris himself wasn't all that odd, when you came down to it. He wasn't even Kelham Island hipster level.

But his family were *bonkers*.

Actually going to this Italian place was apparently an enormous operation. Chris opted for the simpler route, saying John would drive the pair of them and they would meet up later. John genuinely wasn't sure—until they were in the car and Chris leaned over to kiss him—if it was to make things simpler, or to take the pressure off John.

Then Chris said, "You okay?" and John figured it out.

"Yeah. I think so."

"You're doing fine. They like you."

"They do?" Apart from Lauren and her tattoo talk, they'd mostly ignored him.

"Oh, yeah. They're not subtle."

"Thanks...I think."

In fact, they ignored him all the way into the restaurant, and only after orders were taken did Caroline tut and say, "Lasagne, darling? Really?"

"It's traditional, and I like it," John replied uncertainly.

"Traditional," she echoed, like it was a dirty word.

"Yeah, some people like that," Chris chimed in.

"It's limiting!"

"With you around, it's bloody peaceful," Ted muttered.

"Mouth is open, darling, and it shouldn't be!" she sang.

"You know," John said, "I'm beginning to see where you get it from."

Chris raised his eyebrows. "*Your* mouth is open, and shouldn't be."

"Case in point."

Chatter over the main course was easy enough. Basic. Simple. They asked some standard fare questions about him, and he got to work out what the heck was going on here.

Slowly, it emerged that Ted and Lauren had been together since Chris was about twelve years old, and Caroline had come along when he was fifteen or so. Ted lived off his Army pension and spread betting, having broken his back in the Marines when Chris was still a baby. The faint Scottish accent wasn't in John's imagination—he was from Aberdeen. Chris was delicately described as his only living child, and John didn't want to ask a single thing about that if he could possibly help it. Lauren, on the other hand, was from Sheffield and had an ex-husband of her own, less delicately described as a C-word. She was a horse riding instructor, and forever intent on getting Chris to try it.

"No reason for you not to," she said. "Do you ride, John?"

"Hating bloody horses not enough for you?"

"Um, no," John said. "Never tried."

"Oh, *well*—"

He got the impression he might be, soon enough.

Caroline was...well, *Caroline*. She didn't tell him any of the normal things, like where she was from. She told him that she collected amethysts to promote healing, worked at some Buddhist centre, and sold candles on Etsy. She also had another girlfriend in Rotherham and usually spent her weekends with Allison. Neither Lauren nor Ted batted an eyelash.

"So it's a kind of...big, open thing?"

"Caroline's open," Lauren said. "Ted and I, not so much."

"Right," John said.

"Let me guess, traditionalist household? One man, one woman?"

"Well...one and one, I guess. Not so fussed about the genders involved."

"You're out, then?"

And just like that, Caroline's eyes narrowed in on him, and John felt the interrogation part of the dinner open up.

He swallowed. The anxiety balloon inflated.

"Yes."

"Why our Christian?"

John blinked.

Then turned to look at Chris.

"Christian?"

"Yep."

"Why?"

"Christopher's boring."

John left it there.

"So?" Caroline prompted.

"Um. Because...because I spilled coffee on him, and he laughed at me, and my heart stopped beating."

Chris groaned. So did Ted. The sounds were identical. But both women beamed, as if John had said the best thing he could possibly have managed.

"He's...amazing," John said, warming to his theme a little. Chris put his hands over his ears. "He's beautiful and he's funny. When I'm with him, I feel like everything's fine, even the things that go wrong. And he has the worst chat-up lines."

"Excuse me, I do not."

"Oh, like father like son, then?" Lauren muttered.

"Can it," Ted groused.

"You wish."

"Chris hasn't really told us anything about you," Caroline said airily. "I had to get your phone number off his mobile, and then imagine my surprise when Google threw back you were an electrician! I always hoped he'd go for an art student."

"No bloody use in art students, can't pay the bills," Ted groused and earned himself a solid kick under the table from his distinctly artistic girlfriend.

"I, uh, no. Not arty."

"You wax poetic about sex often enough," Chris mumbled.

John's face flamed red. "Chris!"

"Oh, don't be shy, darling, very important to talk about sex," Caroline said. "I trust you do have sex?"

"Oh my God..."

"Don't be embarrassed!"

Chris started to laugh.

"I—yes. We do," John said.

"Are you kinky at all? You know, it could be complicated if you are, Chris's epilepsy doesn't—"

"Caroline, knock it off." Chris cackled, hand over his mouth.

John hid his face in his hands.

"I'm just *saying*..."

"No, you're winding him up," Chris said. "Ask something else if you want to play Twenty Questions."

"And not his damned size," Ted grumbled. "No bugger wants to know that."

"Oh, I don't know," Lauren said.

John could feel himself going beet red.

"Why didn't you want to meet us?"

It was Ted who asked.

It was the first real question he'd asked—apart from the all-important one about what teams John supported—and it felt heavier than all the other questions from Chris's stepmothers. It fell into the room like a lead weight and smacked down on the floor. John paused. He could feel the colour draining out of his face again. The truth? Should he tell these mad but obviously loving stepmothers what he'd been accused of doing? Should he let this ex-Marine—bad back notwithstanding—know?

"I—"

They waited.

Chris's hand carefully gripped his own on the table.

"Parents don't like me," John hedged. "The way I look. Too—big. Scary. Aggressive."

Ted snorted. "Aggressive my fragrant arse."

Chris smiled.

"My last boyfriend used that against me."

"How?" Lauren asked.

"He—he was cheating. Turns out I was the other man. And when he—when he got caught, he tried to say that—that he'd gone along with me because I scared him. That I'd..."

That word.

That *word*.

"That I'd effectively..."

Don't be afraid of it.

"Raped him."

Silence.

John took a gulping breath.

Then battled on.

"I was scared you'd think the same. That I could do that. I needed to prove to Chris—I needed to prove to *me*—that it was nothing but a stupid, ugly lie."

The women glanced at one another. John could see the uncertainty. See the hesitation. See the maybe.

And Ted snorted again.

"Bollocks."

"W-what?" John asked.

"I've seen more aggressive bloody rabbits."

A flower of relief blossomed where the balloon ought to have been.

"You're a bigger pushover than our old dog, and that's saying something."

John's shoulders sagged with relief. Ted believed him. Ted bloody well believed him. They weren't freaking out. They weren't giving each other the look. They weren't demanding he leave, or that they needed to talk to Chris alone.

They believed him.

And Chris's fingers were warm and relaxed around John's own.

John took a deep breath—and there was no balloon inside to restrict his breathing.

CHRIS TURNED ON him at the car and kissed him like they were drowning. Hands on John's biceps, stroking down the sleeves. Mouth caught fast to his own until they were one being. Every inch of that long, beautiful body pressed to John's.

And then, when he let go, he simply said, "I love you."

John ran a hand down the back of his neck and kissed him again.

The curls were thick and heavy against his palm. Their weight was familiar. The taste of rich coffee and richer chocolate cake were sweet and soft around the edges of a mouth that John knew as well as he knew his own. And he loved it. Loved him. Loved every single moment that had brought him here, to this dark spot with this bright man, even the ones that included his darkest days.

He slid his arms down Chris's back. Clasped his waist in both hands and held him close and fast. Held him as though they need never let go, as though nothing could possibly happen that required them to leave.

Because John was in love.

He was in love again. He'd found love again. He'd found trips to the coast, pints at the bar, terrible jokes, wonderful sex, the feel of feet tangled together at the end of a warm bed in the early morning. He'd found laughter, and remembered how to smile. He'd found safety, a voice whispering to him when he freaked out, and he'd found support from the man who never asked what he and Nadia talked about.

He'd found a man who made him want to talk to Nadia.

He'd found better.

And he could recover.

Because Chris loved him. And his mad family didn't think he was a bad idea. And John *knew* he wasn't a bad idea. He could deal with seizures in the street. He could give foot massages, and knew where to get the best takeaways, and drive anywhere Chris wanted to go. He could bring him unimaginable pleasure with his tongue alone, and he could keep away the pain with his fingers. He could keep doing it, all day and every day, as long as Chris would let him.

And when Chris wouldn't let him—when Chris said no, when Chris backed off, when Chris wanted something else—John knew, *knew*, felt, *really felt*, that he would do as he was told.

He wasn't what Daniel had said.

He never had been.

"It's raining."

The whisper was very soft. John felt it more than heard it and smiled against the mouth that made it.

"So?"

"Bit cliché, this. Kissing in the rain."

John leaned in and took the words away.

Chris would just have to deal with cliché.

Just this once.

About the Author

Matthew J. Metzger is an ace, trans author posing as a functional human being in the wilds of Yorkshire, England. Although mainly a writer of contemporary, working-class romance, he also strays into fantasy when the mood strikes. Whatever the genre, the focus is inevitably on queer characters and their relationships, be they familial, platonic, sexual, or romantic.

When not crunching numbers at his day job, or writing books by night, Matthew can be found tweeting from the gym, being used as a pillow by his cat, or trying to keep his website in some semblance of order.

Email: mattmetzger@hotmail.co.uk

Facebook: www.facebook.com/mattjmetzger

Twitter: @MatthewJMetzger

Website: www.matthewjmetzger.com

Other books by this author

Walking on Water
Big Man
Bump
Life Underwater

Coming Soon from Matthew J. Metzger

Coffee

A Cup of John, Book Two

When Chris's stepfather passes away and leaves Chris a house and a wedding ring, it seems like the perfect opportunity to take the next step in his relationship with John.

So, they're both in for a nasty shock when Chris's mother is vehemently opposed to the idea. Despite three years of history to prove otherwise, she insists that John is only a temporary feature in Chris's life, and a man like him can't be expected to stay with someone like Chris in the long run.

Can Chris persuade her that she's wrong in time for the wedding—or will there be an empty space in the photographs?

Also Available from NineStar Press

Connect with NineStar Press

Website: NineStarPress.com

Facebook: NineStarPress

Facebook Reader Group: NineStarNiche

Twitter: @ninestarpress

Tumblr: NineStarPress

CPSIA information can be obtained
at www.ICGtesting.com
Printed in the USA
LVHW112003220822
726563LV00001B/48